BABYJACKED

A PAYNE FAMILY ROMANCE

SOSIE FROST

Babyjacked

Copyright © 2018 by Sosie Frost
All rights reserved. This book or any portion thereof
may not be reproduced or used in any manner whatsoever
without the express written permission of the publisher
except for the use of brief quotations in a book review.

This is a work of fiction. Names, characters, businesses, places, events and incidents are either the products of the author's imagination or used in a fictitious manner. Any resemblance to actual persons, living or dead, or actual events is purely coincidental.

This book is licensed for your personal enjoyment only. This book may not be re-sold or given away to other people. If you would like to share this book with another person, please purchase an additional copy for each person you'd like to share it with. Thank you for respecting the author's work.

Cover Design: Pink Ink Designs
Photographer: Wander Aguiar Photography
Cover Model: Forest Harrison

Created with Vellum

ALSO BY SOSIE FROST

Bad Boy's Series

Bad Boy's Baby

Bad Boy's Redemption (Previously Bad Boy's Revenge)

Bad Boy's Bridesmaid

Touchdowns and Tiaras

Beauty And The Blitz

Once Upon A Half-Time

Happily Ever All-Star

Standalone Romances

Sweetest Sin - A Forbidden Priest Romance

Hard - A Step-Brother Romance

Deja Vu - An Amnesia Romance

While They Watch - A Sexy BDSM Romance

ABOUT THE AUTHOR

Keep tabs on me through Facebook

Join my mailing list to receive updates, news, special sales, and opportunities for advanced reader copies of upcoming novels!

You will **only** receive emails from me and about me—no promoting other authors and cluttering your box!
I'll send **1-2 emails a month** when I have a new release!

You can also receive a **text message** when a new book is live!

Text: SOSIE
to
245-87

Subscribe to text message alerts! Get a text right to your phone! No more wading through all those author emails that clog your inbox. Never miss one of my books again!

I'll only text when a new book is released!
(No more than one or two times a month)

Or
You can always email me at:
sosiefrost@gmail.com

*To L.G.
I'm back, baby!*

BABYJACKED

The classic tale of a lumberjack...
and his nanny.

1

Cassi

The first time I saw Remington Marshall, he stole my heart.

The last time I saw Remington Marshall, he'd just burned my family's barn to the ground.

Arson usually complicated relationships.

Especially afterward, when Rem left our sleepy town of Butterpond in the dead of night without so much as a goodbye. He'd stayed gone for five long years.

Five years with no phone call. No visits. No explanations.

Even worse—no apology.

So, when my brother, Tidus, told me Rem was back in town, I had to make a decision.

Ignore Remington Marshall and forget he'd ever existed…

Or demand an answer for why he'd broken my heart.

I chose the latter, encouraged by the perspective I'd gained over the last couple years. As long as we stayed away from any flammable objects that might've torched what remained of my potential happiness, a conversation would bring me some much-needed closure. Besides, all that time had allowed me to douse the last few embers left burning in my barn, heart, and loins.

But that still didn't make confrontation a good idea, despite my brother's insistence.

He came home to take care of his nieces, Tidus said.

Take him up a box of kids' toys from storage, he said.

Pick me up a burger from Lou's on the way home, he said.

Yeah, right.

Rem wasn't a man who wanted to be found, even in the tiny town of Butterpond—a small cluster of dreams, prayers, and fatty liver disease. Butterpond was where the trees wanted in, the people wanted out, and my family's farm accidentally lynch-pinned the whole place together.

To the town, my family was a fixture. The Payne's farm. The Payne's charity. The Payne's pain in the ass boys who rolled over the town's one streetlight like a plague of locusts. The Payne's adopted daughter in a family of five boys—*bless her heart.*

But Rem? He no longer belonged in the town. Men like him kept to themselves, tucked away inside a cabin in the mountains, hidden from society by gravel roads, the occasional tick, and busted suspensions.

As much as I'd once loved Rem, risking Lyme disease and a punctured tire seemed a bad idea.

I did it anyway.

A box of old toys and children's clothes was jammed in next to my suitcase.

This would be quick. In and out. Hand him the box stuffed with goodies from when my family had foster kids running all over the farm. Wish him well. Make the requisite small talk. And then pretend like my heart wasn't held together with a roll of scotch tape and a smattering of pride.

I wasn't about to let Remington Marshall shatter my barely rejuvenated dignity. Besides, the last I'd heard, *he* was the one crippled with guilt. Rumor had it—and by rumor, I meant the occasional conversation with his sister, Emma—he'd run away to the deepest forests of Canada to join a logging company.

If a heart broke in the forest, did it make a sound? The answer was yes, but it wasn't a thud. More like the noise a sleepy woman yelp in the middle of the night when she stubbed her toe on the way to the bathroom. Less of a *timber!* More like *son of a—*

The box fit snugly against my hip, drawing the hem of my skirt up only an inch. I was fine with that. Showing a little leg would do me good. I'd grown up since the fire. Earned my curves. Managed to fill out my bra without two handfuls of wadded up toilet paper. Things were looking up.

I wound my way over a weed-choked cobblestone path and picked my steps up the rickety porch. The cabin was lost in the woods, and the forest wasn't happy with the new occupant. The little space was so overgrown with brush and leaves that the *trees* would be grateful to be cleaned out of the gutters.

My knock clattered against the cabin door—almost loud enough to drown out the very irritated cry of a baby.

Almost.

The wail might've belonged to a child. Could have also been a mountain lion with a toothache. Sometimes it was tough to tell, even with a degree in early education. Money well spent.

The door flung open. I expected Remington. Instead, a bright-eyed, blonde-haired, puffy-cheeked three-year-old peered up at me, scowled, and belted at the top of her precious little lungs to alert all within a square mile of my arrival.

"Stranger!"

I winced. "Hi. I'm Cassi. Is your Uncle—"

"Stranger!"

This alerted the baby—the real siren of the household who'd missed her calling as the dive alarm for a German U-Boat.

The chorus of screams rang in my ears. I shushed the three-year-old with a wave of my hand.

"I'm not a stranger—I'm a..." Was *friend* the right word? "I know your Uncle Rem...well, not *know* know. We grew up together. I mean, he grew up with my brother—I grew up later. But we were...I'd see him a lot—"

"Stranger!"

I cringed and went to Plan B. The box dropped to the porch. I debated on running, but the tape had loosened enough for me to rip the flaps. An old baby doll rested on a folded pile of clothes. I offered it as a sacrifice to appease the child.

"It's for you!" My frantic words shushed her. "It's PJ Sparkles. All the little girls loved PJ Sparkles!"

The child quieted. She bit her lip, scratched her leg with a foot clad in mismatched socks, and reached for the doll. She jumped as a husky voice caught her in the act.

"What do we have here?"

His voice was a blend of sticky marshmallow and crumbling graham cracker, and I melted like a chocolate bar squished near the fire.

I knew better than to get burned by Remington Marshall, but even the wisest girl sometimes took a big bite before blowing on it.

And, believe me, Rem would go to his *grave* wishing I had blown him.

Rem leaned against the door frame. His broad shoulders were clad in a warm, red flannel shirt. He scratched a wild, thick beard, and might have teased a smile. I couldn't tell. Five years of isolation had obscured his face in dark hair.

A one-year-old baby wailed in his arms.

"Never expected to see you here, Cassia Payne." He grunted as the three-year-old bashed the doll's plastic head into a part of him that regretted meeting PJ Sparkles. He stepped aside and let her go play, but his stare pinned me in place. "Lost in the woods, little girl?"

What had happened to my Remington Marshall?

Gone was the teenage bad boy, strong enough to win his fights but lean enough to make a quick escape once Sherriff Samson flashed his lights. Now, Rem had become a terrifying beast of rugged strength. A *lumberjack*. A man like him could have *punched* down a tree. The Canadian forests never stood a chance.

Muscles packed on muscles. And the beard...oh, the beard. I didn't know if he belonged in an ice fishing cabin or on a Harley, but this wasn't the boy who'd left me behind.

This was a *man*.

And he was in *trouble*.

Rem struggled to bounce the little bundle of pink in his arms. The baby fussed, red-faced and probably wishing her Uncle hadn't given her diaper a wedgie while rocking her. The three-year-old dropped the doll and instead raced over, around, and on top of his feet, tugging on his jeans with an urgent need to tinkle. She tripped over one of the *four* stuffed garbage bags piled in the entryway. One had already blown open, spilling dresses, shoes, socks, and toys into the cabin.

The three-year-old was wearing two shirts. The baby needed a pair of pants. Rem's own belongings had tumbled into the hall—duffel bags and mountain boots.

Tidus wasn't lying. Rem must have come home only hours before to take care of the kids.

The older girl somersaulted around his feet, somehow summoning and then spilling a glass of water. The TV blared cartoons from the den. The baby cried just to be louder than the show. Behind him, every chair had been toppled in the dining room. The cushions stripped off the couch. Something slimy dripped from the sink.

Chaos had descended upon a three-square-foot area of his life…

And a part of me *really* enjoyed the struggle.

"Everyone said you ran away to become a lumberjack," I said. "But apparently you joined a circus."

Rem was a great liar. I'd learned that long ago. He attempted to soothe the baby and accidentally smooshed her face into the wall of muscle that was his shoulder. His wink wasn't fooling anyone.

"Brought the circus home too." He reached down and lifted the little girl to her feet before she somersaulted into the wall. "Got my acrobat tumbling her way into preschool, and the prepubescent bearded lady doing shows before and after naptime."

Cute. "And what's your talent?"

"World's sexiest uncle."

"Ain't no one buying tickets for that."

"Ringleader then."

The three-year-old demanded cookies. The baby, blood. I shook my head. "Guess again."

"Toddler-tamer."

He wished. I crossed my arms. "Better get a shovel. I think you're mucking out stalls and diapers."

Rem grinned, but that was a charmer's smile, part of his bag of tricks. He'd always been the type to sweet-talk his way out of handcuffs just to use them in bed. But maybe he had changed. Maybe the wilderness had straightened him out? Perhaps...the hard work taught him responsibility? Was it possible the time apart had made him as miserable as it had me?

Or maybe *that* smile meant I should've left the box on the porch and ran.

"Do I have to charge admission, or are you coming inside?" he asked.

Dangerous question. "Depends. Got an elephant under this big top?"

"Nah. He's on break. I'm standing in."

"And what are you?"

"The jackass."

Fair enough. I offered him the box. "This is some stuff from the farm—back when we had all the foster kids. Tidus said you could probably use it. Clothes and toys."

Rem easily balanced the baby on his shoulder and the box in his arms. He left the door open. Inviting the little ones to escape or beckoning me inside?

I spoke from the entryway, a promise to myself. "Only for a minute."

"Want something to drink?" he asked.

"That would take longer than a minute."

"Good. I don't have much to offer."

The three-year-old circled the sofa with the doll, tripped over the logs that were once stacked neatly by a stone fireplace, and plummeted onto the hardwood. She whimpered, rolled, and revealed a scraped knee. The crying began anew.

Rem brushed his hands through his shaggy, collar length dark hair and sighed.

"Are you bleeding? *Again*? Really?" He fumbled through a couple drawers. "All right. Here. No band-aids, but…"

Oh, this was a *disaster*.

Rem ripped a piece of electrical tape between his teeth, juggled the baby from one arm to the other, and slapped the silver strip over the girl's knee.

"Good job," I said. "Now she's patched up, *and* she won't conduct electricity."

"She'll be fine." He patted the girl's head. "Mellie, say hi to Cassi. Cas, this is Melanie. And this…" He flipped the baby outwards, finally letting her look around the room. She instantly stopped crying. The chubby cheeks and sniffling nose gave way to an adorable smile with three little white teeth poking out. "This is Tabitha—Tabby. They're Emma's kids."

They looked like his sister—blonde and perky with the right amount of sass that got her in as much trouble as Rem.

I hated to ask the question, but a man like Rem wouldn't volunteer to babysit without a genuine crisis. "What happened to Emma?"

Rem turned somber—a dark, serious glance broken with a forced shrug. "She's…sick. Needed some help."

"Is she okay?"

"Yeah. Just needs time. I came home to wrangle the kids."

"I'm surprised to see you." No harm in the truth.

"It's been a while."

Silence.

I looked away. Somehow, under the heavy flannel, bushy beard, and shaggy hair was the Remington Marshall that still made my chest flutter. My options were to escape or find a defibrillator. My heart was broken, but it could still stop if he whispered the right words.

I shuffled towards the door, but Mellie plucked at the electrical tape banding her knee. The garbage bags of clothes, the injured child, and the quarter inch of dust over the cabin didn't bode well.

"Are you sure you know..." How to phrase it without insulting him or completely terrifying the kids. "I had no idea you liked children."

"They're all right."

"And...they're still alive. So you must be doing...okay?"

Rem snorted. "They're *kids*, Cas. I can handle 'em."

Right. "And...how long have you had them?"

Rem checked his watch. "It's been five hours, and I haven't lost my mind yet."

Yet. "And you're happy to babysit?"

"Sure."

"For how long?"

"As long as she needs." Rem sounded confident. Or foolish. Probably foolish. "Don't worry. It's temporary. A week or two at the most. Shouldn't be too hard. Keep an eye on them until Emma's good, and then I'll head back to the logging company."

I laughed. Sweet Jesus, he was serious. I covered my mouth. "You... you're keeping them *here*?"

"I was going to let them out at night like a cat, but I figured they'd rather get the lay of the land first." He plopped the baby on the ground within range of both the wall outlet, fire place, and his penknife on the coffee table. "How hard can it be?"

And that was all I needed to hear.

I did *not* need to get involved.

Did *not* need to warm at his smile.

Did *not* need to wonder why my skin tingled in his presence.

Rem was a good-looking boy when we were kids, but at twenty-seven, he was absolutely *gorgeous*. A hard jaw from hard work. Toughened voice from a tough life. A strong back strengthened through manual labor. He might've tussled with a baby hell-bent on toddling into the fireplace, but he hadn't left the wilds in the forest.

Rem looked as out of place in his own home as the kids did in the middle of the woods.

I had to help him.

Maybe I made this bad decision because it had been so long since I last saw him. Maybe I let my heart lead because the beard disguised him in a dark, tempting mystery. Or maybe I took pity on him because five years ago I had been hopelessly in love with our small town's baddest bad boy.

Rem wasn't a trouble-maker anymore, but he was still in trouble. Especially now that Butterpond had changed so much. We had cell phone reception. Community events. A giant Facebook group where all the busybodies kept in touch. Butterpond wouldn't let him hunker down in the forest and hide forever.

And it must've terrified him.

"How's the farm?" Even his words were jagged, briars in his throat.

Either he was out of practice with small talk or he knew he shouldn't have asked.

"It's a warzone," I said. "but no fires at least."

"Tidus okay?"

"Is he ever?" I smirked. "Tidus hates this town as much as me."

"What about everyone else?"

Well, they wouldn't be happy to hear that Rem came back home. "Julian is...*Julian*. Trying to rebuild the farm like he has any idea how to manage it. Marius is overseas still—he can't tell us where, and he likes it that way. Varius hasn't been the same since the tornado. Quint...God only knows. Runs around like a puppy, but turns rabid the instant any of my brothers look his way."

Rem rummaged through his fridge and offered me a beer. I shook my head. He popped the cap off but didn't drink.

"About your dad..." he said.

"I know."

"Just...I'm sorry."

So was everyone, but I still nodded and accepted the thoughts, prayers, and Bundt cakes.

"We knew it was coming," I said. "His heart was bad."

"Doesn't mean it hurts any less."

I'd done a fantastic job of smooshing that pain deep, deep down and suppressing the memories of the past few months when I'd taken care of him. My brothers understood, but it felt different for me—the one adopted girl in the family of biological sons.

They'd left me alone on the farm with Dad, and the family slowly tore itself apart. Fight after fight, even during Dad's last days. Each of my brothers swore they'd never speak to the others again.

At least, until *that* phone call had to be made.

"The good news...well...news, I guess," I said. "Everyone is home now. In Dad's infinite wisdom, he left the farm to *everyone*. Every decision on the land must be made in unison, *in person*. No subdividing the farm. No selling our pieces to anyone else. It's World War Three with pitchforks and chicken coops."

"Feathers flying?"

"Bombs dropping like eggs."

Tabby attempted to toddle with Rem's wallet into the bathroom. Mellie giggled from inside. Rem excused himself, swore as the toilet flushed, and returned with a soaking wet wallet. He pitched it into the sink and shooed both kids away.

They stayed glued to him, wrapping their arms around his legs like they hadn't been hugged in years. Rem knelt down and welcomed them into his thick arms.

It wasn't a sight I'd expected to see from a man like him.

"So what..." His words mumbled over Tabby's fingers as she clobbered him in the mouth. "What are you...doing?"

"Anything I can to get out of here."

Mellie slid from his side and skipped back to her baby doll. He set Tabby on the counter. I rushed forward before he realized that the one-year-old was a bit hyper and likely to take a tumble. She eagerly offered me more of his possessions. I accepted the jingling keys and his cellphone, but I stopped her before she lunged for a sheathed bowie knife tucked inside a stack of paperwork.

Rem leaned against the sink, sipping his beer. "You're leaving, huh? Where are you planning to go?"

"Anywhere."

"Been there, Sassy." The nickname rolled off his tongue, like he'd never stopped using it. "Running doesn't get you as far as you think."

"Well, I need to get *somewhere*. I love my brothers too much to start hating them."

"You know they need you, especially with your parents gone."

The guilt was already suffocating me. "Jules says I remind them of Mom."

"Yeah. I can see the family resemblance."

As was the gentle joke which passed around the town. I brushed my dark fingers through the bouncing curls I'd swept away with the aid of a bubblegum pink scarf. Didn't matter if my momma was blonde haired and green eyed or if she shared my mahogany skin and fawn eyes, people in Butterpond knew I was her daughter because she'd taught me how to be a lady.

And how to whoop my brothers into shape if they gave me a hard time.

But mostly how to be a good lady.

Also, a *forgiving* woman. She never thumped the Bible, only used it to swat our backsides when we acted out. What would she say about *this*? The man I swore never to forgive…and the kids tumbling around his house.

Mellie climbed the woodpile. Tabby unsuccessfully attempted to roll off the counter, falling into my arms.

And he thought it was going to be easy.

He wouldn't last the night.

"Do you have everything you need for them?" I asked.

Rem nodded. "I got some of their clothes. They brought toys. I set them up in the spare bedroom."

"Well, that's good. But...do you know Tabby's diaper is on backwards?"

He approached the child, picked her up under the arms, and gave her a quick once over.

"Is that why it keeps leaking?" He whistled in realization. "Thought she was an overachiever."

Fantastic. "Okay, Rem...there's like, six things I can see from where I'm standing that will seriously maim the very young children."

He plopped Tabby on the counter and attempted to twist the diaper to the right position. When that didn't work, he undid the tabs with so much force ripped the Velcro, removed the diaper, and left her tush on the cold counter. The diaper flipped, but he couldn't fasten it.

He grabbed his handy electrical tape once more. "There. Now she's got a racing stripe."

If only he could feed, bathe, and entertain the kids with tape too. At least it wasn't a staple gun.

I finally asked the question. "Do you need help, Rem?"

His lazy smile would've been cute if Mellie wasn't heading for the axe he'd set near the backdoor. "You worried about me, Sassy?"

"Worried you're going to end up on the news..." I pointed to the axe wielding Mellie—one blue ox short of a classic American tall tale. "And now I'll be an accomplice."

"Mellie, you chop my house down, you're building the next one." He took the axe from her hands and searched for a place to put it. The cabin was a mess, so he shrugged and stuck it on top of the fridge, clattering a couple pots and pans out of the way. "They're kids. Sure, I need some time to fix the place up..." Rem batted at a spider web over the kitchen window. I cringed as the spider clamored to hide in the dusty curtains. "But they needed me. Emma asked, so here I am.

Someone's gotta help the girls. Just like what your family used to do for all those kids—including me."

"You're certain you can handle it?"

"Got no problems here."

I should have left. The suitcase waited in my car. I had a full-tank of gas. I'd been threatening to head to Ironfield for *two* weeks now.

Rem had the box of supplies. The kids hadn't set fire to the cabin yet.

They'd be *fine*.

But my feet didn't move. "Do you have food for them?"

Rem took a swig from his beer. A liquid dinner might have suited him, but I doubted Mellie and Tabby wanted to lounge on the couch, knocking back a cold six-pack of Juicy Juice.

"I'll find something," he said. "I think it's cute that you're worried."

"I'm not worried." If I was worried, I'd have to stay. "I'm...making conversation."

"Could have done that a long time ago," he said. "Called me up."

And let him know how *twice* in the past five years I'd actually tracked down a contact number for him in the middle of the Canadian wilds? No thanks.

"I didn't hear from you either," I said. "Not even a *hey, sorry about the barn*."

"I am sorry about the barn. Sorry about a lot of things. Sorry I haven't seen you since then."

I stomped down a betraying warmth. No need to open that Pandora's Box. "You were the one who left."

"You didn't want me around."

"I never said that."

"Cause you were too polite. You'd let Julian's fist do the talking."

"He's quite persuasive."

"And if he knew you were up here, asking about my dinner plans?"

I smirked. "Asking about the *kids'* dinner plans."

Rem glanced over his shoulder. "Mellie, want some dinner?"

The little girl marched into the kitchen, dragging Rem's boots on her feet. She stumbled as she walked, but she raised her little chin as if she wore a tiara instead of steel-toed mud buckets.

"I don't like peas," she said.

"Me either. See?" He winked. "We're fine."

This would be fun. I knelt to her level. "Mellie, what else don't you like to eat?"

Her words bumbled in and out of intelligibility. "Chicken. Broccoli. Green. Yogurt. Cars. Dragons. Shoes!"

The answer became a rambling story about a kitten, dragon, and a spaghetti noodle, but she illustrated my point.

"Any ideas, Chef?" I asked.

Rem had attempted to memorize her preferences and got lost somewhere around *worms* and *green*. "I...have some beef jerky."

"You're going to feed beef jerky to some toddlers?"

"Got some trail mix too. A can of soup beans."

"...How long are you keeping the kids?"

"As long as Emma needs."

I raised my eyebrows. "How long do you think you can keep them alive?"

"At least through the night."

Good enough for me. Now it was my turn to leave him. I'd already survived five years without speaking, without resolving anything, without...

Saying those words.

I'd last another five. Maybe by then, he'd be out of jail for child endangerment.

"Start small," I said. "Do you have milk?"

"Well-water."

"Do you want my advice?"

Rem braced himself on the counter, muscles flexing, eyes brightening with a roguish playfulness that made any game unwinnable.

"It's been so long since I've seen you, Cas...I'll take anything you're willing to give."

"Go into town—"

"*Nope*."

I sighed. "Why not?"

"I've gotten real good at avoiding Butterpond."

"Who's the *real* baby here? Get off this mountain. Take the girls into town. Buy some kid-friendly food."

"Like...chew and whiskey?"

I scolded him. "Battery acid and horseradish."

He grimaced, finally realizing the girls couldn't survive on dried meats and wild onions.

"Okay," he said. "This might be hard to believe, Cas...but I might need some help managing this circus. I mean..." His smile turned wicked. "I can pitch a hell of a tent, but beyond that..."

I didn't need the visual. It'd taken years for me to stop fantasizing about it. "It won't be that hard. Just...*feed* them. Make sure they don't set themselves or the forest on fire. Put them to bed. Repeat."

"Go with me," he said.

"Where?"

"To the store."

Nope. Nada. Not happening. "It's right where you left it, Rem."

"How will I know what to buy? Chicken nuggets or liver and onions? Red jello or red wine?"

"You'll figure it out."

He edged a little closer, grabbing Tabby before she tossed his phone against the wall. "Not asking for much, Sassy. Give me a couple pointers."

"I'm on my way out of town." And this time, I meant it.

That smile didn't just slay me—it pinned me against the ropes, powerslammed me to the mat, then grabbed a metal folding chair from the crowd.

"How about one last favor for me?" he asked.

Not a chance. That well had emptied trying to put out the barn fire.

He read my reluctance. "Okay. A favor to the kids?"

Damn it. Tabby gave me a wave of her chubby fingers. Mellie continued to list things she liked, didn't like, and some sounds the baby particularity enjoyed while shouted at the top of her lungs.

I surrendered. "Tell me you have a car seat."

"No, the kids rode up here on top of a wild boar. Have a little faith, Cassi."

"That's the problem," I said. "I don't have much faith left in you."

"Me either." Rem's voice had mellowed with honesty and time. "Just means I can't disappoint you anymore, huh?"

"You've never backed down from a challenge."

"That settles it." His amusement thudded my heart like an axe missing a tree and striking a nearby boulder instead. "I got nothing else to lose, Cas."

"Why's that?"

"Because I already lost you."

2

Remington

I NEVER THOUGHT ANYTHING COULD BE AS BAD AS THE DAY A SPLINTER had wedged in the cushion of my truck's seat. If only I might have stayed so naïve.

Cheerios made for a worse ride. Or were they Lucky Charms? Some sort of dusted cereal had ground into every square inch of my truck. The seats. The windows. The carpets. *Inside the dome light.*

Five hours.

I had the kids for *five hours.*

Where the hell did the cereal come from? Did it sprout from their pockets? And why the hell were their hands perpetually sticky? They seemed to exude some sort of adhesive. Christ, I could have saved on wood glue and just rubbed a toddler over my furniture instead.

I had braced myself for the diapers and the crying and the shrieking. Wasn't that much different from a weekday night on the snowfields with the other loggers who'd run to the far corner of the earth just to escape whatever caused them to pound beer after beer at night. Vomit. Shit. Piss. Tears. They'd prepared me for the ankle-biters.

But no one had told me about the *crumbs*. The girls had a halo of grime that followed them around. Maybe not dirt or anything gross, but a tornado of food bits, fuzz, and inexplicable chocolate.

I didn't even know I had chocolate in the cabin.

Where in the hell had they found it?

Was it even chocolate?

I didn't have a goddamned clue what I was doing.

And I sure as hell hadn't expected to open the door this afternoon and face all of five-foot-nothing Cassia Payne.

That woman was the embodiment—the em*booty*ment—of my every past mistake. She was a good girl every boy wanted to chase, but I was the bad boy who'd cracked that hard, chocolate shell of hers. Unfortunately, before I could get a taste…I'd crushed her heart.

Probably for the best.

I didn't deserve her then. I sure as hell didn't deserve her help grocery shopping now.

"Is this the store?" Mellie swung her legs with the express purpose of ensuring her mismatched tennis shoes could hit my seat.

They could.

Pink shoe struck first. Purple followed, smacking the seat with enough force to feel it in my kidney.

I'd have to find the matching shoes. *If* they'd been packed. Just another item to add to a growing list for the kids. Find their shoes. Use electrical tape to mend the yellow baby blanket that had ripped on the truck's tailgate. Buy more baby shampoo. Stock up on diapers on top of diapers on top of diapers.

In which grocery store aisle would I find my sanity?

I parked next to Cassi's little red Ford Fiesta and breathed a sigh of relief.

This concluded Mellie's twenty solid minutes of ceaseless questions. Twenty minutes of noise. Twenty minutes of sniffles, giggles, and inquisitions.

If a tree fell in the forest, you're goddamned right it made a thud. If a three-year-old fell in the forest, it'd be a half-hour of philosophical discussion into the hows, whys, wheres, whens, and indignities of the tumble. And then they'd demand a cookie.

I wasn't used to *talking*.

Wasn't used to *kids*.

And I wasn't used to Cassi.

"I'm impressed." She greeted me with a playful tease. "You remembered the way to the store."

I'd sweated in the Butterpond summer for a solid day now, but Cassi's smile was warmer than any record heat. But that hesitance in her voice? The *hurt*? That was a splash of icy water. Like tripping into a puddle in the winter and peeling away the soaked denim sticking to your calf.

"Wasn't hard," I said. "It's the only building in town."

I unhooked Mellie from her seat. Apparently, this was permission for her to bolt across the parking lot without checking to see the rusted Toyota creeping between the lanes. Cassi caught the kid before she skateboarded across the lot on an abandoned cart.

I hated the store—hated the owners more—but I shrugged. "I guess I either get some food here or I pilfer it from the mayor."

Cassi smirked. "I think he's still holding a grudge from the last time you *pilfered*."

One time. I'd broken into his kitchen *one time*, and we got caught. "That was Tidus's idea. He wanted to swipe the old man's ice cream. Just horsing around."

Cassi knew the story. Apparently, all of Butterpond had heard. "And what did you take instead?"

Tabby squealed as I lugged her from the car seat. The kids were too young and Cassi too sheltered to hear the truth about my teenage prank. We'd swiped a pair of panties from the mayor's gold-digging, twenty-five-year-old wife. Some secrets were best left to the past.

"Helped ourselves to his whiskey and cigars," I said.

"Which you smoked and drank in the jail cell."

She made it sound worse than it was. "And where do you think the evidence ended up? Sherriff Samson hadn't had a raise in three years, but he made up for it with a box of Mayor Cowdar's finest cigars that night."

Mellie squealed, stomped, and tugged on Cassi's hand.

"Let's go!" Her little pout would be adorable for the next five minutes...until she had enough of the store and pitched a fit in the checkout. "*Please.*"

"Future bargain shopper." Cassi winked. She helped me settle Tabby into a cart, somehow knowing where the store kept the wet naps to sterilize every touchable surface.

"Do you...shop here?" I asked. "This is Barlow's place."

She didn't tolerate my pouting and shoved me inside the Shop N' Mart with a sigh.

"We're adults now, Rem. We can all shop in the Barlow's family store without it devolving into chaos and bloodshed."

Didn't matter that the store sold six-packs at the entrance or that the rotisserie chickens smelled so damn good. No double coupon could cheapen *loyalty*.

"They're *Barlows*," I said.

"Get used to it...unless you want to drive another thirty minutes to Hunter's Ridge to shop for animal crackers."

It might have been worth it.

"You remember the time the Barlows beat Tidus to a pulp, right?" I asked. She didn't listen, pushing the cart into the produce section. I ignored the chipper colors and decent prices. "Remember how they used to harass Jules? Know how many tires were slashed? Fist fights?"

Her slim finger wagged near my face. "Don't you pretend like you and my brothers were innocent in that feud." Mellie mimicked Cassi's sass and wiggled her hand too. Great. They were ganging up on me. "I've heard the stories, Remington."

"From *who*? Your brothers would never have told you about the shit that went down."

She twisted a curl between her fingers. Those big eyes looked away. Guilty? Or was she *actually* considering purchasing the freshly misted napa cabbage?

"I heard it from Matthew Barlow."

"And what the fuc—" Both little girls stared up at me with innocent eyes. "What were you doing with *Matt Barlow*?"

Cassi shrugged. "He took me out for coffee."

My blood ran cold. Cassi with *that* son of a bitch?

Out for *coffee*?

Doing fucking *god knew what* with a *Barlow Boy*?

I grunted. "What the hell did you do when I was gone?"

The store wasn't big enough for the massive shopping cart, let alone the four little arms that darted out in every direction to smash the fruits, vegetables, and bright candies *inconveniently* located next to the potato bin.

Cassi fumed hot enough to bake every spud into dinners for the next week. She set her jaw, planted her feet, and sunk her hands onto curves she didn't have before I left.

The old Cassi would have stormed away. No bite but enough bluster to blow up her skirt.

This one stood her ground on perfect hourglass hips. She puffed her perky, suddenly full chest. Turned that baby-soft dark skin into armor. And faced me down.

Where had little Cassia Payne gone?

And how could I convince the gorgeous woman standing in her place to go home with me?

"While *you* were gone..." She threatened me with a carrot before bagging half a dozen. "I grew up."

"Don't have to tell me twice." I grabbed the biggest zucchini from the display and wiggled it before her. She had enough class to ignore the metaphor.

Mellie whined and attempted to flee the cart. I helped her to the floor before she cracked her head off the linoleum. And Cassi said the kids would be hard to handle.

"You were just a sprout when I left," I said.

"And now?"

She'd placed a hand on the honeydews. The melons had nothing on her.

"Talk about blue-ribbon produce," I teased.

Cassi didn't giggle. "Well, I wasn't waiting around to get *judged*, thank you very much."

"So you let *Matt Barlow* ring you up?"

She scooted the cart towards the onions and garlic. "*Once.*"

"One time too many."

The potatoes weren't the only ones in the produce section with eyes. I recognized the old bitty spying from around the stacks heads of lettuce. Darla Kaslovski peeked over her cheaters before dropping the chained, pink rims to her chest. The glasses smacked off her bust and narrowly avoided getting crushed in the cavern that was sixty-six-year-old Darla's deliberately low-cut cleavage. That sight had haunted me before I left for the logging camp. Now, the liver spots scarred a new generation.

Mellie pointed at her, gasped, and shouted for the entire store to hear. "*Ursula!*"

I didn't know who that was, but Cassi did. She silenced the girl before Mellie delighted Darla with a medley of Disney songs.

I gave Darla a wave. She huffed, grabbed her cart, and sped off to gossip.

Cassi leaned in. "Hasn't forgiven you for tie-dying her French poodle ten years ago."

"Should have charged the dog for that damned haircut. Beau drank more Kool-Aid than we put in his fur."

Mellie padded to the cart, inexplicably finding a box of Oreos. She'd ripped them open eaten three already. Whatever. It kept her quiet. I plunked her in the cart next to the broccoli.

Cassi gestured to the opened Oreos. "Are you going to say anything?"

Oh. Right. I pointed at Mellie. "Share with your sister."

"Shoplifting is the advanced childrearing course." Cassi sighed and tucked the potatoes under the cart. "So much for her dinner."

"I don't like that." Mellie pointed to the sack. She carefully counted every other vegetable in the cart. "Don't like that. Don't like that. Don't like that."

Cassi pushed the girls towards the fruit. "What about apples? Do you like apples?"

"Nope!"

"I do." I shooed Cassi away from the green ones. "Not those. Got enough tarts in my life."

"That so?"

"I like it sweet." I moved behind Cassi, accidentally brushing her arm. Christ, the woman even smelled like innocence—a soft whisper of vanilla. "Peaches are my favorite. Love the juice."

She pretended she wasn't amused. "Until you choke on the pit."

"I'm much more adept than that," I said. "Gotta use your tongue, hands, teeth."

"*Teeth?*"

I chomped down with a smile. "I could show you."

She hummed. "I wouldn't trust you with a peach—you'd leave it bruised."

"Sometimes that's more fun."

"Ah, right." She tiptoed her fingers over a display of almonds. "Now *these*...these are my favorite."

I winked. "All good girls like a little nut."

"You haven't seen me crush one yet."

"Say the word, and I'll bust one myself."

"Charming as ever, aren't you, Rem?"

"I remember you liking it."

"Oh, to be young and *stupid* again."

Mellie practically leapt out of the cart. I followed her gaze and grinned. "Thatta girl, Mel."

Apparently, we both had an affinity for cherries. I offered the bag to Cassi. She stayed quiet.

"So, what's Matt Barlow got on me?" I asked.

"Nothing you're ever going to find out."

"I like cherries," Mellie said.

"Me too, kid." I shrugged at Cassi. "But it's not a deal-breaker."

"What happens between you and your refrigerator is none of my business." Cassi stole the cart. "Okay, let's get you some chicken nuggets."

Tabby squawked, her face a mess of chocolate cookie. The sugar and excitement practically bounced Mellie into the aisles.

"So much food!" She grinned. "I was so hungry!"

Good thing Cassi drove the cart. My heart lurched. Hard.

"How hungry?" Cassi played along. She didn't know it wasn't a game.

"Mommy had no dinners."

Cassi glanced at me. Great. How the hell was I supposed to explain it with the kids right there?

"Chemo." I guessed a poison was a poison. "Emma would get nauseous. Didn't like anything in sight."

"Poor thing."

Yeah. Right. "Mellie, you can have anything you want. Go ham."

"Ew." She scrunched her nose. "Ham."

"You don't like a lot of things, do you?"

Cassi grinned. "Not going to get any easier."

No. It wasn't, but not for the reasons she thought. I nodded behind her. Her smile faded.

Julian Payne was the very model of a Payne man—an irritating prick with a self-righteous belief in doing what was right for the family, even if it meant pissing everyone off. Which meant I was in trouble.

My best friend, Tidus, had sent Cassi to the cabin, but apparently, he hadn't told his eldest brother I was in town. Or that I hauled two little girls around with me to the grocery store.

Farm life did the boy good—Jules was what now? Thirty-three? Thirty-four?

Old enough to take his shit seriously, and Christ, was he *serious*.

"Hey, Cas." Jules knew better than to call Cassi to his side like a dog. She wouldn't have answered when she was a kid, and she'd probably take out his knees now. He glared at me with those sharp Payne green eyes all the men shared. "What the hell are you doing back?"

No greeting? No small talk.

Yeah. Probably didn't deserve any, especially from Jules.

"Shopping," I said.

"It's fine, Jules." Cassie edged between me, the cart, the kids, and her brother. "I'm helping Rem shop for the kids."

Jules frowned. "They're yours?"

I hadn't become so degenerate that I was knocking up random women. "They're my nieces."

"Emma's sick," Cas said.

Wished she hadn't told him. Last thing I needed was anyone spreading that news. Though anything was better than the story of Julian Payne interrogating me in the middle of the produce aisle like I was a damn criminal.

I hadn't broken a law or a heart in five years. I planned to keep it that way.

Mellie introduced herself by nearly snapping her ankle as she tumbled from the cart. She spotted a display of Cheerios across the store and took off running, arms outstretched, screeching like a banshee until she collided with the boxes. They toppled over her. Mellie *oophed*, but she delighted in the cereal avalanche.

Jules watched her with a cheap ass grin. "Yeah. She's definitely a Marshall."

"Jules." Cassie's scold was noted and ignored by both of us. "He's doing something good."

"For once."

Her voice lowered. "It's been a long time."

"Think that makes it *right*?" Jules snapped.

The Payne boys puffed themselves up when they thought it'd intimidate folks. Always using their strength instead of their heads. I did it too, but I learned a little too late that broad shoulders could withstand everything except the weight of everyone's hatred.

Jules wasn't happy. "You think buying the kids some Oreos makes up for the money we blew and the stress we lived with? We almost lost the farm because of him!"

Good thing Mellie had decided to construct a fort out of the cereal boxes. And Tabby didn't understand much of what was happening anyway. Just thought of me as a giant man with hair on his chin that she could tug. The girls didn't have a clue that I was out of my element, and they knew even less of the past that shadowed me everywhere I slunk.

"Not looking for trouble, Jules," I said. "Just gotta drag my niece out of Fruit Loop canyon over there, and I'll be gone."

"For good?"

"I'm not camping out in Barlow's store. Got a cabin in the mountains."

"Still too close for my liking."

Mine too. "I'm minding my own business."

Jules jerked his thumb towards Cassi. "Doesn't look like it. Looks like you're hanging around some of our business again."

Cassi stiffened. "That *business* has a name."

That didn't please her brother. "Oh, you better not be selling anything...especially to some lowlife like Remington Marshall."

Tabby clapped her hands. "*Rem!*"

Enough was enough. I wasn't much of a man after what I'd done, but I still had to care for my own. No sense letting the kids hear the bullshit, even if it was all true. Mellie gave me a decent escape as she now set siege to the frozen meat case from her cereal castle.

I glanced to Cassi. "Thanks for the help. Go back with Jules. I got it from here."

She frowned. "Rem—"

"I got it. Feed em, bathe em, no fires."

"But..."

"All I need is another pack of diapers for the kid *you* seem to think should be drinking more water and milk. I'll take care of the walking sprinkler and head home. I got this."

She sighed. "Don't forget the nuggets. And some frozen veggies too."

We'd survive.

"It was…" Fantastic. Mind-blowing. *Heartbreaking*. "Good to see you."

"Yeah." Her voice softened. "Same here."

Jules didn't bother looking at me. "Don't let me catch you pissing around with Tidus or my sister. You're no good for them."

It was the truth. Also didn't matter. Only thing I had to worry about now was the baby dead-set on kicking me in the balls from the cart's seat. Also the terror-stricken toddler suddenly weeping over the Cheerios box, fearing she'd hurt the cartoon bee.

The kids were the only reason I was in town. I'd give it a couple weeks, drop them off with Emma, and I'd be done. No need to worry about anything else.

No need to bother Cassi. To see Cassi.

To apologize. To beg for forgiveness.

No need to steal her back.

I'd already hurt her once. I wouldn't break her heart twice.

3

Cassi

One overprotective big brother was a problem.

Two was a coincidence.

Three brothers, and it felt like a conspiracy.

Four was *ridiculous*.

Five arrogant, combative, devoted brothers was a nightmare.

I wasn't a little girl anymore, one who needed to have her bullies silenced or desserts snuck into her room while she was supposed to be grounded. I'd grown up. Probably more than them. Took on the responsibilities of Dad and the farm and my own education.

It wasn't that I didn't need them anymore—in fact, the family needed each other more than ever.

But...

And that was a mighty big *but*...

I didn't need my older brother defending my honor in the middle of the produce section.

Especially as, for the first time since I'd known the man, Rem wasn't looking for a fight. Hell, he hadn't even pushed back. But *why*? Rem had never missed a chance to brawl in a bushel of Brussels sprouts before.

How much trouble did Remington Marshall get himself into by taking in those little girls?

Fortunately, Butterpond had a system for conflict resolution and community outreach. When illnesses struck, chicken noodle soups and chili was delivered to the sick. When a death occurred, the residents mourned over their stoves and baked pastries until the grief passed or arteries clogged. Picnics were potluck, church events casseroles, and Christmas buried us in cookies.

But I wasn't sure what to bring to apologize for my brother almost turning the Shop N' Mart into a cage match. A fruit salad didn't say—*I'm sorry, but my family has decided it's easier to threaten you than admit how much it hurt when you left us.* A pot roast should have been saved for a man who didn't break my heart. And a pie...well, there were terrible connotations there. I wasn't bringing a cream pie within five feet of a man who would think of it as a challenge. Apple was too obvious a temptation. And cherry?

Ha.

No way.

I decided on neutral ground. A sandwich ring. Nothing said cordiality like bologna.

I pulled up to the cabin and frowned. Why did he insist on leaving the front door open? I hauled the sandwich ring to the porch and rapped on the door with my foot.

"Hey..." My voice choked off. I nearly dropped the food.

Rem finished spraying the charred rug in front of the fireplace and set the fire extinguisher on the couch. He tapped out a scorched corner with his boot then kicked the frosted, destroyed rug towards the garbage in the kitchen.

He'd shaved his beard.

Not all of it. Just trimmed it close to his jaw. An immaculately chiseled jaw. The dark beard sculpted his face. Not such a wild, mountain savage anymore. Rem might have been the most beautiful man I'd ever seen.

I tucked the sandwiches on the counter and smiled. "Did I miss the show?"

Mellie used the cushion as a trampoline to careen up and over the back of the sofa. She landed at my feet and grinned. Tabby also played on the sofa, though Rem had foreseen her inevitable fall. A half dozen pillows padded the floor to catch the baby as she rolled off the side.

"I got it under control," Rem said.

"What happened?"

"As best I can tell…" He poked around inside the hearth. "I think PJ Sparkles got too close to the fire."

Mellie shook her head. Her pigtails waggled…one near her ear, the other on top of her head. An admirable effort from Uncle Rem. At least he hadn't used tape.

She pointed at him. "BJ was cold!"

"PJ," he corrected.

"I like BJ!"

He winked at me, but I cautioned him with a wagging finger.

"Careful."

Rem shrugged. "Show me a guy who wouldn't like a BJ."

I wasn't getting sucked into that discussion. "You missed a spot."

Rem stomped on another flickering ember. While he knelt, he examined the fireplace with a poker. "Cas, you know kids better than I do. Is this an accident or a sacrifice?"

He retrieved the melted plastic doll from the fireplace—hair singed away, cheeks charred, eyes a puddle of plastic. Mellie screamed in abject terror and bolted from the room. Tabby, delighted by the new game, mimicked and stormed off down the hall, chasing her sister with an equally shrill squeal.

"You might have some nightmares tonight." I warned.

"Great." He popped the horrific doll into the garbage and tapped a hand over the sandwich ring. "What's this for?"

"They couldn't write *Sorry My Brother Is A Prick* on a cake. Though the bakery did offer to condense the message into a rather convincing doodle."

This gave Rem too much ammunition. He crossed his arms, the green flannel a forest dark against the chestnut of his eyes. He'd trimmed his hair too. Neat and tidy. Damn. Now he knew how sexy he looked. He'd use that to every advantage he could.

His smirk was a blend of playboy arrogance and smug satisfaction. "You were worried about me."

I corrected him before he got too cocky. "I was worried about the *kids*."

"Nah, that's not it." He swiped a dishrag from the sink and attempted to de-goo a puddle of dried orange juice from the counter. His eyes never left mine. "I bet you couldn't stop thinking about me last night."

I thought about him most nights. Last night was no different. "You know it. You're just like a popcorn kernel stuck between my teeth."

"You were lying awake all night because of me."

"Yep. Like a mosquito bite on my ankle."

"Bet you couldn't sleep."

"Know how your sock sometimes flips upside down in your shoe?" I took the dishrag from him and tackled another speck of unidentifiable sticky that had dripped down his counters. "You're *that*. Except there's also a splinter in the toe."

He leaned a little closer, his voice low. "Bet you wished you could have called me."

"Yeah, I wanted you as much as I wanted a never-ending case of the hiccups."

"Bet you wished I'd called you."

My chest tightened. "No way. You'd be the reason my phone dies at fifteen percent."

Too much. Too fast. Rem moved close, and I suffocated in his confidence, his *pride*. One second I couldn't breathe, the next...this broken heart would flutter to life.

"What did you want me to say to you last night?" he whispered. "Tell me what I can say."

Nothing.

There was nothing that would quell five years' worth of rage, disappointment, and *hurt*.

And this tingling mess of emotions wasn't helping. I shoved it down with a sigh, but a deep breath only fueled the confusion. His scent overwhelmed me—a blend of freshly cut wood and salty sweetness like freshly tapped maple. Just the sort of manliness that'd cling to pillows, sheets, and girls who stayed a little too long for their welcome.

I pushed him away with the prod of my finger. "I'm only here to drop off the sandwiches."

"You know the way to a man's heart, Cas."

"Yeah. Now give me the roadmap out."

"Probably vegetables."

A bucket of sponges and rags rested on the coffee table. Rem had found a vacuum from the seventies and parked it near the entryway. I plucked the feather duster from Mellie as she pixy-pranced into the kitchen and used it to brush the dirt off Tabby. No dice. I picked the baby up and stared at the dark streaks over her pudgy cheeks.

"You weren't a dirty blonde yesterday." I held her out to Rem. "How'd she get so dirty?"

"The house has been empty for a long time." He took her from me with a wince. "I'm not sure if she's a baby or a dust bunny."

"Just don't toss her in the garbage."

"Maybe she'd cry less in there?" He looked in her eyes. Her little lip pouted as she shared his furrowed expression. "Maybe I could just put the top on and muffle the sound. Then we'd be quiet again, huh Tabby?"

"*No!*" She patted his cheeks. It appeared to be her favorite word. She giggled as she said it, her face lighting up then going grumpy in an instant for appropriate drama. "*No!*"

The cabin was still standing, but dirt was the glue holding it together. I brushed the duster along the curtains near the window. A plume of dust puffed over Mellie as she rushed to my side, hopped on one foot, and doodled a smiling face into the grime of the glass.

"Rem, I think you need a good spring...summer cleaning," I said. "Your cobwebs are growing cobwebs."

"A little mess is healthy."

"Yeah, but I could grow Jules' planned allotment of corn in the dirt by the entryway." I dusted a bit harder, brushing a year's worth of fuzz and debris from the window sill and wooden planked walls. "Do you need help with this? It's a big job."

"I thought you were just delivering some sandwichs."

Mellie twirled in the golden sparkles drifting through the patch of sun. Then she sneezed.

"Pass me the broom," I said.

"Now Cassia Payne..." He handed over the broom with a low hum. "If you aren't here to let me win your heart...you must be avoiding the farm."

The broom's stiff bristles scoured the wooden floor. It felt good. I pitched the pillows and cushions from my path and swept my irritation into the dust pan.

"Jules was out of line yesterday," I said. "He shouldn't have said those things to you."

Rem shrugged. Did the rest of him ripple too? How much muscle had this lumberjack packed on while away in the woods?

"He wasn't wrong."

I could still be embarrassed for my brother. "It wasn't right to say it. And he knows it. He'd apologize—"

"Jules will never apologize. And that's fine. I'm not looking to earn any respect. I'm only in town to watch the kids."

Nothing had ever sounded so *bizarre* from Rem. When he'd left, he was a bastard. A heartless man who I couldn't believe had hurt my family so badly.

Now?

He'd returned from across the continent to take care of his *nieces*.

What had happened to him out in the wilderness?

"Jules took Dad's death hard…" I stopped. That wasn't right. "*Everyone* took Dad's death hard. Jules especially, since he's the executor of the estate. Marius is guilty because he was overseas when it'd happened. Tidus has all these issues now—he'd said some really terrible things to Dad before he died. Hadn't even come home for three years. Varius…well, after he lost his faith, he lost interest in everything. Hasn't been the same since he quit the ministry. And Quint is trying to keep it together, but he hates it here the most."

Rem offered me a beer. I declined, but he popped off two caps anyway. "And now that the perfect storm of Payne is all gathered in one farmhouse?"

"It's chaos. They're fighting. Constantly. All of them. Jules and Quint. Tidus and Dad's ghost. Varius and *everyone*. Marius hasn't even called from Afganikoreapakiindonesiastan or wherever his classified post is now. Quint is just making it worse for the fun of it. Every day someone is screaming or punching a wall. It's not right." I stabbed the floor with the broom. "We're supposed to be *mourning*."

"What about you? How are *you* doing?"

A lot of people had asked me that. Rem's question felt like the only one that wasn't a platitude, and I hated how it twisted inside me.

"I'm *done*." I punctuated the words with a sweep out the door and onto the porch. Mellie followed, brushing her own pile of invisible dirt with a magazine. "I spent last year taking care of Dad. I lived at home, gave up a teaching opportunity in Ironfield. But I *had* to do it. He was practically bed bound by the end, legs too swollen to walk or do much. And where were my brothers?" I extended my arms. "Nowhere to be seen. None of them could deal with what was happening to Dad. After Mom died, and after the fighting started, none of them could stand to be in the same room with each other. Everything went to hell."

That wasn't the truth. The stress and fighting had started before Mom died—when we lost the barn, the season's stored hay, and two cows. But Rem probably knew that. It'd been his fault.

I plucked the Maxim out of Mellie's hands and offered her the broom instead. Rem had the decency to look shamed, but I *thwapped* it over his head.

"You know, you really ought to babyproof this place," I said.

"What needs to be babyproofed?"

I pointed to the outlets, including the unfinished one near the bathroom. "Oh, I don't know. Those fixtures."

"Do babies really poke things into the outlets? Sounds like an urban legend."

"Not sure you want to rail against helicopter parenting on the issue of *electrocution*."

He reluctantly nodded. "Fine. Electrical sockets. I'll take care of it."

"And the cabinets."

"What about them?"

To illustrate my point, Mellie dove inside the cabinet under the sink, crawled all the way back, and returned to deliver her uncle a present that was either the world's largest clump of hair or a mummified mouse. He frowned, pitched it outside, and set her on the counter to wash her hands.

"Cabinets." He agreed. "I'll nail 'em shut. What else?"

"I...don't know." I grabbed a toddling Tabby to give her a squeeze. She clapped, squealed, and tooted in delight. "I mean, there's a million and one things they can get into up here. What about the big outlay building outside?"

"The woodshop?" Rem shook his head. "Nah. Millie and I went over that. That's off-limits."

"Is it locked?"

"Think it should be locked?"

"What's inside?"

"Woodworking stuff. Saws. Power tools. Hammers. Nails." He winked. "Balloons. Slides. Stuffed animals. A waterfall of chocolate."

"Lock it," I said. "*Trust me*. Keep everything sharp over there. These girls are going to be a handful. They'll need constant supervision. You'll have to make sure they're on a schedule. Breakfast, lunch, dinner, bath time, bed time. Are you sure you're up to this?"

His expression said no, but I'd never known Remington Marshall to admit defeat. "Look, Mary Poppins, if you're so worried...why don't you grab your magic umbrella and stay up here?"

I crinkled my nose. "What?"

"Want a job?"

"Doing what?"

"Be their nanny."

Never knew Rem to have such a sense of humor. I retrieved the broom and stepped over Mellie as she made dust-angels in the foyer.

"Okay," I said. "I charge twenty dollars an hour, and I want benefits."

"Done."

"Did I say twenty? I meant fifty."

Rem didn't blink. "Whatever you want. Name your price."

"You're not serious."

"You said this place is a death trap. And, apparently, I'm unprepared for the responsibility of keeping two kids alive. I agree. When do you want to start?"

"I'm not..." I tapped my nails on the broomstick. "No. I'm not going to be a *nanny*. I'm leaving, remember? Friend in Ironfield. Looking for a job in the city."

"Doing what?"

Damn it. "...Early childhood education."

He poked at Tabby, earning a slobbery smile. "Well, look at that. I happen to have an early child right here. And the other one could probably use some education too before she's adopted into a dust mite society."

"I'm not...I can't be a nanny."

"You know kids. You know what to do for kids. And you like these kids."

He thrust Tabby at me, revealing one pudgy little tummy as her shirt rode up. I gave her a tickle, utilizing my sixty-thousand-dollar education to become an expert in giggles.

"You need the money, don't you?" he asked.

I grumbled. "I do."

"So?"

Out of the question. "Absolutely not."

He lowered Tabby to the ground and offered her a plastic bowl of Cheerios. The cereal immediately spilled, but the bowl made an excellent drum. The baby was content, and he set his sights on me.

"Give me one good reason you'll say no," he said.

I'd give him the best one. "We're not even going to talk about the kisses?"

Wrong reason.

Rem's voice lowered, a dark and caramel growl that layered me with regret and shivers and memories.

"Must have been some good kisses if you remember them after all this time," he said.

I didn't look at his lips. "You mean you forgot?"

"I made myself forget."

"Why?"

"Because thinking of that night when you were almost mine is the reason I had to put three thousand miles of uncut wilderness and five years between us."

In the past twenty-four hours, this man had made my heart ache so much I considered popping some of Dad's leftover beta-blockers. I wasn't about to let Rem twist me up any more.

"No one asked you to leave," I said. "No one told you to go. It's not heroic, Rem. It just hurts."

"Good thing I'm a changed man."

I'd never wanted him to change, only to be *honest*. "How can I trust you?"

"I'll prove it. I got the kids. I got the bank account. The cabin. The responsibility. I'm different."

"You're still chasing me."

His hound-dog grin should have run me up a tree. "Can't blame a man for trying. It's lonely in these woods. Gets real dark and cold at night. I'm looking for someone to warm me up."

"And that's why the answer is *no*. We have a history."

"Do we?"

The sadness kicked me in the gut. "We *might* have had a history."

"Do you think there's still a chance?"

"How could there be, after all that happened?"

He surprised me with a wink. "Then what's the problem? Are you attracted to me?"

"No," I lied.

"Then work for me."

"I can't."

He smoothed that beard. Easier to see his smile. Harder to resist wondering how it'd feel scratching all over me. "What if I show you that this could be perfectly platonic?"

"How?"

"Kiss me."

I poked him away with the broom. "And what would that prove?"

"That there's nothing between us."

"That's like leaving my credit card in the street to prove there are no thieves around."

"Not trying to steal anything from you, Sassy."

That's because there was only one thing left to give him, and I'd mercifully avoided that roll in the hay. "You're out of your mind."

"*One* kiss," he said. "We'll settle it once and for all."

I focused on cleaning as I scrubbed my way into the kitchen, hoping my hips didn't sashay with every brush. He watched, his gaze practically boiling over my skin.

"Why not?" Rem asked.

I didn't have to lie. "Because it took me five years to get over our last kiss, and I can't spend the next five forgetting *this* one."

"*One* kiss." He edged too close for me to breathe, think, or defend my honor. "One little, teensy, tiny nibble of a kiss. I promise—I won't even make it a good one."

"Is that possible?"

"I don't know. I've never kissed badly before."

"Then I can't afford the risk."

"For all we know, every kiss of mine becomes a five-year memory." He towered over me, leaning in, his whisper playful and tempting. "And that's just the kiss. Imagine what I could do with a touch. A lick. One night with me, and you might never forget it."

"Or forgive it."

"Good thing I'm only asking for a kiss." He bumped my chin up with his fingers. "One kiss."

"To prove there's nothing between us...or to torture us for the rest of our lives?"

"You tell me, Sassy."

He leaned in, capturing my lips with a playful, deliberate swipe. I gripped the broom, heart raging, pounding, attempting to crash through my chest and knock my head back into sanity.

Heat swirled between us, suffocating me in that woodsy, fresh-cut pine scent. Earthy and tempting and so much *more* than he was before. Everything was *more*. His words meant more. His eyes saw more. His touch offered more.

And his kiss...

Conquered and overwhelmed. My body pooled into softness. A murmur accidentally parted my lips. His tongue swept in. Gentle. Teasing. Wonderful.

His kiss was every perfect moment I'd imagined in the last five years. Every flirty nibble. Every sensual bite. Every casual, quick peck people took for granted.

In five seconds, he'd revealed everything he might have offered in those lost five years.

And I hated him for it.

And I was grateful for it.

And I melted for it.

Rem pulled away, rubbing a hand through the tickling beard trimmed to his jaw. His eyebrows rose.

"So?"

From behind us, Mellie expressed her displeasure with a drum solo on Tabby's bowl.

"*Ew kissing!*"

This was *not* an *ew*.

This was great. And wonderful.

And the perfect reason to run away as fast as my now jelly-like legs could move.

"I won't be the nanny," I said.

Rem didn't believe me. "Come on, Cas. I was just having some fun."

I handed him the broom, tapped the sandwiches, waved to the kids, and hurried to the door before I melted into a puddle of wistful remorse.

"Good luck, Rem," I said. "I've got to go home and pack. I'm leaving for Ironfield as soon as I can."

He followed me to the door, leaning against the frame as I stumbled over the cobblestones to my car. His voice was a mockingly cruel and lovely tease.

"Was the kiss that bad?"

"No…"

I regretted turning, but I needed that one last look.

How many more times would be the *last time* I ever saw him?

"No, Rem. That kiss was too good."

4

Remington

CASSI'S CAR SKIDDED TO A STOP IN FRONT OF MY CABIN.

She leapt out. Slammed the door. Shouted my name.

"Remington Marshall! Get out here!"

Cassi always did have a temper on her. Her pout could drop a man to his knees. That little cock of her hip was a quick and dire warning to behave. And that eyebrow. That was the worst. As soon as her fingertip traced over that mischievous arch, even the bravest soul knew to surrender.

So, I always used to try to piss her off.

Who wouldn't risk a good tongue-lashing from a beautiful girl like her?

I'd toss a water balloon in her window at night. A firecracker at her feet on the way to school. I couldn't count the number of times I'd let the goats loose just before she had to feed them. Hard to chase a herd of hungry, garbage eating monsters when she was locked in the chicken coup.

When we were young, I'd fucked with her in every way but the best one. Why would I miss a chance to screw with her now?

"Hey, Sassy." I reclined on the porch swing and crossed my legs on the railing. "Couldn't resist the chance to see me again, huh?"

She stomped up the porch stairs. "Rem, I swear to God…"

Tabby gummed on Barbie and waved with four chubby fingers.

Cassi caught herself mid-profanity. "What in the…Harry Potter is *this*?"

The envelope smacked against the railing with a thud. The flap opened, revealing a stack of green as bright as the trees I'd chopped to earn it.

"That's your advance, Cas."

Worth it to watch her squirm. And money well spent to get that fabulous ass back to the cabin.

The two days we'd spent apart had lasted a goddamned eternity. Felt longer than the five years I'd gone without her. It wasn't just her eyes, her voice, the sexy way she'd mewed when I'd finally taken the kiss that had been owed to me for half a decade. I'd spent so long dreaming of this woman that when I finally had her in my arms again, it seemed like yet another fantasy.

I had to see her again.

Her hand settled on her hip, and what a hip it was. The pair of tiny shorts covered her booty, but they were skin tight. She was a tiny, five-foot thing, but her pint-sized legs reached to her chin. Dark. Smooth. Just begging for a hand to run along that perfect skin.

She spat the word. "My *advance*?"

"Yeah." I sipped a beer and pawed through the half dozen rocks, toys, and wood chips Tabby had placed in my lap. I found the coaster and set my bottle on the handmade bench beside me. "I thought you could use it. Get something pretty for yourself and some supplies for the kids."

A wagging finger. Good sign. "What *supplies* for the kids?"

"Whatever you want. Finger paints or tricycles. More diapers. Do you know how many diapers this kid goes through in a day?"

She bit her lip. Now she was really cooking. "Are you even listening to yourself?"

"Yeah, you're right. They're too young for paints. Maybe get them some crayons. Oh, and one of those puffy plastic baby books. Tabby loves to gnaw on them."

All one hundred and twenty pounds of Cassi bumbled onto my steps, seething with frustration, rage, and, presumably, an unquenchable lust that made her quite irritable.

"I *told* you." She spoke through gritted teeth. "I'm not going to be their nanny."

"And I decided I wasn't going to take *no* for an answer."

"That's not how this works."

"You'd be perfect for this job."

It wasn't just a tease. Goddamn it, I needed her help. She'd panicked me into believing the entire cabin was a death trap. Exposed outlets. Cabinets with cleaning products. Wobbly railings. I'd been so fucking terrified, I nearly slept in the truck with the kids buckled up tight in their car seats.

"I'm sure you could handle them yourself," she said.

I couldn't.

"Who wouldn't want an expert around to show them the ropes?" I shrugged. "I also have handcuffs if you prefer. Blindfolds…"

"Rem."

"Cassi."

She crossed her arms. "Look, if you're worried, there's a big ol' woods behind you. I'm sure there's a pack of wolves that can show you how to raise a kid."

"Won't you at least consider it?"

"No."

This was my fault. I shouldn't have kissed her. I knew it'd be a mistake, even if it hadn't felt like anything but the most right, honest, and most perfect thing in the world. For years, I'd hated myself for letting her go. At least in those few seconds pressed against her, I'd found a moment of peace.

"You know the kids would love you, right?" I nudged Tabby with my hand. She babbled and offered Cassi a handful of ground up cereal mixed with a bit of drool.

"*Bababa*," Tabby said.

"See?" I took a breath. "Don't make a baby beg."

"She's convincing." Cassi gave her a big kiss on the cheek. "Where's Melanie?"

I jerked a thumb behind me, into the house. "Playing with her dolls."

"Are you sure?"

"That's what she was doing five minutes ago."

"…But you don't know what she's doing now?"

"There's no houses for ten miles, so I think I'd notice an UBER pull up."

Her mouth gaped. "You left her unsupervised in the house?"

"Relax." I picked up the beer, offered her a sip, and drank the rest when she refused. "I hid my dad's old magazines. No fires today. She can't get into any trouble in there."

Cassi didn't believe me. She marched into the house, searched the living room then returned with a scowl. "Sure, she can't get into any trouble *in there*."

"That's what I said."

"You're right. She's not in there."

"What?"

She rapped her fingernails on the door. "I don't see her."

"She's tiny. Look down."

"I *am* looking down." She headed into the house. "I'm looking everywhere, Rem. I don't see her!"

I rolled my eyes and hauled the baby into my arms. "I'm sure she's playing."

Cassi ducked into the kitchen, checking the cabinets that weren't nailed shut. "Seriously. I can't find her."

Great. This morning we'd played a rousing game of *wake-up-Uncle-Remington-by-jumping-between-his-legs-so-we-never-get-a-cousin.* At lunch, Mellie delighted me with her one-act play, *I-don't-want-to-eat-that-I-don't-like-chicken-even-though-I-ate-it-twice-yesterday*. And just before Tabby's nap, I learned of a new sport, *scream-so-the-baby-won't-sleep.*

Now it was hide-and-seek. I couldn't take much more of this. When did we play my favorite pastime, *drink-until-the-whiskey-tastes-good?*

"Mellie!" I shouted down the hall. "Get out here."

"Mellie?" Cassi checked the bedrooms. The cabin wasn't huge. She scoured the potential closets in less than a minute. "Mellie, where are you?"

Damn it. I shifted Tabby to the other arm and pulled a blanket off the couch. "Mellie, come here so Uncle Rem doesn't stroke out."

"Rem, I don't think she's here."

"Of course she's here. She's just hiding."

Cassi extended her arms. "*Where*?"

Good freaking question. "I wasn't outside for long."

"Why is the backdoor open?"

"I was letting the place air out. Started to smell like Clorox scrubbing pads and baby wipes, and *no*, I didn't mix them up."

Cassi hadn't worried me yet, but that pit of dread bundled in my gut. That *fucked-up* sense when the tree crashed down the wrong way and the widow branches aimed for whoever head was closest.

"All right." I sucked in a quiet breath. "Let's say...*hypothetically*...if a kid happened to wander outside without me knowing...how far could they toddle?"

"Rem!"

"*Hypothetically*."

"There's a three-year-old lost in the *woods*?"

Cassi crashed through the back door and rushed into the yard. The trees bordering my property closed in hard and fast. The canopy engulfed the house, and the thick weeds, ferns, branches, and rocks cluttered the clearing below. The yard was overgrown to the point of strangulation, but a path spread beyond the forest's edge. The evening sun penetrated in spots, long shafts of golden light. Right out of a Disney movie.

Just the spot a princess would love.

"Mellie!" My voice echoed off the trees. "Come here!"

Cassi must have mentally mapped the entire forest. She scoured the tree line. "Okay. She couldn't have gotten far."

"Maybe the wolves took her."

"Be serious."

"She'd probably be better off with them than me."

What sort of man lost a little girl in the damned woods? My gut churned. I wasn't cut out for the baby-sitting gig, but this was a new level of incompetence.

I swore. "I only took my eyes off of her for a few minutes."

"That's all it takes."

"Why didn't you tell me?"

"I thought you knew better than to let a little girl wander off in a freaking forest!" Cassi sucked in a calming breath. "How many minutes is a *few*?"

"Five." A lie. "Maybe ten." Didn't make me feel better. "Fifteen?"

"Jesus, Rem." The temper flared again, but Cassi contained it. Barely. "Fine. We'll go looking. Let's get a flashlight and a first-aid kit."

My heart nearly stopped. "A first-aid kit? *Why*?"

"We don't know how long we'll have to look, and if she's hurt…"

"Don't even say it."

I wasn't hearing it. I rushed to the house. The first-aid kit was easy, some prissy little white box Cassie had insisted I buy at the store. No luck on the flashlight. I hurried outside and gestured for her to follow me to the workshop adjacent to the house. "Flashlight is in there."

Cassi matched my pace. "And so is Mellie, if I had to guess."

"I told her the shop is off-limits."

"But you weren't watching her."

Just what I needed—a toddler stashed away in the most dangerous place on the property. Rusted tools hung from waning pegs. Old machinery with no guards for little fingers waited in the corners. Splinters, spiders, and shards of wood covered the floor. What had been my dad's old shop was now my mess. I'd meant to get some work done on the inside—clean it up, start making some carpentry pieces again. Not like I'd get the chance if I had to balance two little girls around a band saw.

"Mellie?" I slapped the light switch. The old fluorescents flickered, but it took a while for them to hum. I searched between the old machines. No kid. No blood either. That was good.

As long as she wasn't smooshed under an old wood pile.

"Mellie, come here."

I'd kept an old flashlight pegged into a workbench, but the batteries had worn out long ago. I swore.

"Shit." I pointed to Cassi. "Start looking. Check out front again. I'll grab some batteries and search the back of the house. Call me if you find her."

The baby started to cry, but Cassi shushed her as she jogged away.

My stomach plummeted to my feet and tripped over the gravel.

What the hell was I supposed to do in a situation like this?

Did I call the sheriff? Get a search crew?

Did I shout her name to scare her home?

What if she was lost? What if she'd gotten hurt?

For Christ's sake, she was only *three*, and those had been some rough-ass years with her mom. Hopefully she wouldn't remember much of this when she was older—especially when her good-for-nothing uncle lost her in a forest because he was too stupid to check on a suspiciously silent toddler.

I burst into the house, racing for the batteries.

A tiny voice greeted me from the living room.

Mellie sat on the couch, big smile on her face, reading from an upside-down children's book.

"I want chocolate milk," she said. "Read me a story?"

The girl was thirty pounds of absolute chaos, and she'd drop me to my knees. I clutched the wall.

"*Cassi.*" My words were too gruff. I shouted outside. "I found her."

Cassi ran inside, cradling Tabby and sinking against the wall in relief as Mellie volunteered to read her an excerpt of Cinderella even though she held the Frozen book in her hand.

"Oh, thank God." Cassi couldn't catch her breath. "Did you put her up to this?"

If only. Might have worked better than the three hundred bucks I'd stuffed in the envelope. "Nope."

She sighed. "You okay?"

"Twenty-seven is a good age for an aneurysm."

She groaned, her head striking the wall. Tabby liked that. She giggled as Cassi did it again.

"Okay. You got me." Cassi's surrender was as beautiful as it was absolutely necessary. "I think I might stick around for a couple days."

"You won't regret it."

"Already do." She closed her eyes. "You're a bad influence on me, Remington Marshall."

Hell, even I knew that. It was why I left Butterpond in the first place. Cassi Payne deserved better than a man like me. But now I needed her more than ever.

"You afraid of a little trouble, Sassy?"

She approached, handing the baby off and smirking. "You aren't a *little* trouble. You're the worst kind of bad boy."

"Oh yeah? Why's that?"

"Because you're the type who thinks he can turn *good*."

5

Cassi

At 2:01 AM, my phone rang.

At 2:02 AM, a very groggy me bashed the traitorous, *expensive* phone into the wall.

At 2:04, 2:05, 2:06, and 2:07, the once-cute, now-enraging rendition of Aerosmith's *Ragdoll* finally lost its charm.

Considering I'd already cracked its panel, pitching the phone out the window would end the device for good.

I slid out of bed, the sheets sticking to my skin. Was it a hot night or a hotter dream? Did it matter when both ended with a cold shower?

What did he *want*?

Well, the answer to that was obvious, but even Rem had found some class. No way he was he looking to me for a booty call.

The phone blazed against the wall. Even his name on the screen cast a terrible shiver of delight through me.

And that was *bad*.

Every innocent thought, every curious fantasy, every searing hot memory of his kiss tore down my wall, brick by brick. My defenses had been perfected for *five years*. With one word, it toppled over me. I should have used a better mortar than resentment.

I debated not answering, but it was either facing Rem on the phone or meeting him again my dreams. A very sweaty, very *intimate* dream. I prayed those desires came from the trouble between my legs and not the hopeless patter in my chest.

I croaked a hello. Rem didn't greet me. Strangely enough, he didn't make a flirty pass or spread that boyish charm. His voice hardened with a rough and dire demand.

"The baby's sick."

Those weren't words anyone liked, but I'd expected them at some point. Tabby had been a little sniffly when I last saw her two days ago.

I had hoped four days of temporary nannying was enough time to help him wrangle the kids before any more five-year kisses overwhelmed us. I'd left him in charge with all the encouragement I could offer without trapping myself in his embrace.

It wasn't enough.

"Are you sure she's sick?" I faceplanted on the pillow and groaned.

A shout rumbled from downstairs. Jules. A second shout answered. Quint.

Something thudded against the floor. A retaliatory crash shook the windows. Glass shattered. My brothers shouted.

Just a normal Thursday at two AM for the Payne family.

"Of course I'm sure," Rem said.

"Is she *sick sick* or sick?"

"I don't know. What's *sick sick*?"

"Scarlet fever. Pneumonia. Has she lost a leg?"

Rem practically growled. "Her legs are both accounted for. What the hell do I do? How do I tell if its scarlet fever? What if she's really sick?"

She wasn't, but I doubted I could convince him of that. "Is she warm?"

"She's always a goddamned furnace. I sweat buckets when she sits in my lap."

Another threat of violence from downstairs. Quint slammed a door. A string of profanities followed. It would be the third time he'd threatened to leave. His suitcase was parked near the door almost as often as mine.

"Is she sniffling?" I asked.

"Yeah, there's all this gunk in her nose."

"Coughing?"

"Yeah."

"Is it a bad cough?"

"How the hell should I know? Aren't all coughs bad?"

Well, I wasn't getting back to sleep tonight. "Is it a chesty cough? A throaty cough? Post nasal drip cough?"

Rem lost his patience. "I have no clue! It sounds like this…"

The sound he created was no more child's cough than it was constipated donkey.

"If that's the case, you might want to grab the shotgun," I said.

He swore. "Cas, can you just help me before I go insane? I haven't slept all night."

"What a coincidence," I said. "I can't get any sleep either."

Varius was now in on the fight. A clatter rose from the kitchen. The usual frustrations echoed through the house. *You're not Dad. Dad left me in charge of the farm. You're not in charge of us. We have to make these decisions together. You already made the decision and never asked. You never put in the effort...*

My midnight mediations—or *meddling*, as Tidus called it—had never once calmed my arguing brothers before. It certainly wouldn't do a freaking thing now, not with an emptied six pack of beer and four years' worth of repressed rage surging through their veins. Tensions were high after Mom died. They worsened when Dad got sick. And now?

Another broken glass downstairs.

This family wasn't blood anymore—binding contracts and executive directives were all that kept us together. It was Dad's last wish that the family come together, make unified decisions, and become whole again.

That son of a bitch had a sick sense of humor.

"Cassie, I'm out of my element here," Rem said. "I don't know what to do for her."

Damn my heart of gold. Lugging it around really weighed me down. "I'll be there in a few minutes."

"Thanks, Sass."

He shouldn't have thanked me yet. Agreeing to help was easy enough. Escaping the house was the tough part.

God only knew what I'd have to clean up in the morning. Broken glass. Jules' face—again. I never wanted to *spackle* another wall as long as I lived. It wasn't worth wandering into the middle of the fracas to inform them that I was going to visit Remington Marshall.

I'd be back before they'd slept off the buzz. Quick like a bunny. Quick like a bunny who wasn't about to change out of her pajamas or do more than ponytail her hair.

I tossed a windbreaker over the spaghetti tank and my pink fuzzy bottoms, exchanged the slippers for flip-flops, and did what any respectable woman would do when brothers armed themselves with whiskey and dug trenches in the kitchen. I shimmied my booty out the bedroom window and climbed down the rain gutter.

"What the hell are you doing?"

My feet hadn't hit the porch roof before I got busted.

I flattened myself against the roof, shushing Tidus with a quick finger to my lips. Not like he'd ever listen. He hopped the railing and hauled me off the roof before I jumped to the ground.

"Cassi, we have *doors*."

He reeked of cigarette smoke.

I slapped his shoulder. "You promised to quit!"

He snorted and pointed towards the kitchen. The yelling even echoed outside. "*You* head into that hellscape. Tell me what you'd do to escape the insanity."

"I wouldn't *smoke*."

"No. You'd just risk a very breakable neck by climbing out the *window*."

Tidus wasn't as tall as my other brothers, but he made up for it with meathead strength. His muscles were wrapped in tattoos and leather. His hands might've crushed me, but, underneath the petty criminal record and scars, he was a teddy bear pushed onto the wrong side of the law.

And it was Rem who gave him the shove.

"Cover for me," I said. "I'm going out."

No hesitation. "*Nope.*"

"I used to do it for you."

Still a *no*. "That's different."

"How so?"

"Cause I'm...and you're..." His eyes had an electric quality to them, far brighter green than the rest of my brothers. "Where the hell are you going in your *jammies?*"

Who was he to judge me...just because the pink pants had little strawberries embroidered and the word Sassy emblazoned on the butt.

"These are totally real pants," I said.

I never gave my brother enough credit. "You're going to see *Rem*!"

"Fine. Don't cover for me."

"Why are you getting involved with him again?"

I wasn't *involved*. Maybe *mixed-up*. "I'm not, not that it's any of your business."

Tidus scowled. "Drop the attitude, Sassy. I don't want you moping around here for another five years because of that bastard."

"That *bastard* is your best friend."

"That's how I know he's a bastard."

"If you were that worried, why did you have *me* take the clothes and toys up to the cabin?" I frowned. "And why didn't you tell Jules or the others that he was in town?"

Tidus rubbed his face, but the displeasure didn't fade. "I owe Rem for a lot of shit, okay? He fucked up, but I'm not gonna forget what he did for me. But that doesn't mean I'll let him hurt you again."

"He never hurt me."

"Yeah, right. That's why there's a parade of guys here on the weekends, begging to take you out."

"And here I thought that would relieve my big brother."

"We'd rather see you with anyone but him."

I flicked my car keys in my hand. "The baby is sick. I'm going to make sure she's okay."

Tidus let me pass, but he called after me. "And then what?"

What did he think? "And then I'm going to make passionate love to Rem, and we're going to run away to Vegas, spend all of our money on a roulette wheel, and live out the rest of our lives on a sunny Mexican beach."

"Stay out of trouble."

"You can trust me."

"It's not you I'm worried about."

Likewise. Tidus still considered Rem a friend. My other brothers? They'd arm themselves with pitchforks and iPhone flashlights and march up the mountain to save a virtue that wasn't theirs to protect or Rem's to take.

Not that they needed to worry. I'd already told Rem—I was leaving town. Definitely and for real this time. I was only staying long enough to ensure he'd only use electrical tape to fix a broken toy, and then I was gone. Off the farm. Away from the fights, anger, and resentment.

I loved my brothers, but I'd run out of framed pictures to hang over holes in the drywall and lost enough sleep breaking up their fights. Until they made peace, I needed to find my own.

It took me a half-hour to sneak up the terrifyingly windy mountain road in pitch blackness. I sweated by the time I reached the cabin and tumbled out of the car in relief.

Rem owed me big time for this.

The cabin's front door was unlocked. I knocked and let myself in.

Rem greeted me without a shirt.

This night wasn't going to get any easier.

Was he a man...or was he a monster made of pure muscle? His back, chest, arms, abs, *everywhere* ripped with strength. And decorating it all? Tattoos. Bright sleeves down his arms and across his chest.

A snake was his preferred design, coiling over one arm, across his shoulders, and down the other. The bright cacophony of colors practically slithered as his muscles flexed. Bands of red, yellow, and green swept in an almost tribal pattern across his skin. He'd drawn the design himself when we were young, even incorporating trees and foliage to hide the snake. A dogwood tree. Never thought a man could look so fearsome with delicate flowers tattooed over his massive biceps.

He'd inked himself with a new tattoo—a design so out of place, so deliberately positioned, it nearly ruined the aesthetic of his sleeves. The sunflower didn't belong on his skin, especially over his heart. He hated the things.

But sunflowers were my favorite.

Good thing Rem was distracted, rooting through the kitchen drawer. I checked my chin for drool then stopped him before he marched out of the kitchen with a meat thermometer.

"What are you doing?"

Rem frowned. "I think Tabby has a fever, and this is the only thermometer I have. But I'm not sure where to stick it."

"*Back in the drawer!*"

He grunted and tossed it in the sink. "Fine. What do I do?"

I dropped the windbreaker on the couch and peeked into the Pack-N-Play. A bundle of fuss greeted me. Tabby pouted. Kicked. Pretty sure she gave me the finger. She rubbed hard at her nose.

"She's pissed," Rem said. "I moved her here so she wouldn't wake Mellie."

Poor thing. I patted her tummy. "Aw, what happened, Tabs? Don't feel good?"

She declined to answer, preferring to wail instead. This must have been a common sound. Rem groaned.

"I don't know what to do," he said.

Nothing really to do. Tabby calmed a little as I picked her up and cuddled her close. "It's just the sniffles."

"How do you know?"

The little blonde had turned into a mass of frizz. Her hair tickled my nose as she burrowed into my shoulder. I rubbed her back.

"I just do, I guess," I said. "It's instinct. I'm used to kids. I know the signs."

Tabby made a grabby motion with her tiny fists towards Rem. He hesitated as long as a man could reasonably delay before surrendering to the little girl. He took her to the couch, but she still wasn't happy until they settled down together. I perched on the sofa's arm, keeping a respectable and modest distance between my pink jammies and the conniving serpent staring from his wrist.

"Have you changed her?" I asked.

"Yeah."

"Fed her?"

"She didn't really want to eat."

"Did she drink some water?"

"Yeah."

Better than I'd thought he'd do. "Okay. Try to get her to sleep."

He didn't like that answer. "That's *it*?"

"She has a *cold*," I said. "Rest will help."

"But there's nothing else you can do?"

"Short of magic?"

Rem raised his eyebrows. "I'm a desperate man, Cas. Bippity Boppity Boo this shit. If it'd make the kid feel better, I'd shank the fairy with her own wand."

"Let's not hold Mickey Mouse hostage yet." I scooted next to him and nudged his side. Those muscles were hard as a rock. "Tabby has a cold. It's part of growing up. Cuddle her, keep her warm, and pray she doesn't wake Mellie."

"That's it?"

"That's it. Now we can take her to the doctor tomorrow to make sure. Do you know which pediatrician Emma used for them?"

"Probably none."

"*None*?"

Rem bit his words before answering. "I mean, I don't know. She never said what she did when they got sick."

"We'll call Doctor Barlow tomorrow."

"*Who?*"

"Simon Barlow."

Rem fumed. "You gotta be kidding me."

"He opened a practice in Butterpond. He's great with kids."

"Fuck me." He corrected himself as I glared at him. "Sorry, Tabby."

Rem went silent. Poor guy. Not like he knew what to do for a sick baby or a sick sister.

"How is Emma?" I asked.

I thought he didn't hear me. He stayed quiet for a little too long. "Doing okay."

"We could take the kids over to visit. She might like to see them."

"No."

Harsh and quick. I flinched. So did he.

Rem apologized and gestured to the baby. "If she's sick, Mellie might get sick too. I don't want to drag them around Emma."

"Oh, the chemo. Right."

"Yeah. Right." He gave Tabby a couple pats to her bottom and settled into the couch with a heavy sigh. Dark circles traced under his eyes, but his smile could still melt parts of me that had no business warming for a man like him. "You sure you don't want to be a nanny? You're good at this."

"I should be. I babysat enough in high school. Plus that degree I'm lugging around should prove it, even if it doesn't seem to impress any schools in the area."

"So why not do it?"

"It's too much of a risk."

"So, you'd rather stay on the farm instead?" He snorted. "You can either wait for another job to fall into your lap, or you can pray for rain instead."

Yeah. My family had learned that the hard way. "Tell that to Jules. He's dead-set on rebuilding the farm. Crops. Animals. Everything."

"*Why?*"

I lowered my voice as Tabby finally closed her eyes. "Because that's what Dad wanted for us."

"Jules never got along with your dad."

Yeah, I remembered those fights. "I guess he had a change of heart."

Rem shuffled with the baby towards the Pack-N-Play. I helped settle her into the blankets, and we tip-toed away with bated breath while she closed her eyes.

Crisis averted, for now.

I sunk into the couch, unsure why I was even telling them any of this. "The family's not doing so good. Mom's been gone for four years. Dad, three months. None of my brothers even spoke to each other at the funeral. No one came home for holidays. No one stopped by to visit. There's too much hate." I nearly laughed. "And now Jules thinks he'll solve every problem by planting some corn."

"Maybe he will."

"He wants me to stay and help."

"Why don't you?"

I smirked. "You, above *anyone* else, should understand why I want to leave."

He extended an arm behind me, still on the couch, but inviting me closer. "Enlighten me."

"Because I want to be like you."

Rem nearly choked. "Like *me*? You don't want to be like *me*, Sassy."

"Why not?"

"You can't even hold an axe," he said. "Canadian winters aren't for you."

"So I'll buy a coat," I said. "Point is, you got to leave. You hopped in your car, drove away, and started a brand-new life away from here."

"It's a lonely, cold, and miserable life."

"Well, I don't think I'll be a *lumberjack*."

"Don't think I should be one either."

I leaned against the couch, almost grazing his arm. "Then why did you go?"

A dangerous question, especially in the middle of the night when exhaustion accidentally unstuffed all the curiosities and pains and feelings I'd shoved deep into the pit of my stomach, where they belonged. Besides, Rem might have offered a dangerous answer, something neither of us were prepared to admit.

His fingers drifted to my cheek. I craved his touch, but he only twisted one of my curls, pinching it just to watch it spring back in place.

"Why didn't you leave yet?" he asked.

"I had to stay."

He nodded. "And I had to go."

"You didn't even say goodbye."

Rem's eyes had a way of darkening when he got serious. "Would you have wanted to hear it?"

Yes.

No.

It didn't matter because the past was done and we'd all suffered enough for it. Nothing would change what had happened, no matter how many times I'd hit eighty-eight miles an hour on the highway, hoping it'd propel me back five years to prevent everything from falling apart.

"What happened that night, Rem?" I whispered. "*Really*. What happened in the barn? What happened with the fire? What happened when you ran away?"

He teased another one of my curls. "That's all in the past. Who can remember it?"

"I can." I brushed his hand away only to hold it close. To feel him. To enjoy a warmth that wasn't mine to share. "Tell me. Please."

The shadows lifted. He flexed his fingers between mine, light and dark, smooth and calloused. With a little tug, he pulled me closer.

In another world, in another time, and with no less than two glasses of wine, I might have snuggled against his chest. Now, I knew better.

So why did I let his strong fingers stroke the back of my hand?

"Long ago…" He sighed. "An idiot boy met a pretty girl."

"How pretty?"

"Prettiest he'd ever seen. Had all these crazy curls in her hair. Gorgeous smile. And a booty that—*Lord have mercy*—would have driven any red-blooded man to his knees."

I wasn't impressed. "Beauty is such a curse. Can't find any jeans that fit it, can't trust any of the neighbor boys to not be intimidated by it."

"Well, that boy was intimidated. Only thing he could do was run far, far away."

"Why?"

"To protect her virtue."

And now I knew it was a fairy tale. "You honestly thought you were gonna score back then?"

"You didn't stand a chance, Sassy."

"What sort of girl do you take me for?"

"The kind of girl who needed a good roll in the hay."

"Kinda hard to roll when you burned the barn down."

He frowned. "It would have been worse if we'd—"

"You are so *damn* sure of yourself." I rolled my eyes. "You're just as cocky now as you were then."

"No. But I'm every bit as irresistible."

I poked his chest, pretending not to stare at the hard, beautifully tattooed, monster of muscle. "You slick bastard. You lured me here under the pretense of a sick child."

"I'm resourceful too."

"There's a word for men like you."

He grinned. "Give me some credit. This wasn't my plan, but I'm a great opportunist."

"You mean, *scavenger*? A bottom-feeder?"

"Oh, I'll eat anything you want me to, Sassy."

No way. "You'll catch that cold easier than you'll catch me."

"But you're spending the night here, aren't you?"

Oh, now I got his game. "If wishes were horses, Remington Marshall, you could buy back every animal we had to sell for Dad's medical bills."

"You think I'm going to let you drive home this late at night?"

"I *just* drove over here."

Rem gestured to the baby. "Well, that was an emergency."

"And maybe it's imperative that I leave this very moment."

"The temptation too much?"

"I'm drowning in my own lust."

He winked. "Don't worry. I'll give you mouth-to-mouth."

"My *hero*." I stood. "I'm going home and getting back to bed."

"No way, Sassy. Your brothers would kill me if I send you out alone this late at night. God only knows what's lurking out in those deep dark woods."

"I'm more worried about who is creeping in the living room."

"Beware the evil you know." His charm was boundless. So was his confidence. "It's late. Come on. Stay the night. Hell, stay longer. I need your help with the kids. It'd be great."

It would have been great…long, long ago. Now, I was smarter, wiser, and more vulnerable than ever. That old wound was held together with a band-aid and a couple inspirational clippings from Cosmo. Last thing I needed was a new scar to show how stupid I was.

"I'm not the little naïve girl you left behind," I said. "I won't fall for your tricks."

Rem snickered. "What tricks? Offering you good money and benefits to watch the kids? I'm such a monster."

"Slick son of a bitch."

He took my hand. I pointed to his intruding fingers, so easily encompassing my palm.

"You know *exactly* what you're doing, Remington Marshall."

He grinned. That cocky, self-assured smile, framed by the dark scruff of a beard. If a tree fell in the forest, he had probably knocked it over with that smile. How was I supposed to defend myself? If I fell head-over-heels for him, I didn't want to imagine the sound I'd make.

"I might be trying to keep you here." His hand brushed my cheek. I should have pushed him away, but his touch rendered me quiet and lost in the best, most hopelessly fuzzy way. "Five years ago, I thought leaving you would be the hardest thing I ever had to do. I was wrong." His thumb stroked my bottom lip. "Letting you out that door tonight will finally kill me."

I'd go first—my heart had stopped with his touch. "We can't do this."

"Do what?" Rem's lips barely grazed mine. "This?"

Another kiss. Another tremble.

Another huge mistake.

I leaned into his kiss, savoring that commanding and teasing way his tongue swept over mine. A fierce shiver surrendered my body. The warmth spread, binding me in a furious demand that nearly allowed him to push me onto the couch.

Had I learned *nothing* these past few years?

Rem's words lowered, a dark and husky tease. "Cas, I'm not trying to ask your forgiveness. I know you can't give it. And I don't blame you. But now...I need a friendly favor."

Another kiss. Deeper. Hotter. My chest ached, and I sucked in a quiet gasp that did nothing to quench the desire burning through me.

I escaped the kiss with a wavering sigh. "This isn't a *friendly* favor. *This* feels like a seduction."

Rem grinned and licked his lips as if to taste me once more. "Oh, Sassy. Believe me. You'll know when I'm seducing you."

Hopefully he'd let me know so I could build a better defense. Right now, the most I had around my castle was a moat of wetness sticking my pajamas to my legs. A girl needed some cannons or drawbridges or a glass of red wine for this sort of invasion.

A cool rush of air separated our bodies. I froze in the unwanted freedom.

"Favor first," Rem said. "Seduction second."

"So I get to reject you twice?" My voice wobbled as much as my legs. "Sounds like fun."

"I won't put the moves on you if you stay the night."

"Pretty sure there's an Aesop's Fable that would warn me otherwise."

"The bed is big enough for both of us."

He quieted as Tabby fussed in the crib. The charm faded, and the worry returned. The exhaustion plagued us both. It *was* a long ride to the farm. And that baby wasn't likely to sleep much at all. She needed someone to comfort her. So would Rem.

"Fine." I gave up. "I'll stay the night."

He winked. "I knew you would."

"I'll even sleep in your bed."

"Now it's a party."

"Gotta warn you…" I arched an eyebrow. "I sleep in the nude."

"What a coincidence. Me too."

I unwrapped the blanket from the back of the sofa and made an impromptu bed on the couch, complete with swiped pillow from the bedroom.

"You're such a gentleman for giving me the bed. Sleep tight, Rem."

I waved and shut the door tight, savoring his groan.

6

Cassi

I'd planned to put a good fifty miles between me and my shame—aka Remington Marshall.

Now I wasn't sure I'd make it *fifty feet*.

I'd escaped the cabin at five-thirty in the morning. Just early enough to sneak back to the farm and crash in my own bed for, hopefully, the last time.

This was it. After that kiss, I couldn't afford to stay in Butterpond. I'd spent five years getting over Rem. All he'd needed was five minutes to almost get me *under* him.

Tabby's cold wasn't reason enough to delay my trip, and I wasn't nearly drunk enough to let Rem's lips touch anywhere but my tush on the way out the door.

I would not allow myself to wonder *what if*, not even for the teeniest, tiniest fraction of a second.

Just like I wouldn't lose myself in those chestnut eyes. I'd ignore that melted chocolate voice and forget the sweet kisses, the heat of his hands, the tickle of his beard…

Rem texted me at seven. **You didn't stay for breakfast.**

The accompanying picture of a spilled bowl of cereal and half-bitten ham sandwich wasn't the gourmet meal featured on the brochure.

I shouldn't have replied. **Watching my figure. All those Gerber Graduates go right to my thighs.**

Rem wasn't cutting me a break. **You got plenty of exercise running away this morning.**

He was one to talk. **Imagine how toned I'll be once I'm in Ironfield.**

Won't need to imagine if you send me a couple pics. Or if you stay here.

Not happening.

Tell me what I can do to keep you here.

Oh, it was a dangerous, terrible question. Forget the palm fronds, swinging hammock, and Mai Tai. The only thing I needed from Rem were the three little words we'd had the foresight to never admit. Even Superman knew to avoid his Kryptonite.

I smirked. **I'm immune to your charms.**

It was a lie, but if it convinced me long enough to pack my last bag and head to the car, I'd spin a couple other yarns.

No, I haven't gained five pounds since Easter. Go head and splurge on the new purse—what's fifty bucks to your infinite wallet? Your brothers will be fine without you. There's no way they'll murder each other in cold blood over the last Pop Tart in the pantry.

Quint's profanity echoed from the stairs. "Son of a bitch, Jules! Get your own goddamned breakfast!"

The epic battle between Toaster Strudel and Cheese Danish would occupy most of Jules and Quint's morning. That meant I had only one brother to worry about.

The squeaking floorboards didn't fool me. I dove for the towel on the back of my door, burst into the hall, and yelled as Tidus slammed the bathroom door in my face.

"Are we teenagers again?" I pounded against the door. "I'm leaving today. I need to shower."

Life as the youngest of six—and the only girl in a herd of slobbering men—meant I lived on the bottom of the food chain. Scraping together the heels of the bread for sandwiches, growing up to wear Ninja Turtle handmedowns, and waking at all hours to secure a bathroom to myself.

I pounded again. Tidus spoke over the hum of an electric razor.

"Figured you'd use Rem's bathroom this morning."

He thought he was so damn cute. But if I *had* shared some suds with Rem, he'd be the first at the cabin with a loaded shotgun.

"Tidus, I'm serious. Can I please shower first?"

"You're leaving?"

"Yeah."

"What about Rem?" he asked.

"What about him?"

Tidus snorted. "You aren't going to help him?"

"Nope."

"Why not?"

Because life didn't run on hormones and rainbows. "There's too much history."

"So?"

"He singlehandedly torched the barn. The stress sent Mom into an early grave, Dad into a depression, and scattered all of you guys to the far corners of the world. I think I ought to be on my guard with him. Now let me in the shower!"

On cue, the pipes squeaked. His ass wasn't in the water, but he shouted anyway. "Sorry, Sassy. Can't hear you! Get in the downstairs shower before Varius."

Damn it. I pushed off the door and pummeled my way down the stairs. The old wood creaked, and the railing wobbled and cracked—too many years of too many stampeding boys careening down the steps. I crashed through the kitchen. Jules slapped Quint's finger out of his face.

"Stay out of my shit," Quint said. "You know that shelf is mine."

Jules wasn't in a good mood, and he shared that fact with anyone who happened to be near. "Got your name on it?"

Quint slammed the pantry door against the wall and ripped the shelf out of the wall.

Cereals, oatmeals, and breakfast pastries scattered across the kitchen. A jar of pickles crashed to the floor. Good. My shower this morning would include scrubbing the scent of dill and mustard seed off my body.

Quint slapped the hunk of wood in his hand. "Look, asshole. My name's been there since 2002."

Jules kicked a jar of anchovies out of his path. The glass exploded into fragmented shards, and the fish mingled with the pickle juice. Fortunately, the tub of oats had cracked open. At least it helped to sop up the mess. Couldn't say the same for the spilled bottle of whiskey, precariously teetering on the edge of the counter. Varius's breakfast of choice. So much for the floor. And his liver.

"You're twenty-five fucking years old." Jules grabbed the shelf and unsuccessfully attempted to wedge it into the pantry. It immediately collapsed onto the shelf beneath, tore a hole into two bags of chips, then clattered to the floor, dragging with it a bag of opened flour and ripped sugar. They stared at the mess, grunted, then returned to the fight. "Get your head out of your ass. We're stuck here together."

Quint tripped over a wayward can of tomato soup but caught himself before his chin collided with Jules' fist. "And who's fault is that? What the hell do you really expect to happen here? All five of us under a single roof. Just wait until Marius's tour is done. Once he's stateside again, we'll have a real war in this house."

"That's the way Dad wanted it," Jules said. "So get used to it."

"*Dad's dead!*" Quint flinched as his voice carried, but he didn't back down. For the first time, the youngest of my brothers must have felt a bit confident in confronting my father. Too bad Dad wasn't here to defend himself.

"Dad's dead," Quint said. "But we're the ones buried under this fucking farm. We've got no income. No equipment. No goddamned clue how to do it on our own. And *you*—" He pointed at Jules. "You're just as stubborn as he was. You don't know a pitchfork from your prick, and you think we can just *start a farm*?"

The same fight every morning. I could practically quote Jules now.

I sighed. "We have a chicken."

"Yes, we have a chicken!" Jules gestured through the kitchen window to the chicken coop rated for forty. Currently, it housed only a single guest—Helena.

Quint laughed. "That chicken hasn't laid an egg in a year."

"She's working on it!"

"What came first? Bankruptcy or the egg?"

"Would you guys stop it?" I said.

I shooed them out of my way and began the cleanup. I reached for the bag of sugar, not realizing the corner was tucked snuggly under Quint's foot. The bag exploded. Granules of white plumed over the kitchen. Jules sneezed. Quint would probably go into diabetic shock. Fantastic.

"I am not going back to the store for you animals before I leave. You're on your own."

Jules furrowed his brow. "What do you mean, *before you leave*?"

"I'm getting a shower. Packing my bags. And I'm leaving for Ironfield."

Only I had the ability to unify my brothers. Unfortunately, they ganged up against *me*. Quint crossed his arms. His eyes had a brighter quality—a playful sea foam that stirred itself dark when he wanted to get in someone's face. Like now. Big mistake.

"*She* gets to leave?" He turned to Jules. "You're letting *her* leave?"

"She's not going anywhere." Jules didn't bother to fight. He grabbed a handful of soup cans and a bag of chips and tossed them onto the wrong shelf. The rest he kicked into the pantry, wrestling with the accordion doors which refused to shut on the bag of crumbling tortilla chips. "She'll never make it out of Butterpond."

"I'm leaving today," I said.

"I got a fifty with your name on it if you can cross the county line."

"I'll drive over it *twice*, make it an even hundred."

Quint held his arms out, gesturing to the mess. "What about us?"

"You guys don't need me—you need a feeding trough. You're better suited for the barn."

"Don't worry about her," Jules said. "She wants Triumph Farm to recover as much as we do."

Quint pointed at him. "You. *You* want this goddamned farm. Not me. Not Marius. Not Tidus. Not Varius. Hell, I'm not even sure Cas wants it."

"Don't put me in the middle of this," I said. "This has been *my* home the past five years. I'm the one who watched Dad sell equipment to pay for the bills. I'm the one who helped load the last two cows onto the trailer for sale. I'm the one who juggled the water and electric bills while Dad was sick. I did what I had to do, and now I have to get away from you all before you drive me insane."

Jules tore his Pop Tart in half and offered a piece to Quint. "See. She's not leaving."

My phone buzzed. I checked the text.

I'll pay you more.

Not for a million freaking dollars.

I pointed at Quint. "You better get your butt to the grocery store once in a while before you claim a shelf." Then I faced Jules. "And you can mail me my fifty bucks."

"Just set my check on Dad's desk." He laughed. "I know you, Cassi. You can't leave. This farm means more to you than anyone."

That didn't make it right to stay.

I had places to go. A life to live. And brothers to get out of showers.

Fortunately, I knew where to find the hot water heater. Varius and Tidus could do their soul-searching in the backyard pond. I rushed to the basement, fiddled with the controls, and counted the minutes until the profanity rained from upstairs.

Rem's text buzzed in my hand. **What's Ironfield got that I can't give you?**

I helped myself to the upstairs bathroom, ignoring a grumbling Tidus, and locked the door behind me.

I texted back with a smirk. **Peace of mind.**

Nothing more peaceful than the mountains.

Not during mating season.

I'm nothing if not purely professional.

Right. **Sure, you couldn't wait to seal this deal.**

Nothing would deter this man. He immediately replied. **Name the price, Sassy.**

More than you can afford.

What if I promise you a priceless experience?

Then you'd morally bankrupt me.

I could imagine Rem's grin. All the more reason to put the phone away...wherever I could find room.

Colognes, razors, electric trimmers, toothpastes, and boxer briefs of every color cluttered a bathroom that had been *mine* for years. I fished a used q-tip from my peppermint scented candle and cleared a spot for my towel. What had been organized was now destroyed and manhandled. The shelf behind the toilet clung to a single screw with a hope, prayer, and the good fortune of the old farm house. My trinkets—candles, a potted plant, a mirror—were abandoned under the toilet bowl.

Seat up, of course.

Gross. I'd leave them there.

I stripped and sat down to do my business, careful to rest my feet only on the driest portions of the bathmat. Tidus hadn't left me many options, and I *prayed* the moisture was from him leaping out of an icy shower.

At last, I had a moment to take a breath, clear my head, and relax.

Crack.

The shelf behind me creaked and smashed downwards, clocking me in the back of the head. I lurched, crashing onto the floor.

Punched while peeing. I rubbed the concussion away and sighed. Never thought I'd need a Life-Alert necklace just to use the bathroom. *Help, I've fallen, and I haven't mopped the floor in two weeks.*

On cue, Rem persisted. His offers were getting more desperate. Or maybe more fun.

Name the favor…dinners out, foot massages, other sundry and immodest deeds that I'd willingly degrade myself to offer.

I could think of quite a few favors now—a clean bathroom, super glue to recombine the scattered shards of my dignity, and a wild and animalistic night of pure sex like I'd imagined so many years ago.

At least I had a cold shower.

I rushed through my routine, splattering my cheeks with some makeup, tossing on a simple sundress, and gathering my hair in a ponytail. I balled my dirty laundry in the corner of my luggage then sat on top to help it close. The latches whined before clicking, but it was done.

Finally.

I gripped the handle. The loop promptly ripped off the suitcase. The luggage cluttered to the floor, breaking a hinge. The entire mechanism failed.

The spring-loaded compartment burst. The contents exploded from the suitcase. Panties flew everywhere. The rest of my once folded, now knotted clothes followed suit.

Jules shouted from downstairs. "Cas, where did dad keep his tax returns?"

Hell no. One cold shower, a concussion, and a busted suitcase weren't stopping me. I galloped down the stairs to grab a roll of duct tape.

I passed the office and called to Jules. "Bottom cabinet, under *E* for *Extortion*."

"What about his old feed orders?"

"Under *C* for *Critters*."

"It's going to take me a week to find any of his paperwork!"

Probably longer, once he realized Dad opted against sorting his years chronologically in favor of classifying each harvest as *good* or *bad*. Dad had never once touched a computer, and he hated calculators. His business contracts were pre-arranged with lifelong friends who'd provided feed and equipment over a beer, a wink, and gentleman's handshake.

And Jules thought he could pick it up in a season.

I mummified my suitcase with a layer of duct tape and considered tossing a strip over my mouth. God only knew what horrific words would come out—like, *Hang on, Jules. Let me help you.* Or *Sure, Rem, I'd love to stay and watch those two adorable little girls.*

I slung my purse over my shoulder and hauled the suitcase off the bed. I made it to the stairs before my phone buzzed. I reached for it, juggled it in my hands, and then watched as it *crashed*, *banged*, and *shattered* down every single stair.

Jules picked it up at the bottom, whistling as the screen spider webbed and fractured under his hand.

"Looks like you'll have to stay and get that fixed," he said.

"Not a chance." The suitcase had no handle, and now I had no way to get it down the stairs. Screw it. I pushed the damn thing, wincing as it crashed through the bottom railing in a confetti of splinters. "I'll get a new phone in the city."

"With what money?"

"I'll find a job."

"You have a job on the farm."

"I've seen the pay. I'm not working for your five-alarm chili, Jules." I cast my brother a knowing glance. "If I stayed, I'd actually make money nannying for Remington Marshall's two nieces. Would you like that instead?"

Jules kissed my forehead. "I'll tell the others you said goodbye."

I hauled the busted luggage out the door and tossed it into my trunk, managing to crush my favorite pair of sunglasses. My phone buzzed again.

Do it as a favor to me?

The car was loaded. I had plans. Friends waiting for me. Places I could stay. Jobs on the horizon. Maybe even a teaching gig at a prestigious preschool if my networking paid off. I couldn't give up my *one* chance to get out of Butterpond because I still had feelings for a man who redefined the word *flame*.

I slid into my car, regretting my decision immediately. The interior hardened with mud. Flecks of dirt, grass, and hay spewed from the air conditioner. My tank had plummeted to empty. A note waited on my dash.

Borrowed the car to go hiking. Owe you gas money.

-Tidus

I'd kill him later.

Butterpond had one gas station directly in the center of town. The two old-fashioned pumps offered everyone ten minutes of gossip per fill-up. Patricia Martin owned the station, the diner next door, and the debts of at least ten families in Butterpond—including my father's. Kinder than a bank but less forgiving than a loan shark.

Today, Pat wore a garish straw hat with a bird's nest and fake robins. She'd included a cross over her heart and her granddaddy's .38 special on her hip. She grinned when she saw me—a beaming smile that only grew wider when presented with a credit card.

"Miss Cassia Payne…" Pat was showing a bit of shoulder today. Her skin might have been a shade darker than mine, but no one but Jesus ever saw most of it. Modesty was a virtue, and gossip a sin, so Pat kept a close eye on the scales. "I just heard some dreadful news about you, sweetness. Lord bless you, I hope it's not true."

"Hi, Pat."

She ignored my offered credit card. "There's stories about you running around with that Marshall boy again."

Apparently, Rem was the most exciting thing to happen in Butterpond since Billy Bisco accidentally loaded his rifle with real bird shot for the civil war reenactment. The south rose that day, and the historical society was not at all pleased.

"He's just a friend," I said.

"Well, Layne Carlisle said you and that no-good Marshall boy were shopping together last week. Said your older brother had to come down and stop him from pawing all over you."

"That's not exactly—"

"If your poor Daddy only knew—Lord bless his soul—"

I handed her the credit card again. "He wasn't pawing on me."

She swiped the card and frowned. "Heard he had Emma's kids with him."

"Yeah. He's watching them."

"Good thing too. Not sure they're okay with a bad egg like him, but they're better off than with *that* girl."

"What do you—"

The machine beeped. Pat had a way to look both mortified and exhilarated in the same breath.

"Aw, sweetness. Your card is declined."

"*What*?"

Pat practically salivated over the potential gossip. This would keep her high for a week. "Probably just a card error. The bank does that sometimes."

Not often. Just today.

A cold shower. Concussion. Busted luggage. Broken phone. No gas. And now a rejected credit card?

Good thing it wasn't storming. Today was a good day—or a bad day—to get struck by lightning.

I dug through my purse and pulled out the two twenties I kept in reserve. She took my money as well as pity on me.

"Poor thing." She waddled behind the counter and busied herself at the slushie machine. "Seems like you could use this. It's on me."

The Icee drink wouldn't last five minutes in the heat, but it'd be the first and only meal I'd eat until I got my credit card fixed. I took it with a smile.

"Thanks, Pat."

"Heading out to Ironfield again? Think you'll make the county line?"

"How did you…"

"Got me a bet with Julian."

Of course she did.

"Make me proud, sweetness." Pat hooted. "No. Make momma some *money!*"

I was *trying*. God help me, I was doing my best to get out of town. I seized my drink and filled my tank, but I only made it halfway into my driver's seat before a bee buzzed the window. The fuzzy little bastard dive bombed my face, collided with my ear, and gave an angry zzzzzz as he charged my lobe.

It took only a second before his stinger created a fashionable—and painful—new earring.

I screamed. Brandished the Icee as a weapon.

And I defeated the insect in a pool of red, sticky slushie that splattered my dashboard, steering wheel, purse, and clothes.

My ear throbbed. I clutched it, peeking into the rear-view mirror. Yep. Swollen. Little asshole stung me, and the shooting pain radiated from my ear into my jaw.

I couldn't win.

At least, only my phone now buzzed.

Do it as a favor to them?

Rem had posed the girls for the camera—Mellie all smiles, Tabby five minutes too long passed her lunch. Her lip pouted, cheeks puffed, and a tantrum was eminent. Rem probably had no idea. But he'd learn. Slowly, sure, but he'd be able to manage the kids.

All by himself.

With no prior experience.

And no easy way to get a sitter.

And a sick sister doing chemo who would need help too.

I tapped my head against the steering wheel, regretting the sticky decision. An icepack, shower, car wash, new phone, and replaced credit card all waited for me in Ironfield. I was *so* close.

But was it fair to leave him all alone to manage the girls, his family, and his sister's health?

No.

Could I trust myself that close to him?

Absolutely not.

Nannying was just not an option.

I flicked the melting slushie off my keys and stuck them in the ignition. Turned.

The car hummed, buzzed, and then died, clicking when I turned the key.

"You've gotta be kidding me."

The phone vibrated again. Another photo, this one a selfie. Both girls on his lap—him and Mellie making goofy faces, Tabby looking inconvenienced.

I needed to get out of town. To forget Rem. To move on with my life.

But now? I needed money—specifically, fifty dollars for my eldest brother.

My fingers tapped an answer over the fractured screen.

When can I start?

7

Remington

Cassi Payne stepped out of my bedroom in a yellow bikini designed to stop my heart, knot my cock, and destroy the pinkie-promise we'd made when she agreed to become the girls' nanny.

This job was supposed to be *purely professional*.

I'd made a lot of mistakes in my life. Fires. Drugs. Letting this woman get away.

Agreeing to stay *professional* while the most beautiful woman in the world strutted around my cabin in a teeny-tiny bikini?

I was a goddamned idiot.

"I'm taking the kids to the lake," Cassi said. "Why don't you come with us?"

"Swimming!" Mellie bounced into the living room, proudly displaying her frilly pink bathing suit, yellow flip flops, and a pair of sunglasses shaped like two daisies. "Come on, Uncle Rem!"

Mellie's excitement riled up Tabby. Cassi had somehow tucked her little toddler rolls into a spandex suit with a mermaid on the front. She bounded around the floor by bouncing on her butt while chasing Mellie and the last graham cracker. Both girls screamed, giggled, and then tussled in the beach towels Cassi dumped over their heads.

"Pass," I said. "I'll stay here."

"Alone?"

She'd been the girls' full-time nanny for two days. I'd had them for three weeks. That many tantrums, screams, shrieks, cries, and crashes had burrowed a migraine deep into my head. I'd see them graduate before I got rid of the headache.

"I think I'll survive," I said.

Cassi winked and puffed up a pink beach ball. "Aw, what's the matter? Can't brood all alone in your cabin anymore?"

"There's lots of things I can't do by myself anymore." The bikini would kill me. A bright and cheerful yellow caressed her perfect, mouth-wateringly tempting dark skin. Cassi might have been a little thing, but she had curves in all the places that made this world right and good. "There's plenty I could do with you though. What do you say?"

"I say…I better get out of this cabin quick."

"Why? Intrigued?"

"Nope. Just suffering a bad case of cabin fever."

"Sure you're just not hot for me?"

"I don't know." She pitched the beach ball at my head. "Why don't we get out of this stuffy house and find out."

And miss the first and only peaceful afternoon I'd had in a *month*? No stories to read, no diapers to change, no visions of my past waltzing through my kitchen and tempting me with her smile, hips, and vanilla scent?

I had enough to do, starting with a call I'd put off to the project manager of the logging company. He wouldn't like to hear that my *temporary* leave of absence would last another couple of weeks. Plus, I had a load of timber piled high in my woodshed, waiting for me to begin work on a custom new dining room set for a family in town. Most importantly, I had a hard log I was waiting to chop, but I couldn't shout timber without some privacy.

Sometimes, a man needed to be alone.

"Come on, Rem." Cassi nudged Mellie. "Don't you want your uncle to come too?"

Mellie was a sociopath in waiting—the world's cutest master manipulator with golden curls who took no prisoners when inflicting that bottom lip in a pout.

"Please Uncle Rem?" She clapped her hands and nearly tumbled over her sister. "We...can...play...*NEMO!*"

Pretty sure that was the movie about the fish, not the racecar. "Sorry, kiddo. Uncle Rem doesn't have a pair of trunks."

Cassi arched an eyebrow. "When has that ever stopped you?"

"Haven't done it for a while. Believe it or not, we don't skinnydip much in the Canadian wilderness."

Her smile slayed me. "I haven't either...not since that one time."

The woman would destroy me from the inside out. If it wasn't the nostalgia killing me, it'd be the blood pressure surging between my head and cock. The memory blinded me. A night long ago when a beautiful girl slipped beneath the water and cast off a pair of jean shorts and white t-shirt.

It was the night I'd almost had her, when only water and shadow had separated us. Had I known that was my last chance to be with her, I wouldn't have let her out of the pond.

That night, we'd almost made love. Almost said those words. Almost devoted our lives to each other. That was the night before the barn burned down.

Then everything had changed.

"I'll go if you're planning on losing the suit," I said.

"That wouldn't be very professional."

I grinned. "So take the day off."

"And the kids?" Her eyes drifted to the expectant little girls—Mellie with her beach ball, Tabby gnawing a Barbie leg that hadn't survived Mellie's dance party/torture chamber. "You need to think of what's best for them now."

Hadn't I already been thinking of them? All day, every day, for almost a month? Diapers. Baths. Banging my head against the wall at night when they refused to sleep after a dinner of Skittles and juice.

Still, the kids probably deserved more entertainment than making water balloons out of condoms. Not only did Cassi declare that to be *inappropriate,* the damn things never burst. At the very least, I thought that particular demonstration would have convinced Cassi to give me a chance.

I grabbed my keys. "Round em up. We'll take them to the watering hole."

Cassi grinned, shouldering diaper bags and lunches filled with carrot sticks and grapes. The kids squealed in excitement and rushed to the truck—a truck that was once filled with freshly cut wood and hand-crafted furniture. Now it carried freshly filled diapers and home-grown tantrums.

And a diaper blowout? That was a shittier time than a busted tire.

The watering hole had seemed much bigger when I was young. Either I'd grown up, or it'd shrunk. Then again, everything had seemed bigger when we were kids. The town. The problems. The words we never spoke and the moments we'd missed.

I'd never expected to come back to Butterpond. The people didn't want me. The Paynes despised me. And the kids—

Mellie tripped over a rock in the shore and stomped her feet. "*Sockcucker!*"

I wasn't the best influence.

The longer the kids stayed with me, the more likely they'd learn their ABCs in the back of a patrol car and do their first multiplication tables to help calculate bail. Mellie was swearing. I didn't need to be Doctor Seuss to know Tabby was probably behind other girls her age. They had to go home to Emma, but...

No kid deserved to see their mother like that.

At least they had Cassi—someone to play with them, watch them, sing songs with them...

And unleash a hellish scream that curdled my blood.

I sprang over the tailgate and hit the dirt running. So much for a mid-afternoon nap in the sun. I ripped my shirt off as I ran, fearing that a woman's screaming like that could only mean one of the girls was trapped in the turbulent, dark part of the lake with no floaties...

Her second yelp stopped me in my tracks.

No little girl thrashing in the water.

Just a nanny trapped in the tire swing.

Booty first.

Cassi flailed her arms and legs, struggling against the black rubber. The tire swing held her firm, the series of ropes along the sides positioning the tire flat, so a would-be swimmer had a platform to sit, pump their legs, and then jump into the water.

Instead of a gentle swing, the tire engulfed her. Her ass stuck deep enough into the middle of the tire to pin her arms and hips. Her dignity might have dropped onto the dirt below if she hadn't been trapped inside the rubber like an upside down, humpbacked turtle.

"*Mellie!*" Cassi shouted as the devious munchkin slapped the tire round and round, giggling as her nanny spun in frantic circles. Half-naked, those bikini bottoms wedged firmly between those lovely cheeks, Cassi panicked each time the ground bumped that beautiful ass. "Mellie, *stop!*"

I grinned, admiring the view. "Any chance I can get a refund on this nanny service?"

Cassi spun. And spun. And spun some more. "Rem, *help!*"

"What the hell did you do?"

Cassi managed to grab the rope and stop her spinning, but she could do nothing to slow the crawl of the bikini turned thong encroaching on secret regions where I was never permitted access.

She spoke through gritted teeth. "My booty's stuck in the tire swing."

And I had almost stayed home and missed this fun. "Excuse me?"

"I said...my booty...is stuck...in this tire swing."

"And how did that happen?"

Cassi sucked in a breath and attempted to push up on the tire. It did nothing. Her hips and ass were firmly wedged in the luckiest goddamned tire I'd ever seen.

"Well, one day, I was born. Twenty-two years later, the world exacted its revenge." She smacked the rubber. The motion shimmied her deeper into the tire and accidentally pinned her shoulders. "Can you help me?"

I could. I wouldn't, but I could. "What can I do?"

"Maybe if I lose more self-esteem, I can slide out of here."

She wiggled her wobbler and wedged herself in an awkward position against the inner rim of the tire. Her ass was exposed to the dirt. If the bikini bottoms slipped up any further, she'd choke on them.

Cassi groaned.

"Now what would you have to be embarrassed about?" I asked.

"Let's start with the booty."

"Like hell. There's nothing wrong with that booty. That's a perfect booty."

"You're the expert."

"You're goddamned right. And, if anything, that tire swing wants to keep that ass snug for itself."

Mellie gave the swing a push. Cassi grunted as she bounced against the dirt. "Looks like the ground wants it more."

"Can you blame it?"

"Can you help me?"

"Can I get a picture?"

"You can get fu—"

I interrupted with a smile. "The children are listening."

Listening. Laughing. Same difference. Cassi awkwardly humped, pumping her hips and getting nowhere but lodged into my memory. Tabby toddled over to me and pointed.

"*Uh-oh*," she babbled.

"That's right," I said. "Can you say *this would make good blackmail.*"

"*Abababa.*"

"Close enough."

Cassi scowled. "Know what? Forget it. I don't need your help. I'll be fine right here."

"You're gonna sit there all night with your butt in the hole?"

"If that's what it takes."

"Come on, Cas. A booty like that belongs in the world, not attached to a ten-year-old tire swing. Let me help you."

"Oh no." She wagged a finger at me. Her shoulder was stuck, but she got a decent wiggle from her elbow. "You're gonna make fun of me."

"Yes, ma'am."

"And then you're going to hit on me."

"Once I'm done taking pictures."

"My prince charming."

I scooted the kids out of the way and surveyed the ropes holding the tire up. They tugged easily, but so did Cassi. She shrieked as I pulled the tire back and gave the ropes a yank. Her booty didn't unwedge, even as she teetered nearly vertical. I dragged the tire to the water's edge and grinned.

"We're gonna dump you out," I said.

"No, no, no. No dumping!"

Cassi stared into the deepest part of the lake. Her suit was wet, but not her hair. It'd be a declaration of war, but the temptation was as real as sneaking a glance at the most perfect, roundest, absolutely *bounciest* booty on God's green earth.

Right there. Exposed by the miraculous slippage of a very generous pair of bikini bottoms.

I pulled the ropes until the tire swung perpendicular to my hips. Oh, the wicked things I could do.

"Why isn't this a standard feature in every bedroom?" I asked.

"Oh, you *cannot* be trusted." Cassi attempted to spin. She couldn't see me behind her rubber shell, but I had the best view anywhere in the woods. "Okay. I can get out from here."

"All you need is a good bump."

"No. No bumps."

I hummed to myself. "Now how could I give you a good bump out of this swing?"

"You *could* be a gentleman."

"Aren't I helping a damsel in distress?" I grinned. "All you need is one good whack, and you'll be out of there. A solid spank oughtta do it. Get you out of the tire and onto your knees."

"Heaven help you, Remington Marshall, if you do what I think you're gonna do—"

I held the tire firm. Didn't get as good a warm up as I would've liked, but I'd known my entire life that my hand was made for spanking Cassi Payne's gorgeous ass.

It was a solid, joyous whack heard across the pond. The clap struck the fleshiest part of that booty, and the clap that echoed was as if the trees offered a round of glorious applause.

Cassi crashed forward, out of the tire. She face-planted into the dirt. Her language was not appropriate for children.

"You are such a fu—" She swallowed her words and rubbed her behind. "*Bad influence* on these kids!"

Well, yeah. Thought everyone knew that. Cassi marched towards me

—as if a little twig like her could push me into the water. I defended myself with the tire swing, pulling it back.

She raced for me.

I let go of the tire.

The swing smacked her in the chest. Momentum did the rest. Her splash into the pond was impressive, though I once again credited for her booty for the show.

Cassi emerged from the water, hair drenched and covering her face. Her shriek entertained the kids, but she grabbed a plastic bucket from Mellie that I wasn't entirely sure hadn't been filled with rocks instead of water.

So I did what any brave, honorable man would do. I hauled Mellie into my arms and faced Cassi with a grin.

"Is that any way to show your gratitude?" I asked.

The bucket reared back. "Don't use that child as a human shield."

"Tabby!" I scooped the kiddo into my arms too. "Tell Cassi to say thank you."

Tabby waved a pudgy finger at her nanny. "*Dank Boo.*"

"*Thank you*, Remington..." Cassi spoke through gritted teeth. "Put the kids down."

"Now, Sassy...be reasonable. You've been wetter than this before."

"It's like you want to get dunked."

"Just say the word—I'll splash you all you want."

The kids wiggled. My luck ran out. Mellie split first, racing to her own bucket on the shore. Tabby followed, plunking down in the grass and attempted to eat a pebble. Both girls threatened me with the buckets.

"*Ladies...*" I grinned. "I'm sure we can come to an amiable resolution—"

"Get him, Mellie!"

Cassi led the charge, pitching water—and the bucket—at my head. I dodged the attack, caught the bucket, and promptly fit it over my niece's head. Cassi panicked as I stole Mellie's weapon, filled halfway with chilly water.

"Don't!" She pointed at me. "Don't you even dare—"

She bolted. I chased, pitching the contents of the bucket over her torso. She juked, but I captured her in my arms before she could escape.

Her hands flattened against my chest, hand covering the sunflower I'd tattooed into my skin as a permanent reminder of the girl who'd loved them so much. Her breathless smile pounded my heart. She could probably feel it. A thundering, rabid thudding. T

The heat of her mostly bare skin radiated through me. Seared me. I was hot, chilled, drowning, and sucking in the first breath of air I'd taken in five years.

Cassi stared at me with wide eyes and pouting lips.

This was a woman who deserved to be kissed.

A *real* kiss. Not a silly game where I proved to my aching cock how much I wanted her, but the kiss of a lifetime. The kind that curled toes, melted panties, and revealed too much about how I felt. A kiss that would forgive the last five years of foolishness and promise minute-after-minute, hour-after-hour, day-after-day, year-after-year of commitment, honesty, and unrelenting pleasure.

I could have said so much in that kiss.

I should have been the man who kissed her like that.

Instead I was the idiot who'd smacked her ass and dumped her in the lake.

"I'm hungry." Mellie's declarations always came at the worst times. "I want macaroni."

Cassi's fingers dug into my arms. She pushed away.

Hesitantly?

"We should…" Cassi stared up at me, her eyes a dark and simmering in mystery. "Go home. Get them…food."

"And what else?"

"Is there anything else?

I had no idea, but a man could hope. "There might be."

Cassi shook her head.

But I made a decision.

No more living in isolation. No more dreading her knock at my door.

No more wishing for the past and regretting what had to be done.

Five years had passed, and I was ready to reclaim what was mine.

Screw professionalism. Cassi Payne was in my life again. And this time…

I was gonna get my girl—even if I had to trap her in a dozen goddamned tire swings.

8

Cassi

I ALWAYS IMAGINED THE FIRST BARE TUSH I'D SEE INSIDE REMINGTON Marshall's home would be his own gorgeous ass.

Instead, I chased two indecent ankle-biters, running laps around a scandalized sofa.

Mellie led the chanting. *"No bed! No bed!"*

This moment of civil disobedience was brought to me by Osh Kosh B'Gosh. Or...it would be once I got pants on the little buggers. Until then, those pale bottoms mooned me with every ounce of mischief they could wiggle, desperate to end their nanny's bedtime ritualistic tyranny.

"Come on." I kept my voice stern. "You've got to get back in the tub."

"No!"

"Mellie."

Tabby joined in gleeful protest. "*No!*"

The day had been nothing but a series of battles with the three-year-old, ending with a bath-time armada of tantrums, time outs, and tidal waves—her own brand of justice involving a Tupperware container filled with water, bubbles, and possibly a bit of Tabby's pee over my head.

The stakes were high. The kids tested my limits. And my patience. And how far a bottle of red wine could stretch.

"*No bed!*"

Mellie's fight for independence ended when the bubbles of shampoo in her hair trickled into her eyes. Maybe Johnson and Johnson should have developed a No More Tears-Gas. The toddler crumpled into a knot on the living room floor, wailing in a puddle of misery and suds.

"Mellie." We were *so* beyond counting to three now. "You are getting in the tub."

Her words bumbled in toddler hysteria, but I was fluent now. "I don't wanna go to bed!"

"You're not going to bed yet. You're getting in the tub and rinsing off."

"I don't wanna!"

"Come get in the tub, rinse the shampoo out, and I'll read you a story."

"*No!*"

"Now, Mellie."

"Uncle Rem!" Mellie added a series of karate kicks to her tantrum now, spiking at the air, the couch, and a wandering Tabby. "Want Uncle Rem!"

She wasn't the only one.

A week straight of twelve hours shifts—from the time the girls got up until they went to sleep—wasn't just exhausting. It was terrifying.

Sure, they were cute, but Mellie and Tabby were the worst disciplined kids I'd ever met. Sugary sweet when they were presented with trips, games, and food they liked. Shampoo covered demonic screechers when a bedtime approached, a toy was taken away, or anything *green* touched their plates.

A couple of timeouts and some good-behavior sticker magic might have improved their behavior, but good ol' Uncle Rem practiced childrearing in a non-conventional fashion. The *oh dear god, give them what they want, why are they still screaming* school of discipline. A time-tested and effective method of quiet days and nights, but one of the quickest conversions from toddler to sociopath.

"Aren't you getting tired?" I asked Mellie. "It's passed your bedtime."

"Na-uh!"

"All little girls go to bed at eight o'clock."

"Na-uh!"

"Oh yeah?" I placed my hands on my hips. "What time do you want to go to bed then?"

"Want to see Jimmy Fallon."

"*What?*"

"And the Roots."

Mellie plopped to the floor, collecting every carpet fiber, hair, bit of wood, and spec of mud on her wet skin. She whined, but I was too pissed to surrender.

"Does Uncle Rem let you stay up?"

She nodded. Now life made more sense. No wonder I had to lug her out of bed in the mornings. She wasn't just sawing logs in her sleep, she was deforesting entire rainforests.

I offered her my hand. "Let's go. Back in the tub."

"Don't wanna sleep!"

"We're just going to take a bath and read a story, okay?"

Mellie wiped the bubbles from her forehead. The tears remained, but she eyed me with that toddler skepticism that threatened the night's peace with an onslaught of unanswerable, possibly uncomfortable questions. Fortunately, Tabby knew how to create a distraction.

"*Yay!*" The baby stopped where she was running, squatted, and began to pee. "*Yay!*"

"Ew!" Mellie's screams terrified Tabby. "Bad baby! *Yuck!*"

This both intimidated and frightened the child. To escape from her sister's judgment, Tabby bolted across the living room, tinkling the whole way, her chubby legs flailing as her feet slapped a suddenly wet hardwood floor.

I caught Tabby before she raced into the kitchen and held her away from my body as she dribbled her last bit of disrespect with a giggle. Then I herded the girls to the tub for yet another round of baths.

This took an hour. Pajamas took twenty minutes. Another fifteen to bluff my way through Wheels on the Bus, the theme to Friends, and Beyoncé's Halo.

And, finally, the kids slept.

And I, drenched in Tabby's spaghetti dinner, soap, and unmentionables, collapsed on the living room couch. Toys and clothes covered the floor. Dishes mounded in the sink. Food littered the counters.

And Rem was nowhere to be seen.

Just like he'd stayed hidden for the past week.

Well, that was about to change.

I loaded the nanny cam app on my phone and slipped from the house only once both kids slept peacefully. I jogged through the dark and into Rem's chosen sanctuary.

Hiring me meant he'd had the time to renovate the workshop from spider-ridden, dark and dirty storeroom to a spider-ridden, moderately lit, sawdusted wood shop. Boards and timbers, nails and machines, tools and exceedingly sharp implements dotted the shop, just waiting for little hands to pluck a dangerous toy from his supply. Rem had promised to store his equipment in safe places. He'd also promised to be done after dinner, cleaned up by the girls' bedtime, and available for a quick story before his nieces went to bed and I went home.

Why did I ever expect Rem to keep his promises?

So much had changed, but so much stayed the same. The little girls depended on him now. And those consequences scared him. The workshop wasn't a Canadian wilderness, but it was as far as he could run.

He didn't look up when I entered. His attention fixed on a piece of timber he meticulously sanded. He'd carved the maple into a beautiful, artistic arch. It matched the other three he'd cut, shaped, and readied to be assembled.

The wood and dust, tools and equipment suited him. He set the piece with the others and hauled a larger slab of timber onto his work surface, the thick muscles in his arms and back straining against his shirt.

Did men know how good they looked when they rolled the cuff of their shirts just past their forearms? It felt like a conspiracy. Some sort of masculine memo sent out at the boys' secret club meetings. *Tonight's Agenda: Diehard Movies and Muscular Forearms—beef jerky and whiskey to follow.*

It wasn't fair. Rem's body had transformed into total muscle, chiseled as if he'd taken his tools and carved his abs, chest, and that sweet ass from the wood he'd practically crushed with his bare hands.

Annoyingly attractive—that's what he was.

His forehead glistened, slick with sweat. That dazzling smile would've made me sweat too.

"How's it going, Sassy?"

I flashed my phone at him, displaying the grainy images of the two girls sleeping soundly. "You missed bedtime."

"Already?"

"They wanted to say goodnight."

He nodded. "I'll catch them in the morning."

Sure thing. "And…how many verses of *Cat's in the Cradle* do you want me to sing?"

He brushed the dust from his hands, but his clothes were covered in splinters. "If you want, I'll wake them up now…"

Summoning the monsters awake wasn't nearly as hard as banishing them to bed. "Don't you dare."

"Okay then."

"Are you planning to come inside soon?"

He winked. "Is that an invitation?"

"More like a census," I said. "I'm just wondering if you've been scared out of your own home by two little girls."

Rem snorted. "*Three* little girls. The kids I can handle. But you…"

"Yes?"

"It's good to have a refuge."

I arched an eyebrow. "That so?"

"The timber isn't the only wood in here, Sassy."

"And I'm supposed to believe that?"

He dropped the sandpaper. "Want me to prove it?"

"I just want the truth—all of it this time."

"Think I'm lying to you?"

"Yes." I smiled. "But I'm used to that."

"No fair, Cassi."

"Why are you hiding in here?"

He shrugged. "I'm not."

"Don't give me that." I circled the tables, lightly touching carved pieces of chairs and fixtures. "You're hiding in this woodshop. And I can guess why."

He extended his hands. "I'd love to hear it."

"You're afraid of getting close to those little girls."

"They're my *nieces*."

"And they *terrify* you." I stared into his beautiful eyes—a rich, cherry darkness that held me in place as much as I tried to pin him down. "You're afraid of getting close to them because if you do…you'll be forced to stay in civilization again."

He laughed. "Butterpond is hardly civilization."

"But it's your home…and it's the one place you hate to be. Question is…*why*?"

I circled the shop once more before hopping onto a table.

"Cas—*no*."

I waved a hand and interrupted him, crossing my legs and letting my skirt do the talking. "I'm right. Don't try to pretend."

"That's not it."

"I know what your problem is, Mr. Marshall."

He surrendered with a shrug. "And I know what yours will be in a couple minutes."

"Don't worry about me. I've had five years to grow up all on my own, and I've learned a few things."

"Ever varnish a tabletop?"

"I've learned that people will *hide* instead of just coming right out and admitting that they're scared."

Rem smirked. "What are you afraid of, Sassy?"

"We aren't talking about me, Rem. I'm looking into *your* head."

"Don't look too close. It's pretty dirty in there."

"Right now…just looks like there's a bunch of bags packed and a compass pointing north. You want to run again."

"Can't." At least he was honest. "Got the kids to think about."

"The kids you haven't seen all week? The ones who need their Uncle Rem more than ever? The ones who miss their mom so much we spent all day making *Get Well Soon* cards for her?" I sighed. "Why did you come back to Butterpond, Rem?"

"They needed my help."

"And what about you?"

"I've been helped enough, Cas. Your family did more for me than you realize."

"And there's no shame in asking for more help," I said.

"I got you here, didn't I?"

I smirked. "Sure, I'm here…just so you can hide out in this shop."

He pointed across the shed at two hand-crafted dining room chairs. "Not hiding. I'm working every spare minute I can get to build some furniture. I need to bring in some money. God only knows when Emma's gonna…" He frowned. "When she'll recover. So, I better put something away for the kids. In case they need toys or clothes or…tranquilizers."

Oh.

He didn't need to look so ashamed. Nothing was sexier than a man being a man—providing for his family, protecting his own.

"You love those girls?" I asked.

"Of course. They're my nieces."

"Then why are you so afraid to connect with them? With anyone?"

With me?

Rem brushed a hand through his hair, shaking out a plume of sawdust. His voice lowered, heavy and solemn.

"Do you really have to ask why I ran? Why I'm not a part of any *family* anymore?" He snorted. "Take a look out your back window, at the hole in the ground where the barn used to be. You'll get all your answers there."

"That was five years ago, Rem. You've been trapped in the woods for far too long. You're becoming a recluse."

"What's wrong with that?"

Everything. "You're missing out on so much."

He laughed—that solid, rumbling laugh that tickled in my stomach. "What could possibly happen in Butterpond?"

"Lots of things."

"Name *one*."

Easier said than done. "Well…there's the county fair coming up at the end of summer."

"Gonna sign me up for a pie-eating contest?"

"I was thinking dunk tank." I kicked my legs. His attention drew over me, from my toes to my smile. My skin tingled under his stare. "Don't you miss it? All the friends you had?"

"I lost them—and for good reason." He held my gaze. "You know I'm better off on my own."

The question slipped out before I could stop it. "Aren't you lonely?"

"Nope." His words darkened, wicked. "Though I do miss a couple of the good things."

"Like what?"

"Getting a little personal, aren't we, Sassy?"

Oh. I rose to the challenge. "No hot dates in the logging camps?"

"…Not the good kind."

"Well, now you're home. You could have any girl you want."

"And what if I told you I wasn't interested in any of those Butterpond girls?"

His steps drew close. My heart skipped one too many beats, but I refused to let him see how much he affected me. My chin rose, and I studied his bearded jaw, the way his smile teased the corners of his mouth, the darkness of his eyes.

"What if I told you…" His voice warmed. "I rather grab my girl fresh, right off the farm?"

We weren't easy pickings. "Farm girls know better than to entertain the local wildlife."

"Never stopped you before."

"Had to learn my lesson—don't let that loathsome coyote chase me."

"Won't chase you if you don't run."

He stood before me, unwilling to approach the table, careful to keep his hands away from mine. I tightened my legs, crossed so hard at the ankles I'd fracture my foot. That only encouraged him. Urged him closer. Drowned me in his shadow.

I licked my lips. Whoops. Too much of an invitation.

"What would happen if I stop running?" I asked.

"I'd eat you up."

"Doesn't sound like a happy ending."

"That's because it would be the beginning."

His kiss came quick—a dizzying spiral of anticipation, desire, and doubt. A shiver guided each wayward emotion. The frantic pattering of my heart. The tender submission of my body. The raging protests of my mind. The more I fought against myself, the harder it became to focus on anything but his nibbling, tender, deliberate kisses.

I stopped him before the heat traveled too far, too quickly.

"This won't ever happen, Rem." It might have been more convincing if my voice hadn't trembled. "Not now."

"You want me to *reconnect*, to get back into the *world*?" He tucked a lock of hair behind my ear. "Give me a reason. Give me a chance."

I wanted to do nothing more, and that's why I couldn't. "I already did, once. Years ago. It wasn't the barn that hurt me. You left, and you broke my heart, Rem."

"I'm not proud of it."

"Doesn't matter now," I said. "Besides. It was for the best. I'm smarter now."

"I know."

"Wiser."

He nodded. "Of course."

"I know what's best for me."

"So that means no fun?"

I met his gaze. "It means no *you*."

Rem liked the challenge. His smile turned wicked. "You know, we're the same, Sassy."

"I doubt that."

"You've grown up. So have I. I'm a different man."

"Then why are you alone in the woods?"

"Not alone anymore. I've got you."

"You're paying me."

"I couldn't take advantage of your kindness. You'd have stayed, regardless of the paycheck."

I pushed his hands away from my knees before they teased the hem of my skirt. "That's not true."

"Now who's lying?"

"I wouldn't have stayed unless you tied me to a tree."

"The night is young, sweetheart."

He just didn't quit. I hummed, knowing his game.

"Rem, I've learned my lessons. I know when a bad boy is just looking to score." I tapped his nose. "And that's all you want."

"So you've got me and the world figured out," he said.

"That's right."

"No surprises." He smirked. "No disasters."

"Absolutely."

"Look before you sit, right?"

"That's…" I frowned. "What?"

Rem backed away with a laugh. "You just sat on wet varnish."

Damn it.

I pushed from the table. I didn't make it that far. The sticky varnish wasn't yet dry, but it wasn't nearly that wet. It'd formed the perfect consistency to cling to my cotton dress and fuse my butt to the table.

Good old sensible me, wise beyond my years, ass made of adhesive.

"Help me down?" I asked.

Rem surrendered, his hands up. "God no. I'm such a bad influence. One touch and I might just ravish you right there on Mrs. McMann's brand-new dining room set."

"You're such a jerk."

"Right now, it's your booty undoing a half-hour's worth of polishing. I hope they make panties out of microfiber cloths."

"*Rem!*" I twisted. The dress didn't move, stuck to the damn table like he'd painted the piece with Gorilla Glue. "What can I do?"

"Well, if you can hold a bowl of fruit, you'd make a great centerpiece."

He was hopeless. I grunted, grabbed the edge of the table, and pushed.

I fell forward.

My skirt did not.

It was the rip heard around the woodshed, and it'd occurred on the one day I'd concerned myself about panty-lines. Mercifully, the thong stayed on my body. Unfortunately, it had wedged so far up my booty it'd tuned my voice to the g-string.

Rem laughed as I fumbled for the skirt, giving it a hard yank. Half of the material sprung free of the table. I tossed the scrap at his face as he howled in hysterics.

"There." I spat. "You've always wanted in my pants. You can keep them."

"I got some glue if you want to lose the thong."

I had nothing to cover the panties except a chunk of 2x2 near my feet. It'd have to do.

"I think I need some glue to keep this damn thong in place," I said.

Not the encouragement Rem needed. "I won't tell if you drop em."

"Doesn't seem very workshop safe."

Rem practically flexed. "You afraid of a little wood?"

"Only the *low-grade* lumber."

He smirked. "But that's the best to screw."

"Rotten to the core."

"Nothing a good drilling can't fix."

He thought he was cute. I rolled my eyes. "If only we had a stud finder around here."

"Look no further, baby."

I uttered a wistful sigh. "Must be broken."

"Gotta give me a chance to nail you first, Sassy."

My turn to laugh. "Yeah. Good luck polishing the rest of your knobs, loverboy."

I backed towards the door, careful to gather what remained of my modesty as I tip-toed away.

"Don't go." Rem called. "I haven't even showed you my caulk yet!"

He was sweet as 100% Grade-A maple syrup, and just as a dangerous as a falling branch. "I will *not* end up another notch in your bedpost, Remington Marshall."

"Cas, I'd build a whole new bed for you."

"Keep the skirt." I met his gaze with a challenge. "Think about me tonight while you're doing your...*whittling*."

"Always have, Cas." He sunk onto his chair with a sigh. "Always will."

9

Cassi

I told Rem it'd take an act of God to get me in his bed.

So, of course, the heavens opened, the rain poured, and the weather service issued a county-wide flash flood warning.

Too risky – Julian had texted.

Tidus agreed. *It's dangerous.*

How did you get my number? – Quint didn't care.

You're working for Remington Marshall?? – Varius rarely came out of his room.

And then there was Rem—arms loaded with the two little girls, all three of them giving me a pouty lower lip.

"Dark and rainy, Sassy," he'd said. "Why not have a slumber party?"

A slumber party with the girls was fine. But did I trust myself with him?

Not a chance.

That's why he took the couch.

Not that his bed was any better. The soft sheets caressed me with his scent. The mattress held me tight. The pillows ached my head…and everywhere else.

For five years, I'd imagined myself in his bed—and the tossing and turning was usually a precursor to a much more satisfying night's sleep. Now? I stared at his ceiling, inhaled the earthen pine clinging to his blankets, and counted the crashes of thunder in the distance.

One.

Two.

My eyes drooped closed just as a terrifying crash echoed from outside the window.

"What the…"

Thunder didn't topple trashcans. Lightning didn't creak the wooden boards of the porch.

I bolted upright, darting for my phone. The trash cans rattled again. The sky streaked with brightness.

Was that a shadow passing the window?

Who was on the porch?

I dove from the bed, skittering passed the window. The bedroom door stuck shut, and I grappled with the knob as I stared into the night.

The middle of the woods was easy to find, but Rem's cabin was in a backass corner of nowhere, surrounded by trees, dirt roads, and hidden from any and all civilization. Only by a miracle of science did we get phone reception, and even that was influenced by the clarity of day, the wind in the trees, and a daily prayer to the cell tower positioned on Krieger Hill.

The forest was dark and scary on the best of days. But if someone lurked between the shadowy trees, who could help us? No one in Butterpond would know that we'd been turned into a cannibal's hamburger until my brothers ran out of Pop Tarts and came looking for the grocery checkbook.

I wasn't taking a chance with two little girls sleeping in the other room. I half-shimmied, half-crawled into the kitchen, ducking under the windows.

Rem slept on the couch, one arm over his eyes, the blanket low on his chest.

His bare chest.

And bare hips.

Of *course* he'd sleep naked. That was real practical. We *ate* on that couch.

At least it was a great sight to see before we'd be brutally murdered by a crazed serial killer during the summer's worst storm.

I searched for a weapon. Rem's kitchen contained one dull chef's knife, a stock pot, and a broom. I grabbed a lid to the largest frying pan as a shield and wielded both the broom and knife in the same hand. No more crashes from the porch.

Did the intruder know I was awake?

"*Rem.*" My hissed whisper wasn't loud enough to carry over the rain pounding the metal roof. "Rem, wake up!"

A good slap to his chest startled him awake. I groped the floor to find his jeans crumpled near the couch. I handed them to him before pushing the knife into his hands.

He blinked, bleary, staring at the pants and weapon. "Is this…is this a seduction?"

"It might be a burglary."

Even half-asleep, he grinned. "You don't have to steal it. I'll give it up willingly."

"I'm serious."

"So am I."

"I hear something."

"A racing heartbeat and murmured longings?"

I jabbed him with the broom. "A crash. From outside."

"Okay."

"Something is out there."

Rem rubbed his face. "It's the *woods*. There's a lot of things out there."

"It could be a murderer."

"Who the hell would come all the way up the mountain to kill us?"

"What better way to do it? We're so far out in the boonies. No one would know."

"Boonies? Sassy, you grew up on a *farm*. It's probably an animal."

"I grew up with domesticated animals—horses, cows, chickens. Not whatever might be out there."

"Nothing bad is out there. Just a coyote. Maybe a bear."

"On your *porch*."

"Be glad you're inside."

"We'll check together."

Rem sat up. The blanket fell low. I tried not to look.

Failed.

What was I afraid of outside? The biggest animal twitched to life right beside me.

Rem didn't notice. He grunted and checked the time. "You want us to go outside and see if there's a bear on the porch."

"Or a murderer."

"*Why?*"

"So it doesn't get in *here*."

He glanced at my impromptu shield and staff. "Is that why you're wielding half-assed weapons? Christ, Cas, you *are* the Dollar General."

Another crash. I flinched, but enough was enough. I aimed the broom for the door. Rem hauled me away, tossing me onto the couch while he hobbled into his jeans as quickly as he could without causing permanent damage to his manhood or pride.

"You stay here." He scratched his beard with a lazy swat of his fingers. "I'll check it out."

I offered him the broom. "Take it."

"Yeah, I'll sweep him off the porch." He handed it back. "You keep it in case I get eaten."

He flung the door open and braved the torrent of rain outside. A still second passed. The light of his cellphone swept across the yard.

Then his shout echoed over the night.

"Cas! Get in the house!"

I leapt away as he rushed into the cabin, slamming the door and twisting the lock with a profanity.

"*Seriously?*" I clutched the broom. "I thought the storm just freaked me out."

"No." He peeked out a window. "I saw him."

"*Him?*"

"Yeah. He's a sneaky son of a bitch. Hiding in the shadows. Knocked over the garbage can."

My heart lurched. I glanced to the kids' room. Still sleeping, but they were entirely too far away from us to feel safe. "Who was it?"

"Some little fat guy. Real chubby."

"You saw him?"

"Not that it'll help." Rem gestured over his face. "He wore a mask over his eyes."

Damn it. Our options were limited. Sheriff Samson never responded to anything outside the bar after midnight—and only because he was usually the last customer served. He'd never make it up the mountain in the middle of the storm.

That meant it was up to us.

"We've gotta go out there," I said. "Confront him. Fight him off."

Rem nodded. "Good plan. I can't let him prowl around. My luck, he'd get into the attic."

"Is there a window?"

"A pest like that? He'd chew right through the damaged shingles."

"What?"

Rem shushed me with a finger to my lips. "Okay. We'll go outside. You distract him. I'll circle back and grab his tail."

"His…*tail?*"

"I'll swing his ass into the woods. That'll teach him a lesson."

"What the hell are you talking about?"

"Or maybe I'll make a hat out of him." He grinned. "It's a goddamned raccoon, Sassy."

I aimed the broom for his gut. "You son of a—"

He dodged the attack. "Shh. Don't wake the kids."

Oh, I didn't need words. I slapped his shoulder once, twice, then another time just to make it hurt. My hand stung. Rem's muscles hadn't even twitched.

"You scared the hell out of me," I said.

He dodged my fourth slap and folded his fingers into mine. One tug, and I was trapped against his chest.

"You think I'd let anything happen to you?" he asked.

"Well, you just gave me a heart attack."

"Nothing to fear, Sassy. I'm your big strong hero, here to keep you safe all night."

I snorted. "I'll take my chances with the bandit outside. At least he's only stealing trash."

"Yeah?" Rem's smile melted my irritation. Wasn't sure how the bastard did it. "And what do I steal?"

"Anything you can get."

"Like..." He leaned in quick, holding my cheek as his lips brushed mine. "A kiss?"

I batted at his chest. "And worse."

"What? Like a touch?" He swatted at my behind.

"Knowing you? You'd take a girl's virtue."

His words mellowed. "And her heart, if she'd give it to me."

My chest fluttered a little too hard. I swallowed. "I think the most dangerous animal in these woods is standing right in front of me."

"You know it, little girl. Better run. I do worse things than bite and scratch."

"You wouldn't dare."

He lunged. I giggled and twisted away, batting his hands from mine and diving around the couch. Rem followed, easily seizing me in his thick arms as I attempted to escape into the bedroom. We tumbled to the couch, my body tangled in his, my legs twisted under his weight.

And like a fool, I'd ended up exactly where I swore I'd never be caught.

Beneath him.

Breathless. Panting.

Staring at the only man who had ever made a raccoon attack actually seem *romantic*.

"We should go to bed," I whispered.

"I agree."

Bad boy. "*Alone*."

"Where's the fun in that?"

His fingers trailed over my arms, pushing my wrists over my head. I debated reaching for the broom. A good swat might have stilled his hands.

But it did nothing for his lips.

Rem leaned in, seizing me in a kiss so sudden, so perfect, he didn't need to hold my hands. My body puddled right there, a mess of indecision, denied urges, and dreaded desire. He nibbled at me, a swift and commanding kiss that threatened my surrender right then and there.

No one was sexier than this man.

I'd fallen for him since the first moment I knew my heart could belong to another. And he knew it was always his. He'd carried it. He'd teased it. He'd broke it. Now it beat with such a fury that I had no doubt he could feel every last thump.

A kiss, and I was lost. A gentle caress of my cheek, and I submitted.

A nip to my neck, and I was in trouble.

Rem moved over me, wedging himself between my legs as his hardness pressed against my thigh. The denim did a poor job of containing that strength. And I did even less to discourage it.

I'd wanted to feel him.

For so long. So many years. So many broken promises.

And now? He kissed me, deep and dramatic, as if proving that I wasn't the only one lost to those memories.

My shirt rode up. My dark tummy exposed to him, and his hand tickled upwards, brushing against the swell of my breast. Heat spread from his fingertips—a wonderful magic that shivered and delighted. It washed over my body and ignited every part of me.

My hips accidentally bucked against his.

He liked that.

So did I.

"You have no idea how much I've wanted this." Rem's words caressed me, sweeter than his hands. "My biggest regret was never getting to touch you. To taste you. To hold you." He kissed me once more, his words a low growl. "To be with you."

"It was for the best." I wished I hadn't arched as his hand tickled downwards. "We wouldn't have worked together."

"Maybe not then…" He teased over my thigh, but he never shifted his gaze from mine. Instead, his eyes widened as his fingers drifted down, over the borrowed pair of boxers separating his skin from mine. He pressed hard. A dozen intoxicating shivers rose from his touch. He smirked as I gasped. "Things have changed, Cas. We're different now."

Who could concentrate when a master of pleasure rolled his fingers over that delicate secret?

"You're all grown up." He teased me with quick circles. "And I know the kind of man I am now."

"What kind?"

"Not good." He didn't apologize for it, only tightened and quickened his pace. "I've never pretended to be a good man. I left because I had to, but I've never wanted to hurt you."

He wasn't hurting me now. Just the opposite. My fingernails sunk into the couch. I didn't dare speak.

"You're the only woman who's ever made me regret the man I became. You're the reason I want to be *better*."

Sweet words and dirty touches. He traced the most sensitive part of me and watched as I tensed and panted for him. Too intense. Too new and amazing. I moved against his hand and struggled to piece together enough thoughts to break my heart.

"You know this is too complicated," I whispered.

"Doesn't have to be." He caressed a little harder, stealing a mew from my parted lips. "This is what we've always needed, Cas. Just to feel each other. We need to be together. To touch and kiss and just…"

"I can't lose you twice, Rem."

"You *never* lost me the first time." He kissed me once more. "I left you, but I never stopped—"

"Don't say it."

"Then let me show you."

He leaned over me, his heat and strength and the wild promise of his touch capturing me within his arms. I sucked in a breath as his fingers tangled in the waistband of my shorts. Our gazes met.

And the door squealed from the kids' room.

"It's thundering. What are shadows made of? Can I have some water?"

Mellie had little tact when it came to entering a room.

Rem swore, panicked, and accidentally rolled off the couch. He struck the floor with an *oof*, but was on his feet and offering his hand to Mellie before she got too close to the sofa.

"You okay, kiddo?" he asked.

"Thirsty." Mellie tilted her head at him. "I want Jimmy Fallon."

"Aha!" I pointed at him. "I *knew* you let her stay up after her bedtime."

Rem sigh and led the little girl into the kitchen. He cracked open a bottle of water for her. "No TV tonight. Go back to bed."

"You're not sleeping."

Rem cleared his throat. "We were *almost* sleeping."

I smirked. "Hopefully not *that* quick."

"Well, in a good two hours."

"Two?"

He grinned. "At least."

"Must take you a long time to get tired."

He eyed me with a terrible, wonderful hunger. "Stamina for days. Need some proof?"

Mellie tugged on Rem's hand. "Can I have a story?"

The cuteness pained him. He glanced from the girl to me.

"I'm off the clock," I said. "This is all you. I should get to bed."

"Sure you don't want a story too?" His smile was wicked. "I can tuck you in."

And then where would we be?

Exhausted. Deliriously happy. Hopelessly confused.

And possibly more hurt than I'd been five years ago.

"I think I'll tuck myself in tonight," I said.

"Afraid of what would happen?"

No. Because I knew *exactly* what would happen.

I wouldn't just fall for Remington Marshall. I'd hit absolute rock bottom.

But I'd *so* enjoy the tumble.

10

Remington

Nothing had felt greater than waking up with Cassi...

Though it might have been a hell of lot more fun if we'd have awakened in the same room.

Beggars couldn't be choosers, and I was begging. *Hard.* I'd have no problem convincing her from my knees, but I needed her to listen first. Or spread her legs.

Damn, I'd gotten close. Didn't deserve the brief kisses and touches I took, but nothing was going to stop me now.

I was going to win Cassi back.

Why the fuck did I ever leave her in the first place?

Because I didn't have a choice. I couldn't offer her an explanation, but at least I knew I'd done what was right. I'd hurt her, but running had caused less heartache.

Three days. That's how long her scent stayed on my pillows. Sweet, floral, and intoxicating. And if I planned to make that a permanent perfume, I had to work hard.

Fortunately, I had an idea.

Her text had been frantic that morning, so I dressed the kids, loaded them in the truck, and met her at the municipal center at her request. We waited at the playground for fifteen minutes before Cassi jogged up the sidewalk, greeted the kids with a wide smile, and offered me another round of apologies.

"I'm so sorry I'm late." She'd wrapped her hair in a vibrant pink scarf. The knot came loose as she ran, and she reached back to tighten it, scrunching her nose as she picked a piece of floss off of her arm. "You have no idea how *frustrating* it is fighting over the bathrooms every single morning. Adult siblings are *not* supposed to live together. I love my brothers so much that I just want to strangle them all very, very slowly."

I grinned. What a perfect opportunity. "So move in with me."

I hadn't expected a complete silence to befall the municipal center. Swings stopped creaking. Water fountains dried. Birds practically dropped from the sky.

And Cassi laughed her ass off.

"*Move in*?" She patted Mellie's behind and sent her running to the sandbox. "You've gone insane."

"You could be a live-in nanny."

"You can't afford a regular, full-time nanny."

I could do one better. "I'll guarantee you a bed, a bathroom, and a fresh box of wine in the fridge every day."

"Well, damn. Marry me now."

Would if I could. "Limited time offer."

"Are gonna find some other easily manipulated early-education major to seduce?"

"What can I say?" I hauled Tabby up, kissed her cheek, and realized then that most of her breakfast had ended up in her diaper. "I have other interested parties. These kids are usually quite cute."

"Usually?"

"Yeah..." I held the baby at arm's length. "This one has done something decidedly not cute. Did you clock in yet?"

Cassi tapped her chin. "Yes, but I like to watch you squirm."

"Rather watch me change her in the grass? A couple kids turned the changing table in the men's bathroom into a trampoline."

She gestured for the baby and grunted as Tabby bounced in her arms. "You win this round."

"Enjoy your prize."

Cassi whistled, calling for Mellie. "Potty break. Come on, kiddo."

Mellie promised me she hadn't needed to go before leaving the house. Now she danced in the sandbox. "I don't gotta."

Cassi snapped her fingers. Mellie pouted, but she wiggled cross-legged to her nanny and hobbled towards the bathrooms.

Just in time too. I stared across the playground towards the municipal building. Part county offices, part sheriff station, part take out hotdog stand, the parking lot was almost bigger than the governmental seat of Butterpond. The space was just small enough so everyone's dirty laundry aired in front of the town.

And this laundry was real dirty.

Chad Bilcon hit the bottle like he hit his women—hard and often. The slimeball was old enough to be Emma's dad when he'd knocked her up. He left her after Mellie was born. Waited two years.

Then came home to finish the job. Out popped Tabby, and off he ran.

Just like me, the bastard wasn't even supposed to be in town. Last I'd heard, the potbellied, balding asshole had spent time up at State, earning the tattoos staining his rotten flesh. He wasn't good for anything, least of all child support. A man like that deserved to be hung from his ankles until every last cent he owned struck the floor.

Wasn't bad enough the kids didn't have a dad.

But to know that *he* was their father?

Revolted me.

Chad tore a yellow citation into three pieces and shoved it into a nearby garbage can. He staggered towards the parking lot. I didn't let him get far.

"Who the hell said you could come back here?"

Chad turned, eyes bloodshot with whatever drug of the month he'd decided to shoot into his veins. He stared at me, unrecognizing, and spat a lug of chew onto the pavement. The bastard marched a couple steps closer before he realized he should've kept walking.

"*Remington*?" He wiped a hand across his sweaty forehead—a pale slug of skin that now extended to the crown of his head. "I could ask you the same question. The fuck are you doing here?"

Chasing toddlers. Avoiding the gaze of the mothers who shuffled the children to the opposite end of the playground from us. Consoling Mellie once she realized no other kids were allowed to play with her.

"Patrolling the gutters to find slime like you," I said.

"Get your ass outta my business."

"Your business is my business nowadays." I squared my shoulders as he encroached. "You chasing Emma again?"

"A man has some standards."

Classy. "Then you here to see your kids?"

He held his arms out. "Got no kids."

"I know those girls are yours. You know they're yours. Bout time you acted like it."

"Only birth certificate with my name on it is my own." Chad sucked the spittle from his lip. "Emma can't remember who knocked her up anyway."

"Well I got a good memory."

"Last I heard…she was in a bit of trouble."

His fault. "Yeah. Feel bad for that?"

"Emma made her own bed. Got more dicks than mine in it too."

"You mother fuc—"

"Emma got her own problems. Ain't mine anymore. And those…" He pointed over my shoulder as Cassi returned, Tabby in her arms, Mellie racing to the sandbox. "Those ain't my problems. Keep the brats away from me."

"They aren't brats."

"And they ain't *mine*." He spat once more. "So don't come reaching for my wallet when Emma finally kicks it."

I reared back, fist balled. Cassi caught it, spun me, and forced Tabby against my chest.

Not many men could fight with a squirming one-year-old in their arms. Cassi knew it.

Cassi banished Chad with a frustrated wave. "There's no trash on this playground. Move it before we shove you into the garbage."

Chad seized the opportunity and stumbled away. I should have followed—should have showed him how shit was settled in the middle of the wilderness with no police or laws preventing a man from solving matters of disrespect.

Tabby tugged on my ear and punched her enthusiasm.

"Ba!" She pointed over my shoulder at the kids playing with an inflatable ball. "Ba!"

If I wasn't careful, Cassi was about to rip my *ba* off. She stared at me, bewildered.

"You are twenty-seven years old. Are you really gonna have a fist-fight on a *playground*?"

I stared as Chad started his beat-up Chevy and sped away. "Someone has to take responsibility."

"And beating up some burnt-out junkie is the way to do it? Rem, you're better than that."

"Am I?" I let Tabby down, holding her arms as she toddled across the grass. "Don't pretend, Cas. You look at me, and you still see the same fuck-up from five years ago."

She frowned. "Only because you swear in front of the kids."

That wasn't the reason she hadn't welcomed me into her bed. Why she was resisting me. Why she denied the feelings we both shared.

"I'm serious," I said.

She sighed. "So am I. I know things are different now. My dad's gone. My brothers are back. The farm has turned on its head. In five years, a lot can change. We're not the same people we once were."

"You are."

It seemed to offend her. "I am not."

"Didn't say it was bad. You know I always liked you. Probably too much."

"Well, I am quite lovable."

"More than you realize."

She looked away. "You always were a sweet-talker."

"Only with sweet girls."

Mellie ran over, babbling and pointing with such enthusiasm she fell, face-planted in the dirt, rose, stomped her feet in a pout, then resumed her excitement. Her blue eyes widened, bright and pretty, as she practically foamed at the mouth.

"They. Got. *Balloons!*"

At three years old, Mellie's life had never been and never would be the same again unless she could possess a poorly twisted balloon animal haphazardly strung together by a burnt-out college-aged punk in oversized shoes, a red nose, and smeared makeup. She bounced in place and tugged on our hands.

"*Balloons!*" She squealed, supersonic over the playground. "*Kitties!*"

As if anyone could resist.

As if anyone had a choice.

Pretty sure if Mellie had a sharpened stick she might have held it to my throat for a crack at the balloon animals. A dozen or more kids had already formed a mob around the clown, climbing over each other Walking Dead style to wrench the animals from the stoner clown's hands.

Tabby whined for a snack, so I braved the crowds with Mellie, letting Cassi go sit with the baby on a viciously guarded table, patrolled by a rash of mothers on the lookout for a place to park it.

And I thought the kids were malicious trying to get their grubby hands on the balloon animals. The mothers practically flung their babies at the picnic tables to reserve a spot for their families. Purses swung. Cell phones cracked. Coffee cups splattered.

Butterpond might have been small—every family knew each other, no news went ungossiped, no family unjudged—but all was fair in war and playgrounds.

I returned with a snail-turtle-frog for Tabby. Mellie spun in circles on the grass with a cat that looked suspiciously like a rabbit. And I poked Cassi with my personal favorite.

She stared at the shaft and two orbs with a gasp. "What the hell is that?"

I grinned. "Supposed to be an elephant. See the trunk?"

"That's vulgar."

"Pretty impressive, huh?"

Cassi rocked Tabby and kept her delighted with a stash of grapes. "Oh, you *wish*."

"Like looking in a mirror, Sassy."

"I doubt that."

"You never thought to check."

She baited me with a quick smile. "Oh, I thought. I thought about it a lot."

"Did you?"

"My brothers thought about it too."

I frowned. "That's...not as flattering."

"They just worried about me and..." She poked the balloon. "Your elephant."

"Why? Nothing to worry about. I would have shown you a good time."

"Glad I didn't," she said.

"I'm not."

She arched an eyebrow. "And if I had...there you were...running off to chop down trees and be all reclusive."

"True." I grinned. "But you *did* think about it."

"Is that all that matters?"

"If you're not stroking anything else, at least give the ego a tug."

"And *that* is why I didn't." She tossed a grape at my head. "You were my first crush. My first kiss. I thought you'd be more. You meant a lot to me."

"And if I said you still meant that much to me?" I asked. "And it would have meant just as much five years ago?"

"Good to know."

Tabby attempted to eat her frog. She gnawed on the balloon, made a face, and tried to spit out the bad taste. Cassi popped a teething ring into her mouth before she fussed.

She was a natural at this. So why didn't she have a kid of her own? Butterpond's usual pastime was breeding. Some even raced to get started—fourteen, fifteen years old. Most popped one out as soon as they had a high school diploma.

But Cassi was different.

"What'd you do after I left?" I asked.

She gave me a sidelong glance. "If you're expecting a sob story about how I wailed, gnashed my teeth, and tried to set myself on fire aboard a Viking burial ship, you're only partially right."

"Once you got off the pyre, what did you do?"

"Went to college. Came home. Took care of my dad."

"Not what I mean." I gave her a shrug. "Who...did you *see*?"

"Everyone I looked at."

"Very funny."

"Well, you gotta be joking too," she said. "I'm not answering that."

"Why not?" I pretended the jealousy wasn't searing my heart to ash. "You're a beautiful girl. Someone must have snatched you up in college."

"I *studied* in college like a proper student, not like any of the girls who *you* ever chased."

"Only ever chased you, Sassy."

"Yeah, the others threw themselves at you."

"And I stopped catching when I realized I had a shot with you." Easiest decision I'd ever made. "So come on. You can tell me."

"Nope."

"Why not?"

She bit her lip. "Because it's none of your business."

"Oh." I got it now. "You're *embarrassed*."

"Am not."

The edge slipped into my voice. "You hooked up with one of the Barlow boys, didn't you? The only guy who'd be worse for you than me."

"I did *not* hook up with a Barlow boy." She poked my chest. "And I'd always thought you'd be good for me. For my first time."

That I liked to hear. "Yeah?"

"I've always wanted you to be my first."

"I'm flattered."

"You should be."

She paused. Stared at me. Eyebrows rising.

Holy shit.

My heart dropped to my balls. Everything hardened, and it didn't help the situation.

"Don't tell me that you waited for me, Cas."

"You broke my heart."

"Jesus Christ. You didn't..." I edged my words around the baby. "You mean you haven't..."

"I'd like to say that you frightened me off of men." She didn't look ashamed. Instead, she seemed rather at peace with such a revelation. "But I think it was the opposite. No one compared to you."

My heart would have stopped if the blood weren't all draining to my cock. I rubbed my face, exhaling a dozen silent profanities so I didn't corrupt *both* girls sitting before me.

"Shit, Cas."

I needed to stop imagining her. Pure. Innocent. Untouched. Begging for me. In my bed, in my arms, in my *life*.

What the hell was I doing? This wasn't right.

I wasn't a good man, but indulging *that*?

Then I would be a monster.

"You know what I want," I said. "But I am *not* good enough for you."

"I didn't say *hop on*." Cassi laughed. "You asked. I answered."

"But there's so much you don't know. So much that happened. It's a good thing we never..."

"Why?" Her voice never wavered, but she stared at me as if trying to understand a day, a life, a decision I couldn't explain. "Why not? What are you hiding that's so bad?"

"You heard the story."

"Not from *you*," she said. "I never heard it from *you*. Only Tidus. Why don't *you* tell me what happened?"

A dangerous question that I sure as hell wasn't answering. I swung my legs from under the table and watched Mellie destroy a bush leaf by plucked leaf.

"You already know everything," I said. "I was smoking in the barn. Wasn't paying attention. The cigarette must have caught on the hay—everything was so dry that year. It went up. I tried to put the fire out. Couldn't. Tidus ran in and got me out of the barn before I died. He saved me." I didn't look at her, though I kept my voice firm. "I was careless."

"And that's all that happened? That's why you ran?"

"Isn't that reason enough? I was no good back then. Pissing around. Drinking. Drugs. What else was there for a fuckup like me to do? I got into trouble, I got Tidus into trouble, and I was good at it. You didn't need me chasing you."

"I don't think that's true."

It was. "Your family lost so much in that fire. It wasn't right to stay. I had to get away. Better myself. Try to be…*something*. If not a good man than just…someone sober who could control himself."

"Did it work?" she asked.

"I don't live in the woods because I'm ashamed of myself," I said. "I stay away from town and people and civilization because that's the only way I trust myself. When I was logging, I had to stay clean. Out there, I had to be smart so I wouldn't freeze, starve, or get hurt. So I did it. And I recovered. And I've stayed clean." I looked away. "Never wanted to come back to Butterpond, especially after the last time."

"When was that?"

Not a time I wanted her to remember. "I came for your mom's funeral."

The pause of grief. It only lasted a breath. "I didn't know you were there."

"I didn't want you to know." I hated every minute of this confession. "I came home for a couple weeks and immediately fucked it up again. Got into trouble. Got into drugs. And I *knew* that wasn't what I wanted for myself. That's when I realized I couldn't be a part of *this*." I waved a hand over the wholesome park. "I had to stay away. By myself. Isolated. And it worked. I've been clean for four years."

"That's good."

"I got some money. Had a good job until…" I nodded to the kids. "But I have enough to get by. I finally found a place in the world, even if it's outside of it."

"And you like it?"

I'd spent the better part of an hour last night begging the project manager to keep my position open. "Yeah. I'm good at it. Responsible. If only you had met me now. We might've had a chance."

Cassi snorted. "Are you kidding? If I didn't know who you were, I would have assumed that you were a crazy hermit living off in the mountains. Someone who'd kidnap me and whisk me away to do terrible things in that cabin."

"I still might. You never know."

Cassi shuffled closer. "I guess I'll have to take my chances."

"With the kidnapping…" I brushed her hand. "Or with me?"

She didn't look at me, but she smiled. A beautiful, hopeful smile.

"Like I said, Remington Marshall…" Her words were a velvet promise. "No one compares to you."

11

Remington

The promise of a free bathroom with complimentary bubble bath was the key to a woman's heart.

Better than chocolate, wine, or sex.

Well, maybe not sex.

All it took for Cassi to pack her bags and move her gorgeous ass into my cabin was a fight between Tidus and Quint. One busted showerhead and five hundred dollars' worth of water damage to the downstairs bathroom, and she was mine. I had a tub, some bubble bath, and a pledge to give her all the time she wanted to soak without interruptions.

Once the kids went to bed and Cassi's bags rested in the corner of my bedroom, I banished myself to the couch like a gentleman. But the thought of her naked, sudsy, and hot in the tub? Not my most wholesome of fantasies.

The image would torment me the rest of my life. What the hell was I thinking? *Move in with us. Be a live-in nanny. Torture me every night until I've got calluses on my hand because I can't stop thinking about you.*

I was a monumental idiot.

Cassi screamed from the bathtub. A clatter, crash, and problematic splash followed.

But I was a *useful* idiot.

I hopped the couch and rushed to the door, busting inside as heroically as a bastard could get while hoping to save his lady and catch a glimpse of her goods.

"Are you okay?" I asked.

"*Get the axe!*"

Cassi wove herself into the shower curtain. She sunk deeper into the bubbles of the tub, armed only with a rubber ducky and toilet scrub brush. Two shampoo bottles scattered across the bathroom. Only one had the decency to not splinter against the ceiling and explode lavender scented soap over the room. A wadded washcloth slid down the wall like a half-assed spitball, and enough bath salts crumbled over my floors to get most of Butterpond high as a kite.

"What the hell are you doing?" My house was a *disaster*. "No fucking wonder your brothers didn't want to share a bathroom with you!"

Cassi's bubbles thrashed under her kicking feet, but she cautiously floated them back in place to regain her modesty. Her words sputtered under the water line.

"*Spider!*"

Oh Christ. "You really don't belong in the woods."

"Get it before it eats the kids!"

I mourned the tube of toothpaste floating in the toilet. "It's just a spider."

I regretted my words when the hairy beast scurried across the bathroom floor, hesitating near a fallen toothbrush as if it wished it arm itself. Easily the size of my hand, the little bastard practically snickered as I stepped away.

"It's *huge*," Cassi said.

"Everything is bigger in these woods."

"Well, kill it! If that thing bites you, I'm *not* sucking the venom out."

"That's snakes, Sassy."

"If there's a snake in this bathroom, Lord have mercy on you, Remington Marshall."

I wadded up a couple squares of toilet paper, checked the spider once more, and realized I needed heavier artillery for that bad boy. Paper towels maybe. Quilted and four-ply. Hell, maybe the mop. I had big feet, but my boots would have only stunned the beast.

"Oh, God." Cassi reached for me, realized it put her within another foot of the spider, and retreated under the water. "Do it quick. Don't let it get angry."

Fucker needed a chair and a whip. "He's already angry, Cas. Think you pissed him off when you doused him with shaving cream."

"Be careful!"

My shoe rose up.

And Mellie's scream echoed through the house.

"*No!*" The little girl sprinted inside the bathroom and attached herself to my leg. "Don't!"

Cassi nearly launched from the tub to move the child away. I didn't blame her. Mellie was the right size for a midnight snack. I should have probably checked on Tabby too, just to make sure she wasn't cocooned in the corner of her room.

"It's a *spider*, Mellie," Cassi said.

"Mommy says they eat bad bugs."

"That *is* a bad bug, kiddo!"

"*Uncle Rem!*"

Damn it. I dropped the shoe.

What the hell was Emma doing with her kids? The only time she was ever a mother to the girls was to ally them with every creepy crawlie that lived in the basement. Then again, they probably didn't have a choice. I saw the state of their house. A couple spiders would have made it more hospitable.

Mellie burst into tears. I sighed.

"Hold on."

I grabbed one of the Dixie cups on the side of the sink. No way. Bastard needed a soup bowl. Fuck it. I'd make him fit. What was losing a leg or two when he had six other hairy haunches?

Even I fought a shiver as I crashed the cup over the fat thing. I slipped Cassi's handheld mirror under the rim and captured the thrashing arachnid.

"You realize there's creepier things living in barns?" I said.

Cassi covered her eyes. "I never looked in the barn."

"Mice. Rats. Spiders. Snakes."

"Don't tell me."

I grinned. "You should be thanking us for torching it."

"What?"

I paused. So did she. Her bubbles went still.

Damn it. "Bad joke, I know."

"No…" She frowned, her eyebrows furrowed. "You said *us*."

"What?"

"You said, thank *us* for torching it."

"Did I?" *Shit.* "I meant me. And you can thank me any way you like, Sassy."

I nodded to Mellie. She tugged on my arm, uncomfortably close to the crawling captive scurrying around the cup.

"Is he okay?" Mellie asked.

"Better than you'll be if you don't get in bed."

I escorted both to the front door, thought better of letting the beast that near the house, and released him at the tree line with a diligent Mellie waving at him from the driveway.

"Bye, Spider!"

I pointed at her and gave chase, earning a quick giggle as she darted into the cabin. A quick scoop in my arms, a toss into her bed, and a begrudgingly read a story about a hungry caterpillar—what was it with this kid and bugs?—and Mellie was out.

I returned to the bathroom with a cautious knock. Cassi struggled to align the few bubbles still in her tub to cover all the good parts I'd only ever dreamed about. I grinned.

"How's your bath?"

Cassi raised an eyebrow. "*Crowded.*"

"The spider is gone. Girls are asleep. Now I gotta take care of you. How's the water?"

She shrugged. "Cool."

"Allow me…"

Cassi rolled her eyes, but I carefully adjusted the faucet, trickling in a new wave of warmth to the water. Beneath the bubbles, her sculpted legs twisted. Dark. Tempting. Just begging to be spread.

A goddamned virgin.

Waiting for *me*.

And I'd blown it.

We had to make up for five years of sinful, delicious excitement, and I wasn't missing a single moment anymore.

Another hit of bubble bath made her smile. She welcomed the bubbles over her skin.

"You know, after all that hard work with the spider…" I said.

She shook her head. "No more talk of spiders, please."

"I need to warm up after those shivers too."

I reached for my shirt.

"You wouldn't," Cassi said.

It landed in a heap on the floor.

"Oh my God." Cassi gasped. "You aren't really…"

I unbuckled my belt. The pants kicked off. She hid her eyes.

"You're gonna get me dirtier," she groaned.

I stepped into the tub behind her. "That's the plan."

She scooted forward, sloshing the bubbles over the edge. "You're getting everything wet!"

"Get used to it, Sassy."

I grabbed her by the waist and hauled her onto my lap, letting my legs stretch out as she nestled against on my chest, in my lap, in my arms.

I hardened to the point of pain. She could feel it, but hell, wasn't like it'd surprise her. She knew what I'd wanted—what I'd felt for her.

"Better?" I asked.

She cautiously used an arm to block any unsanctioned peeping. "Well…I'm not as cold now."

"Believe me, you're gonna get hot."

"Why do I get the feeling you're trying to seduce me?"

"No way." I lied. "You were adamant. Can't take this any further. Broken hearts and promises and five years of lost opportunities. I missed the chance to seduce you."

She cuddled closer, watching as my fingers traced a soft line over her shoulders. "So you're just naked and in the tub with me…platonically?"

"Yeah."

"And that bulge back there?"

"Platonic bulge."

"Sounds painful."

"I've learned to live with it."

Her smile would have boiled the water. I reached for a new wash cloth and dunked it into the bubbles. She lolled her head to the side, and I lathered the sensitive skin around her neck.

"And now you're washing my back…just as a friend?"

"I live to serve."

"So, if *this* isn't seduction…" She wouldn't turn without revealing more of her perfection to me. I willed every last bubble to pop. "What exactly *are* your moves?"

"Damn. I've got so many."

"And how many would work on me?"

"Just one." I murmured. "Just a kiss."

"You've kissed me before."

"Not the way I should've kissed you."

I envied the washcloth as it caressed the softness of her skin. With a bit of encouragement, I moved her arm from her body and rewarded her bravery with a gentle stroke of the cloth down to her fingertips. She sighed and nestled deeper against me, the swell of her breasts barely peeking over the water.

"You've always kissed me good," she whispered.

"Nah. This would have been a *real* kiss. Just you and me. A gentle touch. A million heartbeats. A kiss so good no fire would've ever separated us."

She didn't tense as the washcloth crossed over her chest.

Over the swell of her breast.

Tickling her hardened nipple.

Then below.

She shivered against me. "Why didn't you ever kiss me like that?"

I pressed my hand against her belly, the washcloth teasing her with a slow massage. "I knew what would happen."

"You must have known I fell for you."

"That didn't make it right. You weren't supposed to be with me."

"Says who?"

"Your brothers."

She hummed. "They're just overprotective."

"They were right to be. I was a bad influence. On Tidus. On you."

"I hope you weren't doing these things with Tidus."

I nipped at her neck. Her giggle transformed into a mew.

"Even he knew I was no good for you. The things I might've done to you…"

Did she realize she'd ground back against me? "Like what?"

The washcloth drifted lower. Cassi's breath quivered in a quiet coo. How could such a tiny, sweet noise drive me so crazy? My cock twitched, pressing against her back. The heat didn't make this any easier.

I dropped the washcloth.

Held her tighter.

And my fingers demonstrated just how much I'd missed her.

"I might have touched you, Sassy." Regret punished us both. "Might have teased you in all sorts of special, beautiful places that weren't mine to touch."

Her legs opened—not enough to sate five years of denied passion, but just enough to slip two fingers over her slit and revel in the velvet softness. The water only made her slicker.

So fucking tempting.

I parted her folds and circled that sensitive, perfect button. She flinched as my fingers rolled over her, but her head sunk against my chest. I claimed that chance to give her every pleasure I'd imagined since I last held her in my arms.

Too long ago.

"I might have teased you," I whispered. "Petted and stroked and kissed all those secret spots a good girl like you kept hidden from a man like me."

Her lips parted. "*Kissed?*"

My mouth watered at the thought. "Kissed. Licked. Sucked. There's not a part of you I wouldn't have devoured. You would've had to fight me off, Sassy. Once I finally got a taste of you, I would have been insatiable."

My fingers circled her clit quicker, pulsing a quiet rhythm with the softness of her breathing.

"I never told you how beautiful you are," I said. "Not back then. Not now. Never told you how much I wanted you. How much you deserved someone to hold you…" I wrapped an arm around her waist and drew her closer. "Touch you." She glanced back to me. "Take you."

I captured her kiss and overwhelmed her with quick flicks of pleasure to her quivering folds. The heat destroyed me. She wasn't just ready—she was *eager*. Hot and frustrated and so desperate for my finger, my lips, my cock that she ground back against my teasing hand.

"You shouldn't have left me…" Cassi's words broke with quick and sudden gasps.

"I couldn't have stayed."

"We could have fixed it then."

"Can't we fix it now?"

She stared up at me, eyes wide, body trembling on the verge of absolute pleasure. "I…I don't know. I thought it was *over*."

"We were never together, Cassi. Give me a chance to do it right."

"So much has happened, Rem."

"So forget the past."

"Can you?"

She twisted for me, pinching her eyes shut, gripping my arm. A sudden shudder quaked her body. Then a second. I rubbed her clit harder, watching as each sharp graze wracked her in dozens of shivers. She gasped my name. Clutched my hand. Braced herself against the tub.

And I delivered her every passion and pleasure I'd promised.

But it was too late.

She'd lived through five years of lies. Five years of silence. Five years of idiotic regret.

I'd lost her.

And here I thought I was protecting her. Protecting her family. Protecting myself.

Secrets and lies and deceit ruined everything—including how her heart might have softened for me.

"*Rem...*" Cassi breathed my name and shook her head, still shaking from my touch. "I..."

I didn't need to hear it. Couldn't handle the words. The apologies. The *end* of it all.

"I'm going to bed," I said. "Enjoy your bath."

"*Wait...*"

I pushed out of the tub, hating the hardness that made wrapping a towel around my waist impossible.

I didn't look back, couldn't see what I was losing once again, what the past had taken from me.

What good was hiding the truth when I was the one getting hurt?

12

Cassi

THIS WAS A MISTAKE.

I escaped from the tub with shaky legs.

This would be a *terrible* mistake.

I wrapped only a robe around my body, dripping with soap and desire and every aching urge to be close to Rem once more. Wrapped in his arms. Surrendering to his touch, his voice, the promises we never made and would never have kept.

Rem wasn't in the house. I grabbed my phone and set the nest cam to keep an eye on the kids, both sound asleep. That meant no interruptions. Nothing to stop me now.

He'd gone outside. Rem leaned against the porch railing, staring into a cool, dark night with only the moonlight above. The thick canopy of the trees rustled with a quiet breeze. Everything was still. Waiting. Listening.

But I had nothing to say.

Nothing that I hadn't longed to speak and knew better than to voice.

He hadn't put on a shirt, just barely had buckled his jeans. Droplets of water rolled over the muscles of his back. The drips teased low, chasing the colors of his tattoos before gathering at the hem of his jeans. His solid abs tightened as hard as the bulge in his jeans. He ran a hand along the trim of his beard.

His eyes stared—hungry, but so *sad*.

Why were we doing this to each other?

The teasing. The flirting. The denial.

It meant everything and nothing. It pulled us apart only to slam us together with unquenched need. He'd asked to forget the past, but it wasn't the past that scared me. It was the future.

What would happen if I never let him close? If I never got over him?

What would happen if I walked away from this, our last chance?

This was a mistake.

I dropped my robe to the porch and kicked it away.

His gaze feasted over me, but he shook his head. "Cassi..."

I didn't let him protest. Not now. Now when I knew what we both needed. More than words. More than excuses. More than stories about a past we should have shared.

The only thing that mattered was *this* moment.

And I wouldn't let anything take it away from us.

I didn't have to say a word. Rem was on me within a single breath. A ragged, guttural growl surged from his throat, and he took me in his arms.

I'd waited years for *this* kiss.

And I surrendered completely to it.

His lips nibbled over mine—a commanding and raging excitement that shuddered us both in a thrill of conquest. His hardness pressed into the bare skin of my belly. The thought sizzled through me, reigniting the pleasure still smoldering from the last explosion.

Nothing had ever felt as good or as right as his touch.

At least, nothing until now.

I'd waited far too long and lost entirely too much time. Tonight was ours, and the shadows of our past would forever fade in the glow of our passion.

He walked me backwards, aiming for the porch swing. I didn't let him push me down. Not now. Not after the pleasure he'd already delivered to me. If I savored any more touches, kisses or teasing, I'd be lost in my own demanding need. The only thing I wanted was him—his taste, his desire, the feel of *him* finally in my hands, in my mouth, inside of *me*.

I pushed him down. He sat with a grin, all too eager and yet patient.

"You have no idea what you do to me, Cas."

"I can take a guess."

I unzipped his jeans and stared at the most wild, uncivilized part of him. I swallowed my own amazement. His hardness jutted upwards, thick and pulsing so intensely it must have been painful. I'd felt him in the tub, pressing against me, heated and raw.

How many times had he almost taken me now?

How many nights had he gone to bed just as demoralized, just as desperate and aching as me?

No more.

I knelt before him. Rem breathed a soft profanity.

"You don't have..."

Oh, but I wanted to. I grinned and took his cock in my hands. First one I'd ever held, and the only one I'd ever wanted to touch. Rem flinched as I curled my hands around the base. He didn't fit, even with both fists stacked.

That probably should have scared me away. But this curiosity would get me in far greater trouble.

I leaned down, unsure but encouraged by the rasping hiss of his breathing. My tongue darted out, circling the head of his cock. Rem swore. Good enough for me. Another lick. A soft kiss. I glanced up at him, voice a soft whisper.

"Am I doing this right?"

"There's not a goddamned thing you could do wrong now."

"So...this is good?" I popped the head in my mouth. Salty and warm. He tasted like raw, primal excitement, and his shiver traced over my own body and centered in my core. I mumbled over his length. "That's what you like?"

"*Fuck...*"

I took that as a *yes* and dipped lower over his shaft.

How in the world was a girl supposed to take a man like him? He was thick. Hard. His cock was almost an angry, fierce spear of flesh. It pulsed in my mouth, waiting for a chance to strike a lot lower and far deeper. My tummy clenched. The wetness should have shamed me, but my body only did what came naturally when so close to this man.

This perfect, sexy man.

His body tensed, every muscle tight with a thrilling need. His abs flexed. His biceps flared as he gripped the chain of the porch swing with his huge, callused hands. Skilled hands. Hands that knew *exactly* where to touch me, how to tease me, and how to shatter me in a quick and unbelievably intense orgasm that should have left me in a puddle in the bathroom.

Except I wanted more.

I *deserved* more.

Five years of waiting. Of longing. Of wishing things had been different. But only a fool wished for change. If I wanted him—if I wanted the past we should have had and the future we both dreamed about —then I had to take it for myself.

I had to forgive him.

Or at least...forget what had happened.

One of these was far easier than the other with his cock in my mouth, his hands in my hair, and his groans filling me with desire.

His hardness twitched. A quick pulse shot through his body. Rem pushed me away, his smile a wicked and knowing tease.

"Need more than your mouth tonight, Cassi," he said. "And I know you do too."

He pulled me to my feet, but he didn't let me stay still. He swept me into his arms and carried me to the porch railing, setting me down and spreading my legs so he could slip between.

"No more games," he said. "No more imagining."

"I want you," I breathed.

"I've *always* needed you." His finger trailed along my slit.

I didn't hold back this time. The pleasure crashed over me, and I bit my lip to keep from groaning.

The slickness opened my petals, and he circled my clit once more

"But you're…you waited," he said.

"For you."

"Are you sure you want to give me this?"

"I've always wanted it to be you."

He stared down at me, voice hoarse. "I don't deserve you."

"Not true. We deserve this. Maybe just once. Maybe forever. It doesn't matter." I reached for him, my fingers tickling the tattooed sunflower over his heart. "Let's have tonight. Now. You and me. Forget the past. Forget the future. Forget everything."

Rem grinned. "There's no way in hell you'll ever forget this night."

He kissed me, edging closer, drawing my hips towards him. His beard tickled my cheek as my head rolled back, granting him access to the soft skin of my neck. He nibbled along my collarbone and stroked himself. I flinched as the head of his cock teased my slit. The sensations burst through me.

"It's…you're…big." I whispered. "Are you certain it'll fit?"

"That's the fun of it."

Sure…but I was me, and he was…

Huge.

Rem had become a mass of muscle and strength and raw power born of the wilderness. He'd not only lived within nature, he'd conquered it. Nothing about him was *tamed*. His kisses were gentle, but that wasn't him anymore. He'd lived a tough, hard life.

Now, he was rugged. Strong, fierce, and commanding. He stood before me more animal than man with a hardened cock and years of pent up aggression and desire that twitched the thick shaft jutting from between his legs.

"I've wanted you forever, Cas," he said.

"Then take me. Make me yours."

His grin faded. A dark sensuality masked his features, wild and ravenous. "If I take you, I won't be letting you go. Not tonight. Not tomorrow. Not ever."

Nothing had ever sounded so wonderful. "I'm yours, Rem."

"Waited forever to hear you whisper that."

If this was a mistake, it was the best mistake I'd ever made.

Rem held me close with one arm, his other hand stroking the length of his pulsing cock. Once. Twice. He stared down at me with a quiet, possessive growl.

He pushed.

Slow at first. Oh, so slow and carefully. A gentle, tenacious pressure that opened me to him. Just a slight movement at first. He rubbed the head along my slick folds and moved his hips inward.

He filled me. Inch by inch, a dangerously intense pleasure of fullness that impaled me. I gasped, gripping his shoulders, his arms, any of the strong, knotted muscles that might have protected me from the delicious shivers racing through my core.

I tightened as my body ached with a sudden pinch.

Then...

Completeness.

His length slowly eased inside of me. His head. The shaft. Until finally our bodies met, slick with sweat and trembling in amazement. The entire length of him stretched me. My breath shuddered. My body ached and cried out and crashed again and again with a newfound confusion and excitement and dizzying sensation.

Too much?

Too big?

Yes and no. I needed more.

I craved a movement he hadn't given. Instinct or greed? My hips bucked as I tried to emulate the motions I knew would come. In and out. Harder and quicker. Anything. But I earned no more than a mind-blowing inch.

"*Rem...*" My hoarse whisper shattered us both. "Please..."

He leaned in, capturing my kiss with a rugged, husky laugh. "Christ. Now that I have you, now that I'm inside you...fuck me, I don't think I can move."

"That's no fair."

"Neither are you..." His kiss turned feverish, frantic. "I could stay here forever. This close to you. This deep inside of you. *Finally*. After all this time...you're *mine*."

I arched into his hands as he explored the curves of my body. My heart raced, aching with every passing moment that frustration flexed my hips. I needed him as much as he needed me, but now I ached for something more. What'd he'd promised. What we both craved.

We'd waited for too long to be romantic.

Suffered alone for too many years to be gentle.

Denied ourselves too much pleasure to be cautious.

And together, as our bodies pressed and our kisses muffled our groans, we'd finally taken everything we'd ever wanted.

"Please..." I pleaded with my own desire. "Don't hold back."

"I'm barely holding on, Sassy."

"*More*, Rem..."

With an agonizing tease, Rem pulled from me. Only a few inches. Only a brief crest of hips. But that was all he needed to drive inside me. The fierce size of him should have scared me, but I'd never felt so complete in my life.

A part of me had been missing for so long, filled by the part of him I'd so long denied.

Every trust became a promise. Every kiss the first truth we'd spoken in years. Every shivered bolt of pleasure, a fantasy come true.

I took him deeper, arching to let him within my tightness. My words panted. My breath trembled. Wrapped in each other arms, desperate for each other's desire, we murmured words we'd never said and feelings that neither of us were ready to admit.

He rocked inside me, hands squeezing my hips. "Should have done this long ago."

I would have let him too. Would have welcomed him. Offered myself to him. Given everything to him.

I'd loved him before. I loved him now.

And that made me reckless and foolish and so incredibly desperate for him. This wasn't fair. We belonged together. We couldn't change the past, but what had it done to him? The once playful, excited puppy of a boy had turned into a reclusive, gruff, bear of a man. Alone. Miserable. Struggling so hard to see the good in himself.

But I saw it. I knew it was there. And I fell for him with every breath, every stroke, every minute of every day that he denied the past and struggled to imagine a future where he belonged.

His future was in mine.

No more hiding. No more wilderness.

Just me and him.

Tonight was only the beginning.

Breathing was hard. Thinking impossible. A rushing, intoxicating intensity built so deep inside of me it actually *ached* with every hardened thrust. I gripped his arms. The muscles beneath my fingers tensed. He fought with himself, with me, with everything. Each drive inside me struck through him with the same shivering realization.

I hardly recognized the wild, rasping warning that growled from his throat. But the words stirred in me. I tensed, nodded, unable to speak.

"I'm not pulling out." Rem stared at me, daring me to protest. "Now that I finally have you, I've gotta come inside of you, Cas. I gotta make you mine."

And I would have fought him if he'd even dreamt of pulling from me.

I clung to him, tensing as my own excitement unwound every part of me.

He struck first—a hard, powerful thrust straight through me. He bottomed out as deeply as he could get, a solid and uncompromising mark of strength. He pinned me against his hips. Clenched his jaw. Sweated.

I arched as the heat of his seed burst within me.

My core first, then every muscle, every inch of skin. The tingles became shocks and transformed my breath, my words, my weakening strength into jagged and fierce energy. Every tremble rocked through me, a strike to my most vulnerable and sensitive secrets.

I came for him again and again, clutching at his shoulders and chest as our bodies still quaked and moved together. The heat and mess between my legs only hardened him more. A captured kiss, and he was on me again, wrapping me into his arms, threatening me with even more pleasure.

I giggled as he held me against his chest and swept me into the house.

"No cuddling?" I teased. "And here I thought you'd be a romantic."

"Fuck cuddling." Rem tossed me onto his bed and shut the door behind us. His cock hardened again, slick and intimidating and so very delicious. "I've been without you for five years, Cassi. Little girl, you're in for a rough night."

13

Rem

I didn't wake up next to the woman of my dreams.

We never went to sleep.

Sticky, exhausted, and utterly spent, we crawled out of bed once the sun rose.

Cassi reluctantly dressed, smirking as she tucked her hair into a ponytail and borrowed one of my old shirts and a pair of boxers. She so easily fell into my arms now.

"I don't want this to end," she whispered.

God, the woman was beautiful. Sexy and dark and wild enough to ache me in all the best places.

I stroked her cheek, earning a smile. "Good thing this is just the beginning."

No end in sight, but plenty of interruptions. The bedroom door crashed open.

Mellie sprinted into the room, diving into Cassi's arms. "Yay! You're home!"

Tabby followed close behind, escaping her crib even though she was groggy and wielding a heavy diaper. She gave her nanny a mischievous grin. Both girls pinned her in a hug.

Cassi arched an eyebrow. "Nothing like a toddler catching you on the walk of shame."

"Nothing shameful about last night."

She disagreed with a giggle. "Well, maybe *some* of it was shameful."

"You liked it." I had proof.

"You encouraged it."

"You teased me."

"You begged for it."

I grinned. "I'll beg again."

Mellie smooshed Cassi's face between her hands and drew her attention back. "I'm hungry."

Cassi spoke through puckered lips. "Okay. Lemme get coffee first."

"Why?"

Her glance to me wasn't sly. "I'm kinda tired."

Mellie cocked her head. "Why?"

I took credit. "We stayed up late."

"Doing what?"

"We played a lot of games," she said. "That's all."

"Cassi won." I winked. "About ten times."

Cassi gave me a pinch and shooed the kids from the bedroom. "Who wants *pancakes*?"

"*Mememememe!*"

I raised my hand. "Me me me."

She baited me with that smirk. "You had enough to eat, Mr. Marshall."

Bad girl. "And you tasted like maple syrup."

"Sweet talker."

I licked my lips. "Your fault."

Cassi hoisted Tabby into her arms and led Mellie into the kitchen. "Okay. I'm going to make you guys my mom's super-secret family pancake recipe. But you have to *promise* not to tell *anyone* what goes in it."

Mellie's blue eyes widened. "What is it?"

"Bisquick," I winked.

Cassi smacked me again. "Don't insult my mother's cooking. God knows you ate enough of it growing up."

"Had to. There was never any food at my place."

"So, instead you ate us out of house and home?"

"All the Bisquick I could stuff in my cheeks."

"She made them from scratch!"

Never insult a woman when she's got her hand in a bag of flour. A plume of flour burst in my face. Bad, bad girl. Shouldn't have started a fight so near heavy artillery. I grabbed a wooden spoon from the drawer and countered, giving her bottom a quick smack. She squealed and threatened to topple the flour bag over my head.

"And here I offered to make you breakfast in bed." I patted the white dust from my shirt.

She waved a hand over the screaming girls. "And what would we do with the hungry kids?"

"It's a big woods. Let 'em scavenge."

Cassi let loose the hounds. "Mellie, Tabby! Get him!"

Mellie needed no encouragement. She bolted at my legs, giggling and striking my thighs with little balled fists I'd learned could actually inflict some hurt on defenseless places. The kids laughed as I led them through the kitchen and across the living room. No longer was the couch a safe refuge. I no sooner dove over the back when Mellie roared, charging over an end table to get to me. Blocks ricocheted off the ground. A sippy cup bounced into the hearth. The remote to every electronic device cracked against the ground. Batteries plinked away.

A little destruction never stopped a toddler. She charged with a ferocious giggle and tugged the blanket off the couch. All the better for me to use as a net. I twisted the kid inside the knitting, nearly breaking a lamp as I rolled off the sofa. I returned to the kitchen for a chance to sweep Cassi into my arms.

Denied by Tabby. The baby whimpered and reached for me. I kissed her cheek instead.

She liked that. "*Unc Hunk!*"

Cassi patted her bottom. "You little rat."

"Uncle *Hunk*, huh?" I grinned. "What's Cassi been saying about me, Tabby? You think she likes me?"

Tabby nodded as I nodded.

"You think she *really* likes me?"

Tabby's smile grew.

"Do you like her?"

Didn't even need to mime it. Tabby's slobbery grin spoke for us all.

"Do you like her more than your favorite and only uncle?" I asked.

"Yep," she babbled.

Cassi grinned. "Oh, the betrayal! Good girl, Tabby!"

A furious scream echoed through the kitchen. When left unattended, Mellie tended to cultivate glasses of water. She cackled and pitched the water at me. Unfortunately, the glass flew too.

"*Got you!*"

The cup shattered against the floor. Water spilled everywhere. The baby wailed in fright.

And I was soaking wet.

I reflexively shouted. "God *damn* it!"

The words echoed off the walls. Mellie, eyes wide and face pale, crumbled to the floor in terror. Tabby cowered against Cassi.

Fuck me. I'd scared them.

"Sorry." I gentled my voice. Didn't help. The irritation still hardened the words. "Are you okay?"

Cassi's gentle scold was a lot more suitable for a kid than my idiotic roar. She knelt to face Mellie and shook her head.

"Oh, Mellie, that wasn't nice at all."

Mellie's eyes glistened with tears. She tried to bolt, but Cassi took her hand. Only made me feel worse.

Great. The kid wanted to *hide* from her damned uncle.

Her words hiccupped as she sobbed. "S—s—sorry."

"It's okay," I said. "I just…I lost my temper. It's okay."

Mellie wasn't convinced. She nibbled her fingers, face red with tears.

So how many doll babies did I have to buy to make up for this mistake? I'd already plumped her up with chocolate when I accidentally stepped on her foot a week ago. Before that, I had to score her a three-foot teddy bear when her tantrum got me so pissed off that I slammed the bathroom door and broke the hinge.

The stories were all true—kids *were* expensive. Especially when a man had a bad temper and limited patience.

"Go sit down." Cassi sent her to the couch. "There's glass in here. It's dangerous."

"Same for you." I handed Tabby to Cassi before the kid waddled over the glass. "I'll clean up. Just gotta get a towel."

The laundry room had become a secondary wardrobe for the kids. Piles of socks and shirts, panties and leggings. None of them clean, of course. Like an idiot, I'd told Cassi I'd handle the chores. Figured little clothes would make for a little load of laundry. Lesson fucking learned.

A knock rattled the cabin. I dropped the towel.

"Shit." My words echoed inside the dryer. "Fuck me."

What was the date? I checked my watch.

"Shit, shit, *shit*."

How the fuck did I forget?

I rushed to the living room just as Cassi opened the door.

The county representative wore a scowl. It looked better than the pantsuit. Chubby, irritated, and one coffee short of a good morning, the woman had already marked an unsatisfactory box on her clipboard. She eyed Cassi's shirt and boxers with a huff.

"I'm Theresa Raymond, CPS. And you've obviously forgotten our appointment."

Cassi's eyes widened. She glanced from the woman to me, hackles immediately rising. "God damn. I know Rem's new with babysitting, but that's why he hired me."

Shit.

The *one* fucking time my best laid plans actually got me laid was the *one* morning I shouldn't have welcomed Cassi in my bed.

"Mr. Marshall..." Theresa clicked her pen and scribbled more notes. "I understand our meetings are infrequent, but I'd hoped for something of this magnitude you'd understand the responsibilities expected of you..."

She stared at my bare chest. Not quite drooling. More...judgmental.

Yeah, the snake and sleeves inked on my fleshed didn't inspire confidence in everyone.

"Wait." I grabbed a shirt from the back of the couch, dodged the upended table, and approached the door. "Hi. Yeah. I remember. We were just—"

"My goodness." Theresa stared at the living room, the kitchen, and the broken glass. "What in Heaven's name are these children being subjected to?"

"Whoa. *Wait.*" Cassi turned momma bear in an instant, and I prayed she wouldn't maul the one woman I desperately needed to keep the kids safe. "What's going on? Who are you?"

Theresa didn't offer her hand. She stepped through the entryway, shooing Cassi from her path, and surveyed the rest of the house.

"The home matches the owner..." She frowned. "*Unkempt.*"

"Hey, I'm kempt." Sure, the shirt was covered in wet playdough or *something* damp and purplish, but I looked good in all manner of toddler gunk, goo, and garbage. "We're just running behind this morning."

Theresa stared at me through meticulously hair-sprayed bangs that framed her expression into a limited range of irritated, frustrated, or pissy.

And shock.

She now looked *shocked*.

She clutched the clipboard to her chest. "Mr. Marshall, I expected drug use from your sister, but not from *you*! Have you no shame, taking in these children only to subject them to the same environment?"

"*What?*" I rubbed my face. The white powder dusted away. *Flour?* "No, no! That's not—"

"Absolutely unacceptable!"

"You don't understand!"

"I'll have to report this immediately. I'll send a car for the children—"

Cassi panicked and blocked her path. "Ms...whoever you are. Wait. That's not...it's *flour*. We're making pancakes. It's *flour*. Rem, what's going on?"

Theresa's mouth edged into a hard line. "I see."

This was getting out of hand. Mellie wailed from the couch, and Tabby now joined the chorus. Sobbing children didn't promote the image of a safe and nurturing environment. Neither did shards of glass and overturned end tables.

At least Theresa hadn't found the spider living in the hall closet—pissed that I'd exiled his buddy.

I guided her out of the house. "Let's talk. Away from the kids."

Theresa snorted. "That will be best."

I didn't dare glance at Cassi.

Christ, how was I going to explain *this* to her?

One thing at a time. First priority—*keep the kids*.

I led Theresa to the porch, closing the front door behind me. The morning was crisp, clear, and a perfect opportunity for fate to fuck me over once more. Theresa stepped over Cassi's robe, discarded by the porch swing. Her eyes read most of everything and her judgment put together the rest. This didn't amuse her.

She folded her hands and waited for me to dig a deeper grave. Joke was on her. Now that Cassi knew I'd lied to her? I was already six feet under.

I sucked in a breath. "Look, Ms. Raymond."

"Mr. Marshall, I placed these children under your guardianship as I believed it was better for the girls to live with a direct relative. Have I made the wrong decision?"

"No. Not at all."

"I find that hard to believe, given the evidence of this morning. A forgotten meeting. A thoroughly unkempt house. A dangerous situation in your kitchen. Crying children. And..." Her gaze darted down. "A scantily clad woman in the house."

"Scantily clad?" Christ, I *wished*. "She's in her pajamas."

"Yes. Another...*concern*. I was not told you would host unrelated women in your home. Frankly, I fear this placement may not be the most suitable arrangement for Melanie and Tabitha."

Goddamn it. "Look, *you* said it was going to be temporary, so I took them in. It's been three months now, and I had to do something. We're adjusting. We're getting along. The kids are happy and healthy. I even hired a damned nanny to help take care of them."

"Ah, so...she's the...*nanny*. Of *course*."

I didn't like the tone. "What's that mean?"

"Well, she's bla—" Theresa stopped herself before she gave me reason to toss her off the property. "She's suited for a service role."

I stepped too close, my voice low. "Lady, it doesn't matter if she's the nanny or my wife. Don't you ever fucking presume *anything* about her based on her...*suitability*."

Theresa frowned, but at least she didn't check off some racist ass box on her chart. She held the clipboard to her chest and nodded.

"Your sister has completed her rehab," she said. "She will be returning home soon."

"Good."

"Until that time, you are responsible for the wellbeing and safety of those children."

"Have been for three months."

"And if you're lucky, it won't be for much longer...which, in my professional opinion is a good thing."

"Lady—"

"We must think of what's in the best interest of the children." Her interruption rivaled her stare. Sharp. Uncompromising. Absolutely honest and undoubtedly correct. "I have your records, Remington. I've conducted interviews from long-term residents of this town, and I've noted your behavior in our prior meetings. Believe me, I placed those girls with you because of our internal policies, not my own preference. We both know you are not a man who should be responsible for those little girls. You aren't just a bad influence, you're entirely toxic."

She wasn't wrong.

"But I did it. I did what was right. I took them in."

"Then let us hope you did not traumatize them any further." Theresa wrote a new date and time on the back of her business card. "Clean your house. Calm the children. And be responsible enough to remember our future meetings. I'll return in a week. I'll expect more of you, Mr. Marshall, though I'm not sure I could be any more disappointed than what I've seen."

"Yeah. Feeling's mutual."

Theresa stormed off my porch. Good riddance. I grabbed Cassi's robe and headed inside, slamming the door behind me.

The kids flinched again. Little lips quivered, and their eyes widened with tears.

"Uncle Rem is mad at me..." Mellie sniffled.

Christ. Theresa was right. I *did* traumatize the girls.

"No, I'm not mad at you." I mussed her hair. "Everything is okay. I just had to talk to our...friend outside."

That placated the kids.

Cassi wasn't as easy. She stared at me, even her curls shaking in a quiet rage.

"Rem, what was that?"

Glass still littered the kitchen floor. I knelt and swept it away. "Very unfortunate timing."

"Rem."

"It's not a big deal."

"Don't." Cassi blocked my path. "Don't do that."

I tossed a chunk of glass into the garbage. "Do what?"

"Don't you dare lie to me."

"It's *nothing*."

She offered me a roll of paper towels. I wished it were an olive branch.

"You're doing it again," she said.

"I told you—"

"You shut down, Rem. *Every time.* When something bad happens, when life gets a little complicated—you shut down. You'd rather run and hide and *lie* than confront what's really wrong." Cassi took my hand. "Don't do it this time."

And do what instead?

Confront this?

This wasn't my battle to fight. I wasn't the one on the front lines. Hell, I didn't even know what was happening until I got the call in the middle of the night from a phone number in a town I swore I'd never see again.

Within a day, I'd traveled across the country, landed at my family's old house, and had two little girls tossed in my arms. They didn't even pack their shit. Just jammed their clothes and toys in *garbage bags* and pretended like that night wouldn't scar them forever.

Mellie called from the kitchen, still sniffling. "I'm hungry."

I tossed Cassi a box of Cheerios, and she delivered a bowl to Mellie, setting her in front of the TV. Both girls giggled with excitement, thrilled to be allowed to watch a movie so early in the morning.

"I gotta clean the kitchen, but we'll have pancakes, I promise." Cassi kissed the top of Mellie's head. "Just watch Nemo for a bit, okay?"

"*Kay.*"

Mellie devoured her cereal, even tossing the occasional piece to her sister—or at her sister—as she giggled from her bouncer. The last of the debris tumbled into the garbage.

Now what?

And why didn't I save a piece of glass for my wrists?

I leaned against the counter and rubbed my face.

"Should I get the whiskey or make a pot of coffee?" Cassi asked.

"Why not both?"

Neither was strong enough for this conversation. It wasn't like the kids would understand, but I lowered my voice anyway. Looked away.

Shame was a lot easier to hide when I was three thousand miles away.

"Em's not sick." A lie was so much better than this truth. "She's got problems."

"CPS took the kids?"

"Yeah."

"Why?"

Why else? "Drugs. Em's…gotten worse the past few months. Since Tabby was born. Had some complications. I guess the oxy helped too much. Easier than heroin…for a while at least. CPS called and said they needed someone to take the kids. Said they wanted to put them with a family member first. If I couldn't take em…" I exhaled. "They would've gone to foster care."

"That's terrible."

And nothing I'd ever put my nieces through. "I took a leave of absence, flew home, and grabbed the girls. You know the rest."

"You never told anyone?"

"Why would I?" I laughed. "Everyone in Butterpond knows the Marshalls are fuckups. Last thing I need is to give anyone confirmation."

"You didn't tell me."

I frowned. "No. I didn't."

"You lied to me."

"It wasn't my lie." Like it made a difference. "What was I supposed to do? Tell you my sister's such a hardcore junkie that she put the girls in danger?"

"You don't think I'd understand?"

No. She wouldn't have understood.

"Cas, I haven't seen you for five years. You're the only person in this whole damn town that matters to me. You know how rotten my family was—that's why I stayed with yours for so long. Last thing I wanted was to come back, see you, and make you think nothing had changed."

Because it hadn't.

I couldn't handle some spilled water without losing my temper. Couldn't impress a lady from CPS. Couldn't take the kids into town without *my* name overshadowing them.

Good thing they were so young yet. Once Mellie got older, once she understood what the whispers and the looks and the gossip meant, she'd follow the same path as me. Withdrawn. Bitter. Getting into trouble.

At least I had the option to run. They were innocent and stuck in this hell.

"Just…" I hated that I had to ask it. "Keep this to yourself, Sassy. Please."

Her hand grazed my cheek. I brushed her away.

"No one is judging you, Rem," she whispered.

"Everyone judges, Cas. And if they look close enough, they're going to see a bastard who doesn't deserve you."

She planted her feet and gave me a smile.

"Well, guess what, Remington Marshall. I know who you are. I know your family, I know your past, and I know *everything* you've done. And I'm not going anywhere."

Poor thing.

She sounded so sure of it too.

Like she believed it. Like she honestly thought the past could be forgotten and a future created right there in the middle of the kitchen over some pancakes and cartoons for the girls.

She didn't know the full truth about that *past*. About everything I had done.

Some secrets were worth the isolation.

I'd lied five years ago and lost her once.

The truth would lose her forever.

14

Cassi

Nothing said family celebration like the threat of bloodshed.

Today's menu: roast beef with a side of mashed potatoes, vegetable casserole, and a knuckle sandwich.

Rem parked the truck outside the farmhouse and grunted. "This is a shitty idea."

Mellie agreed with a giggle. "*Titty!*"

"That's...not what he said but it's still a bad word." I eyed them both. "Neither of you should say it."

Tabby coo'ed with a wicked grin. "*Sitty!*"

Rem sighed. "Fantastic."

"Don't worry." I squeezed his arm. "This is *just* what we need."

Rem didn't believe me. I didn't either, not really. A dinner with my family wasn't a pleasant occasion on the best of times—whatever those were anymore. But my brothers were still his best friends, despite whatever circumstances had pulled them apart. Maybe reconciliation was all they needed? Some food, wine, and laughter to rid Rem of whatever shame, torment, and secrets prevented him from looking towards the future.

A future with me.

One we should've started long ago.

"Really, Cas…" He kept his hand on the gearshift, like he'd actually toss the truck in reverse and speed back to his mountain. "This dinner is a private…family…*thing*."

"It's a dinner to honor my mom's birthday," I said. "And you loved my mom just as much as I did."

"It's not my place."

"You were in our lives for *twenty years*. It's only right you come too."

His voice lowered. "At least you believe that."

I took his hand. "I do. I'm not going to let you rot away all alone on that mountain anymore. What's done is done. The past is behind us. It's time you be a part of the world again. See what you've been missing."

"I can guarantee they're not missing me."

"Doesn't matter. All this self-exile and isolation isn't good."

"Neither is getting pummeled by your brothers." He glanced at me. "Julian made his feelings on the matter pretty clear."

"Well, Jules will have to deal. I want you here. And so does Tidus. And so would Mom. We've gotta work through this bad blood sometime."

"I'd rather it not spill."

"I promise. I won't let my brothers get all brothery."

Rem smirked. "Oh. I see what this is. You want me here as a buffer between you and *them*."

Busted. "You're one hell of a distraction."

"You owe me."

I winked. "A hundred kisses, a dozen touches, and one very, *very* satisfying night."

"Hope I survive."

"The dinner or me?"

Rem snorted. "One and then the other."

"Come on." I hopped out of the truck and unfastened, unbuckled, and untangled the kids from their car seats. Rem unsuccessfully dodged Tabby's thrown sippy cup. The first and, hopefully, only blow of the night. "At least the kids will have fun."

Even that was optimistic.

I led Rem into the house...

And panicked.

Since I'd left to stay at the cabin, the house had transformed from uneasy borders to all-out trench warfare. Disputed territories in the den and dining room seemed a particular source of contention—marred with new cracks in the walls and broken furniture from what I presumed to be the fist-fights of thirty-year-old men. Even the fridge wasn't immune. A wall of aluminum foil divided the shelves, separating out four individual gallons of milk, four cartons of eggs, four pizza boxes, and a variety of multicolored Tupperware containers with scribbled names staining the lids in permanent marker.

As far as I could tell, no one was speaking to each other, but the lights and water were still on. Bills were paid, even if my brothers were slowly tearing the house apart.

Tabby needed a quick diaper change, but one glance in the downstairs bathroom flashed me with memories of mucking out horse stalls. I was better off changing the baby in the middle of the floor than dealing with the mountain of dirty laundry Quint collected next to the tub.

I'd left the house to take care of the children. Good thing CPS hadn't gotten involved when I'd abandoned the biggest babies of all—*my brothers*.

I helped myself to the living room floor, casting Tabby's baby blanket over the bits of Cheeto dust and flecks of mud. No truce and no vacuuming. I should have imposed sanctions on my warring brothers. Unilateral peace talks, mandatory meal time, and Pledge for the wood and furniture.

"We're here." I called into the house. "Please tell me the smoke isn't coming from the roast."

Tidus jogged in from the kitchen. "Hey, Sassy—"

My tattooed, leather bound, bad boy brother took one look at the wriggling baby on the floor and diaper in my hand and crashed into the wall.

"What the hell are you doing?"

I smiled. "My job. This is Tabby."

"I...hadn't expected to meet that much of her."

Mellie was fearless while denigrating her sister. She made a face. "She's a *baby*. She wears diapers. You smell like Mommy."

He did smell an awful lot like smoke, the bastard. "And that's Mellie. She just busted you. What did I tell you about smoking?"

"Needed it for today."

"You'll need your lungs later."

I buckled Tabby into a fresh diaper and tucked her into a pair of pink leggings. The diaper wasn't the only thing mortifying Tidus. He stared at Rem, jaw set.

"Hey," Rem said. "Been a while."

Tidus groaned, reluctantly shaking his hand. Their matching tattoos practically melded into one.

"What the fuck are you doing here, man?"

Mellie and Tabby delighted in the one word they heard so often and were forbidden to repeat.

"*Fuckfuckfuck!*" Mellie curtseyed and spun in her princess dance. "Fuckyfuck."

Tabby flailed her legs and stomped, bending down to pick up a lost Cheeto. "Fookfookfook."

"Great." I glared at Tidus. "I'm gonna beat your…bottom if you swear in front of the kids one more time."

Tidus winked at Mellie. "Why don't I teach you a new word? It starts with a *B* and ends with—"

"My fist in your mouth," I snapped. "Stop it."

"Gotta have some fun today." Tidus eyed Rem. "God knows we'll need it."

"Hey, what's burning?" Quint's footsteps echoed from the hall. He peeked into the living room, bandana around his head, mismatched pot holders on his hands, bearing a casserole dish brimming with a marshmallow encrusted goo. He glanced over the room, grinned when he saw me, and just about shit as his eyes passed over Rem.

"*You!*"

The casserole dish teetered in his hands. Tipped. Fell.

Tidus dove for it, but the glass was still hot. He shouted as both of his palms bore the brunt of the casserole.

"Son of a—"

The dish clattered to the floor, and the kids learned a variety of unique and flavorful words they'd undoubtedly share the next time we met the lady from CPS.

Molten sweet potatoes splashed everywhere—carpets, drapes, over Quint. He batted at the superheated specks dotting his legs with a yell.

"Those were my sweet potatoes, you prick!"

Tabby burst into tears. Mellie, emboldened by the scent of toasted marshmallows and sugary sweetness leapt forward to investigate the mess.

"Uh-oh," she said. "Gotta sing the cleanup song!"

"I didn't knock over your damn bowl," Tidus said. "What the hell are you doing with that in here?"

"I didn't have room in the kitchen." Quint swore. "You left your potato peels and bowls all over the counter, asshole."

Mellie belted out her song. *"Clean up! Everybody clean up!"*

"So move them."

Tidus accepted a rag from Rem, but the damage was done. Marshmallow coated his shoes, the carpet, and—he groaned—now hardened on the TV screen.

"Not my responsibility." Quint grunted. "Great. Dinner's ruined."

"Time to clean up!"

"It's only the sweet potatoes and whatever is burning in the oven," I said. "I can help you make something else."

Tidus snorted. "Open a can. Pour yams in bowl. Smother with sugar. Melt in the oven. Done."

"Pick up. Everybody pick up!"

"What is he doing here?" Quint didn't even look at Rem. "Why the hell would you bring *him*?"

Quint only had about two-and-a-half years on me. Young enough to miss most of the trouble Rem had caused. Didn't hate him like Jules and Marius, but our family had a decent amount of loyalty, not matter how much they currently despised each other.

"I wanted to bring him," I said.

"You clear it with Farmer Brown?"

"Who?"

"Pick up the toys. Put them away!"

Tidus snickered. "Jules."

"I don't have to clear it with anyone—least of all Jules." At least, that's what I'd told Rem. "Jules won't care. Marius is still overseas, and I don't think either of you are going to say a damn thing, isn't that right?"

Quint still hadn't looked at Rem. He sucked in a breath. "Whatever. Is that kid all right? The mess is like...distressing her or something."

Mellie and Tabby danced, bumbling through the rest of the song. Rem smirked.

"She's good," he said. "Em's kid."

Quint frowned. "Think they'd be used to a mess then."

Tidus seemed to understand more than he'd ever told me. "How's Em?"

"Getting better," Rem said.

I sucked in a breath. "Okay. Where's Jules? Let's get this over with."

Quint jerked a thumb over his shoulder. "Dad's office. Buying equipment."

With what money? Dad's medical bills didn't leave much in the farm's budget for new equipment, buildings, animals, feed, and seeds. Julian couldn't get a damn tomato to bud. How did he expect to grow money on the trees?

I guided the kids into the dining room. Mellie strode in first, happy as can be. With no hesitation, she plunked down in the chair right next to an amused Varius, picking at a loaf of his freshly made bread.

"Hi." Mellie grinned at him. "Wanna play?"

Tidus, Quint, and I tensed. For the past two years, Varius had withdrawn from everything—the family, the town, his congregation. Abandoning a life was hard. Abandoning a faith? That changed a man. Hardened a gentle soul.

Mellie still saw the old Varius. And maybe, for just a moment, in the smile he gave her, Varius had felt like himself too.

He glanced at Rem. "Come seeking forgiveness?"

"Only if you'll give it, Preacher."

"I'm not a minister anymore."

Rem shrugged. "Got any forgiveness left?"

"Some." Varius's hair had grown longer, brushing over his jaw—more gaunt that chiseled anymore. The Payne family green eyes were lost on him now. Dark and sullen, he'd lost so much of the light that had once brightened his features. "I budget it out for special occasions."

"Is today special?" I asked.

Varius motioned to the stoic figure in the doorway. "We'll find out."

Julian wasn't pleased with our dinner guest, but was he ever happy anymore? Stress and responsibility and his never-ending quest to seek Dad's approval from beyond the grave had taken its toll. He ended his phone call and shoved the cell in his pocket.

"What's he doing here?" Jules grunted.

"Eating," I said.

"Says who?"

"Says me."

Rem kept his voice low. "That gonna be a problem?"

A tense moment of silence passed, broken only by Mellie as she crawled beneath the table to retrieve a dropped fork and spoon.

"*Clean up! Everybody clean up!*"

Tidus knew better than to let me and Jules stand-off. We might not have been blood, but we fought like we'd shared the same womb.

"Just dinner, Jules," he said.

Jules was too handsome to frown. He did it anyway, and often. "This is our *mom's* dinner."

Varius still kept the peace even if a war waged in himself. "And Rem stayed here more than he ever stayed at his home."

"What home?" Quint snorted. "It was as broken then as it is now."

"Hey." I stared each of my brothers down. "We gave *everyone* a home. Mom's orders. No one goes hungry. No one goes cold. No one is alone. *Ever*. Our family is family to everyone. So what's changed now?"

Jules got smart with me. "You really gotta ask that question?"

"Do I really gotta ask you to be *forgiving* on mom's birthday?"

A grumble. A pause.

A truce.

Guilt was an excellent motivator. Jules backed down, heading into the kitchen with a fire extinguisher to tackle the burnt roast. My other brothers began setting the table. I patted Rem's arm with a wink.

"Get the girls washed up?" I asked. "I'll talk to Jules."

"Won't do much good."

"It'll take time. We knew this."

Rem took the kids, shaking his head. "Don't expect a miracle."

I joined Jules in the kitchen and helped load the table with platters of veggies and sides. A feast Mom would have loved—especially since all of her kids, including her surrogate son, Rem—were home to enjoy it.

So much had changed after she'd died, since Dad had died. Our family had been through hell for the past five years. It had to get better at some point.

Right?

The roast had shriveled. Jules attempted to poke it with a fork. I stopped him before it deflated.

"We'll...call it blackened." I crinkled my nose. "Cajun."

"Should I add some spice?"

"Doubt anyone will taste it over the char."

"Right." He nodded. "Gravy then."

"About Rem..."

He interrupted me. "You know the kids are welcome here."

"What about the uncle?"

Jules set his jaw. "What about him?"

"I'm not asking you to be his friend again."

"You're asking too much."

"*One* dinner." I followed him to the kitchen as he unsuccessfully searched for the butter. I dislodged it from a chunk of potato peelings and set the lump that remained in the dish. "We just need to talk."

"There's nothing to talk about."

"There's *so much* to talk about. It's been five years."

Jules wasn't listening. "And you know most of all what those years have been like. What the stress did to Mom and Dad and us."

"Tidus is willing to talk. Quint will come around if you do. Varius doesn't care about anything anymore. And if Marius were home—"

Jules laughed. "If Marius were home he'd be talking with his *rifle*."

Probably, but that's why I was almost relieved he was half a world away, doing God knows what in the middle of God knew where.

"Do this for me," I said.

"Why *you*?" Jules saw right through me. "Don't get involved with him, Cassi."

"It's not like that," I lied.

"He broke your heart."

But now he was fixing it. "He did a lot of things that he regrets. Give him a chance."

"You moped around this house for weeks. Didn't eat. Didn't go out. Didn't date. You weren't the same after he left."

"But I'm me now, right?" I smiled. "Don't be so protective."

Jules wrapped me in his arms. "I'm your big brother. That's my job."

"You don't have to do it so well."

I dragged him to the table just as Rem returned with the girls. After rummaging in a cabinet, Tidus returned with a mound of Playboy magazines.

"What..." My head would explode. "What are you doing?"

"Making a booster seat."

"Out of *playmates*?"

Quint snickered. "I think that was a centerfold pose last year."

Varius pitched a napkin at Quint's head. Tidus covered the magazines with a cloth napkin and patted the seat for Mellie to climb up.

Oh, Lord. We were all going to hell before we even ate.

My brothers took their seats. Rem kept Tabby in his lap, mostly as a human shield. That was fine. Enough sharpened cutlery rested around the table. A long moment of silence passed.

"Should..." I shrugged. "Should we say grace?"

We pretended to not look at Varius.

He said nothing, only shook his head. A *no* from the man who used to have more faith than all of us combined.

"Should we say...*something*?" I offered.

Mellie took the initiative. The collective asses around the table unclenched.

"This is a farm?" she asked.

Some people called it that. "Yep!"

"Where are the cows?"

A common misconception. "Well...we don't have any cows."

"*No cows?*"

Quint winked. "Got some on your plate."

"Hush," I said.

Mellie's eyes widened. "Piggies?"

"No piggies."

"Horseys?"

Once upon a time. Those days were gone. "Nope, sorry."

Mellie pouted, but Jules saved the day.

"We got a chicken," he said.

Varius choked on his beer. "Only cause no one would buy her."

"That chicken isn't for sale!"

Tidus frowned. "That's not a chicken."

Jules usually kept his temper in check. Not when it came to Helena. "She's got feathers, don't she?"

"She's no chicken." Quint pointed to Rem. "Now see he...he's a chicken. But that bird out there? No eggs, good for nothing."

"Good for expense write-offs," Jules said.

"Yeah, corn thrives on tax deductions."

"Look. The farm needs some maintenance, but we'll get there. It's not hard. Dad did it his whole life, and his dad before him."

Quint wasn't convinced. "Just toss a seed in the ground and cover it with dirt, right?"

"As long as you don't piss all over it."

"See, that's what you've been doing wrong." Quint didn't wait for anyone else. He stabbed a hunk of roast beef and tossed it on his plate. "Plant it and then add the salt. That'll do the trick."

"Screw you."

"Guys." I scolded. "There's kids here. Language?"

"Oh, Rem can handle it." Jules fixed a heaping plate for himself. "I'm sure he's heard worse. Done worse."

Rem tensed, saying nothing, but he often turned the other cheek only to parry an incoming blow.

He was getting pissed.

And I didn't have a clue what to do.

"Can you pass the..." I regretted peeking into the dish. "Neon...green...liquid?"

Tidus crowded half of his plate with the potatoes, the other half with butter, and pointed to the pitcher of green with a knife. "That's supposed to be Jello."

Varius stared in horror as the liquid attempted to coagulate. "What happened to it?"

"Nothing. It's jello."

"Why isn't it *set*?"

"Think I added too much vodka."

And I moved the little cup of it away from Mellie. "Good job, Tidus."

Food smacked the plates. The girls stuffed their faces.

And conversation ceased.

I shifted the veggies on my plate, avoiding the ashen roast and bourbon glazed carrots that needed only a tumbler and ice cube to transform into my after-dinner drink. The silence fell, broken only by the clinking of forks against plates. The minutes dragged. My stomach twisted.

Why was it always so damned *hard*?

A lifetime ago, we'd have dinners like this every weekend. Our family.

The foster kids we'd take in. Rem. Sometimes Emma. Kids from the town. Friends of my parents. The house was always alive and buzzing and full of...

What was it?

Warmth? Family?

Happiness?

Whatever it was, it'd ended with Mom.

I tapped Mellie's plate and pushed a piece of broccoli towards her. She refused, but at least this was a familiar battle. Mellie, sly as she was, attempted to pawn her broccoli off on Varius.

"Cassi?" she said.

I replaced the floret with another. "Yes, sweets."

She pointed to the table. "Your family?"

"That's right."

She poked my arm again, a pale hand against my chocolate skin. "You're different."

My brothers never saw those differences. The rest of the town did. Not that it mattered. I smiled at her.

"Well, they all came from my momma's tummy, just like you and Tabby came from your mommy's belly," I said. "After my mom and dad had so many boys, they wanted a little girl. So they wished and prayed and..." I shrugged at the others. "Paid a tremendous amount of money in fees. And here I am."

"Tried to send her back once," Tidus said. "They'd only give us store credit."

Varius winked. "Wouldn't even replace her with a new model."

"Oh, hush." I pitched my dinner roll at his head, but stopped Mellie before she repeated the motion with the damnable broccoli. "What would you do without me?"

"You tell us." Jules was the only one who ate the roast. "You were halfway to Ironfield before you...took your current position."

Silence again. Rem tried to break it this time.

"Food's good," he said.

Jules didn't miss a beat. "Couldn't get some of your own at home?"

I dropped my fork. "I invited him. Can't you guys just have a civil dinner for *once*? Give him some credit. He came back here—"

Rem waved a hand. "Cas, I got it."

"No." Enough was enough. "He's doing *good* for himself now. He's taking care of two little girls, and he's doing it without complaint, which is more than I can say for the four of you who can't spend ten minutes together without putting a new hole in the wall."

Quint pointed his knife. "We fight because we're *family*. And every problem in this family can be traced to *him*."

"That was five years ago!"

"And it drove Mom to her grave. Dad went after."

I couldn't believe them. "You all spent the last *three* years avoiding anything and everything that had to do with this family and Dad. Coming home for Christmas doesn't count. The rest of the year? You guys were *nowhere* to be seen. Who took care of Dad? Who looked after the farm? Who had to mediate conversations between you guys and *our father* because you were too pissed off to call him yourself?"

Varius helped himself to another piece of bread. "Great dinner, guys."

Jules agreed. "So, did you bring Rem here just to berate us, or is your contribution to the night a case of indigestion?"

"Let it go, Cas," Rem said.

Jules wasn't about to peacefully transition into dessert. "We got rid of you once while you were sniffing around Cassi. Now you're home again. What do you expect out of this...*job?*"

Rem didn't back down. "I needed a nanny."

"Is that all you got?"

For Heaven's sake. "Enough guys. It doesn't matter."

"Sure, it does," Jules said. "He hired you. Lured you up to that mountain. Now you're spending your nights there too. All alone. All isolated."

Rem nearly laughed. "I don't need a mountain cabin to get laid."

"No, not when you can fuck a nanny." Quint scowled. "You hired her to get in her pants. We shouldn't have let Cassi take the job."

Oh, hell no.

"*Let me?*" My sharp tone wasn't nearly the punishment they deserved. "Excuse me, but I am an adult—more than I can say for half of you. I can choose where I want to work, what I want to do, and who I want to sleep with."

Silence.

Uh-oh. That was the *wrong* thing to say.

Rem leaned in, his voice low. "*Take it back, take it back, take it back.*"

Jules stood. "You *slept* with him?"

My stomach flopped. The food didn't go with it, choosing to evacuate to my throat. "There are kids at the table."

That meant nothing to my brother. "*You slept with him?*"

I had a split second to either deny everything and reassert my virtue or to sit in awkward silence as inevitably the image of me and Rem together spawned in each of my four brothers' minds.

The results were predictable.

Their chairs scraped against the floor. My brothers stood. Rem clutched Tabby a little closer to his chest.

But it was Tidus who launched first, thrashing over the table, upending the mashed potatoes, crashing into the gravy, and flinging roast beef against the wall with a gooey slap. Quint dove for Tidus, holding him back before he flung the container of broccoli at Rem.

"You said it was over with her!" Tidus pointed at him. "Jesus Christ, Rem! You can't keep it in your pants for a goddamned summer?"

"Hey!" I grabbed Mellie before her fistful of butter also splattered against the wall. "It's not a big deal."

Wrongo.

Tidus lunged again. Quint grasped only at his shirt now.

Rem stepped away from the table, voice low, baby in his arms. "You wouldn't hit a man with a kid, Tidus."

Tidus didn't blink. "Cassi, take the baby."

"Come *on*." I pleaded with Varius. "Can't you calm them down?"

Nope—not when Varius was equally pissed. "Was this your plan all along, Rem?"

"The hell do you think I am?" Rem's jaw tensed—the first time he'd let himself get angry. Mellie crossed to his legs, wrapping her arms around him. He tussled her hair, but even she couldn't prevent his voice from rising. "You all knew how I felt about Cassi."

Tidus scowled. "You said you'd never touched her. I believed you!"

"I hadn't." Rem shrugged at me. "It just…happened. And I'm glad it did. You all know how much I…care about her."

"I *trusted* you," Tidus said.

"Yeah…" Rem stared him down. "I think I earned that trust."

"Earned the chance to *fuck my sister*?"

"I earned a chance to be *forgiven!*"

Chaos erupted, and Mellie quickly learned no less than five new vocabulary words that would be sure to prevent her acceptance into any decent preschool. Tabby began to cry, her hands reaching back to the table where her forgotten sippy cup dripped milk onto a mashed potato stained carpet.

Rem shouted. Tidus yelled back. Quint reluctantly prevented a fist-fight. Even Varius couldn't keep the peace. He resigned himself to picking far-flung peas and bits of yams out of his dinner plate. Above it all, Jules cell rang. And rang. And rang.

"You don't deserve forgiveness," Quint said. "You set the *barn* on fire. We lost *everything*. Animals. Feed. Equipment."

"I can't undo what I did." Rem stared only at a silent and seething Tidus. "But maybe *one* of you could have a little understanding."

"There's nothing to understand," Tidus said. "It happened. It's done. None of us give a fuck about the barn."

"Bullshit. That's what this is all about."

"No, this is about you taking advantage of our sister!"

"Taking advantage?" Now Rem got pissed. "We have feelings for each other. Always have. Always fucking will."

"Hey!" Jules shouted, hand over the phone. "Quiet down."

"You think you're *good* enough for Cassi?" Tidus laughed. "How many drugs did you do as a kid? How many times were you arrested?"

"You tell me—you were there too."

"Guys!" Jules pointed to his cell. "This is important!"

"But I never pretended to be something I *wasn't*." Tidus growled. "I never pretended I was a *good guy*. I never took in babies so I could convince myself I wasn't a sack of shit. I never chased after a girl who was too good, too nice, too sweet for me. *I knew better*. I thought you did too."

"People change," Rem said.

"Not men like us. Especially not men like *you*."

"Jesus Christ." Jules threw a glass against the wall. The crash silenced everyone. He held the phone in his hand, covering the speaker. "Everyone shut up!"

His face had paled. He clutched the phone, nodding every so often with a grunt.

"Is he conscious?" he asked.

My stomach dropped.

Jules glanced over us, his eyes wide. The question reluctantly drew from his lips. "Is he gonna live?"

The fight was forgotten. The uneasy quiet turned my stomach.

And somehow—I *knew* what Jules was going to say.

My brother ended the call with a wavering breath. He met my gaze first, heart-broken.

"It's Marius. There was a firefight. He was hurt. They're flying him to a military hospital at a bigger base—couldn't tell me where. He's going into surgery."

A long pause.

Heavy, terrible silence.

Jules answered the question none of us wanted to ask. "They don't know."

The weight of it all crushed us into our seats.

Another crisis. Another sleepless night.

We couldn't handle another fight. Another emergency. Another *funeral*.

This family couldn't survive another death.

15

Remington

"*I hate you!*"

Mellie had first declared it at eight o'clock when I'd asked her to go to bed.

She repeated it at nine o'clock when I physically placed her in said bed.

When she screamed it at ten o'clock, I gave up.

Night number seven of complete failure.

Couldn't even put the kid to bed at a reasonable time. Couldn't get her to eat her dinner.

Couldn't get her to do *anything* but tear my heart in half.

Three little words.

How the hell did those three little words cut so goddamned *deep*?

She was just a kid. A three-year-old didn't understand *hate*. Did she?

So why did it feel like a test...a goddamned Olympic trial.

On Tuesday, she'd loved eggs. On Wednesday, she wailed, pouted, and threw them to the floor. Took an ice cream sundae to calm her down. Yesterday, she'd liked her bath. Tonight, it was an unrelenting torture, as if I was scrubbing her skin off instead of the dirt.

How could a little kid grind down every last shred of patience? Mellie was thirty pounds of adorable cuteness and criminal deviant. A master of manipulation with a set of lungs on her that could be heard all the way to Butterpond.

I was out of options. Out of energy. Out of fucking patience.

With Cassi stationed at Walter Reed Hospital while Marius underwent his multiple surgeries, I had to deal with the kids myself. And I was *failing*.

I'd always thought myself *capable*. Give me an axe, point me at a grove of trees, and, after a time, I'd build a fire, create a goddamned house, and craft all the furniture I needed to survive.

Put me in a cabin alone with these girls for a week?

Chaos.

Nothing shattered a man's confidence more than begging a damned toddler to eat her favorite grilled cheese sandwich.

Cassi had made it seem so effortless.

"*Damn it! I hate you!*"

Mellie picked up steam and a few vocabulary words. Great. I was rubbing off on her. How was I supposed to fix *that*? Timeouts did nothing. She screamed over stern lectures. If the kid wasn't crying, she was fighting with me. Sometimes at the same time. Most times, right after she'd been beaming ear-to-ear.

I gave up. The child was unknowable. She fought with me through the night, and, as a result, Tabby hadn't slept either. She started crying, her wails echoing through the house. That must have made me the biggest piece of shit outside of her diaper.

"What do you want?" I knelt before Mellie. "Just...tell me. What do you *want*?"

Tears streamed over her face. She spoke through four fingers in her mouth, garbling every word.

"Elsa watch eat I'm hungry why want to color."

Fantastic.

"Do you want mac and cheese?"

She shook her head yes. "No."

I couldn't take much more. Wasn't like I had the instincts, inclination, or basic human decency to handle the girls. According to Cassi's family, I didn't deserve Cassi and I sure as hell shouldn't have fostered the kids.

Glad the Paynes saw it so clearly. I'd been deluding myself for the entire fucking summer.

"You're getting mac and cheese." If I bargained with a three-year-old, neither of us would win. "Then bed."

"*No!*"

"Whatever."

The pot clanged on the stove loud enough to shake the cabinets. I measured out the water and turned up the heat, hoping I could distract the kid with twenty minutes of TV while it boiled. No such luck.

Within a minute, Mellie had enough of the waiting. She trudged into the kitchen, dropped her doll on the ground, and reached for the pot.

"*Mellie, no!*"

I stopped her before she dragged it from the stove, but not before her hand touched the hot metal.

She screamed, flailing away from the searing pot. Her little hand flushed red, but I didn't get to see it before she cradled it against her body, sunk to the ground, and started to cry.

"It was *hot!*" I yelled. "Why the hell did you grab it?!"

My shout terrified her. She rolled on the floor, screaming louder.

Was she trying to get away from me?

My heart lurched into my throat. Why didn't it just make the final slice and end my misery then and there?

I hoisted the kid onto the counter and checked her hand. Red, but not seriously hurt. Still painful. What was I supposed to do for a burn? Butter? Worked on toast, probably not on kids.

Water first.

I stuck her hand under the faucet and forced her to open her palm. Her face had turned as red as the burn, and she kicked while I tried to help.

"Mellie, stop. Sweetheart." I slowed the stream of water. "I know it hurts."

"I hate you!"

"You gotta let the water cool it down."

"*I hate you, Uncle Rem!*"

"I'm trying to help!"

"I want *Mommy!*"

Now that was a first, and it kicked me right in the gut.

Maybe I'd been wrong.

Maybe the kid did know what *hate* meant.

Hell, if she wanted to risk the drugs, the neglect, and the hungry nights to get back to her mom...

Christ, how bad of a parent was I?

That answer was easy. I couldn't even last a *week* without Cassi. The kids were cranky, hungry, and fighting. Discipline didn't work. They'd refused any entertainment. They no longer respected me.

Little hard to demand respect from someone when I didn't respect myself. Cassi's brothers were right. Chasing her was wrong. I'd done it anyway. I'd seduced her, knowing she had unresolved feelings for me. Hell, I didn't even try to mend her broken heart—just fucked her until she forgot about it.

She deserved to know the truth, but I was too chickenshit to give it to her.

And why?

Because then *she'd* be the one to leave.

It wasn't just the barn that complicated *us*. The fire had destroyed more than an old building. It'd destroyed me. Burned friendships and bridges. Consumed futures and reputations. I'd never once redeemed myself for the lies. How could I?

Maybe the kids saw through the smoke. Maybe they sensed the real me.

Maybe they knew they were better off with Emma. Hell, she was out of rehab. Found a part-time job in town. I'd even talked to her, amazed by the clarity of her voice and mind.

Emma was getting better.

And I...

I was getting worse.

The cool water helped Mellie. I dosed her with some Children's Tylenol and covered the burn with some gauze and about six different Barbie band-aids until she was satisfied. After an hour, she went to bed. I tossed the macaroni in the garbage, loaded the baby monitor app on my phone, and sat outside on the porch to drink a beer. I had second. Then I had another.

Around midnight, headlights appeared on the horizon. I hadn't expected her until the morning. Cassi dragged herself out of the car, exhausted. Hair in a bun, sweats low on her hips.

Absolutely beautiful.

Her purse thudded onto the porch. "Hey, stranger."

I'd planned to save the fourth beer to knock me out. She needed it more. I popped the cap and handed it over.

"How's Marius?"

She sunk down on the swing next to me. Eager to cuddle or looking for answers? I wasn't the right guy to comfort her. I did it anyway. Selfish. Desperate for her. Missing her touch, her kiss, her laugh.

All the things that should have never been mine.

She rested her head on my shoulder. "They amputated his leg."

"Shit."

"He'll be in the hospital for a while, but...at least he's alive."

"What's he gonna do?"

She hummed. "No idea. He can't go back in the SEALs. He'll be in rehab for months. And someone has to take care of him. Jules didn't want to talk about it there. They had him pretty doped up, but if he heard us talking about eventually bringing him to the farm, he'd induce himself into a coma."

I didn't envy that fight. Jules and Marius only ever saw eye-to-black-eye, even when they were kids. Then again, wasn't like Quint got along with Tidus. Or Tidus and Varius. Or Marius and anyone else. Fortunately, they all had Cassi to rely on, but how much could one woman handle?

"He ran away from us too, you know?" Cassi didn't rub it in. She twisted the knife. "He couldn't stand anything on the farm. Hated Jules. Fought with everyone. The SEALs were his way to get half a world away from us. He didn't even come home for Dad's funeral."

"Probably couldn't make it."

"Just when I thought things would settle down…" She tangled her fingers in mine. "I'm so sorry about what happened."

"Don't worry about it."

"I didn't get to talk to you."

"You had to go see Marius. It's okay."

"It's not." She kissed my shoulder. "I know you've changed. My brothers will see it too, but now everything is even more complicated. The guys hated each other, but with Marius coming back…"

"From one battlefield to another."

She looked away. "I don't care if we don't have their approval."

"Hell, Cas. I'm not even sure I approve."

"Don't say that." She squeezed my hand. "How are the girls?"

Living on processed sugar, but at least I hadn't spiked their juice with Benadryl. Considered that a victory.

She scrunched her nose. "That bad?"

For once, I was completely honest with her. "I'm not cut out for this, Sassy."

"Of course you are."

"No. This week was…" I didn't have the words, but I had a beer. I chugged it. "The kids hate me."

"They don't."

"I can't make them eat. Can't give them a bath. Pretty sure Tabby has diaper rash. And Mellie…I fucked up. Lost my temper. Fought with her. Tonight she burned her hand on a hot pot. Cried for an hour."

Cassi sat up. "How bad?"

"Just red. But enough to scare her." I finished the beer. "Probably the highlight of the week."

"They're sleeping now?"

"Yeah."

"And they're safe?"

No open flames or heated pots in their room. "Yeah."

"Then you did good."

But was that all I should have expected from myself?

Getting overwhelmed was pathetic enough. I already knew I was a bad influence. A bad uncle too. Last thing I wanted was to do was traumatize the kids.

Good thing Emma was finally clean.

Cassi gave me a sly grin. "I take it I have job security?"

"You get a raise."

Her eyes darted down. "So do you…apparently."

She stood, stretching in that perfect way that arched her back and showcased every delicious inch of her body.

I shouldn't have wanted her. Shouldn't have let those terrible and degrading images run through my head. Shouldn't have listened to that dark, selfish part of me that hungered for a woman who deserved so much better than my hands on her curves, lips on her skin, and cock buried deep inside a surrendered innocence.

She knew better than to lick those pouty lips. "I take it you missed me?"

I was on her in a moment, pulling her into my arms, one hand gripping her hair, the other clutching her waist. I dragged her against my body and punished her smile for daring to tease me.

Her giggle was all the encouragement I needed. A quiet, timid, thrilled sound that hardened my cock and shattered my soul. I'd capture it. Kissed it. Sealed it away inside me forever. Her mew was a perfect sound of surrender and desire and longing. I'd dreamt about it, fantasized about it, and, for five years, mourned its loss.

But now it was *mine*.

This woman. This beautiful, exciting, absolute sweetheart of a woman was *mine*.

Her kiss ravished me as I devoured her. My name caressed her lips, but I claimed her gasp as I trapped her on the porch swing.

This woman wasn't supposed to belong to me.

I'd chased. I'd flirted. I'd even tempted her.

But that was in the *past*, when I'd made the decision to run because I knew what my life was worth. Back then, my future was as dark and twisted as my past. A girl like Cassi needed someone stable, reliable, and *good*.

I had the strength then to recognize what her brothers saw now. What the town believed. The part of my name, of my life, that had driven Emma to drugs and me to the wilderness.

What made me think I had the right to touch, savor, and mark this woman?

Maybe we all wanted to change who we were.

Maybe we all believed the lies about ourselves, feasted on the best parts in the worst of us, and pretended the rest could be ignored, mended, or forgotten.

Didn't make me any different from the rest. Just made me hate how hard my cock pounded and how my mouth watered for her.

Why change who I was?

A liar. A disappointment. A bastard.

Cassi wanted me. I wanted her.

What harm was there in taking exactly what I'd always wanted again and again and again?

Love always had consequences.

A man just had to chance how much he was willing to hurt.

I knelt before Cassi and pushed her onto the swing. Her legs pressed together. I kept them that way, reaching only for the waistband of her pants. God bless the man who invented yoga leggings. A goddamned genius.

The stretchy material slipped off her butt and down her hips, but I left it to bundle over her thighs. The material bound her legs together. Perfection. Every curve on display just for me. I pushed her legs back, knees nearly to her chest.

Then I dove for the perfect little secret of wetness peeking from between her thighs.

Heaven was made of chocolate sweetness and sticky pleasure.

I lapped at her slit and seized her clit. Screw subtlety. Why bother with formalities and sensual touches when we could rage together in reckless desperation?

It'd been a week since I held her, touched her, tasted her—and that was seven nights of a searing, wicked torment that had isolated me longer than the five years I'd been without her.

Tonight wasn't about soft caresses or tender moments.

This was about us.

Taking what we needed.

Forgetting every trouble.

Ignoring every responsibility for as long as I could last bottomed out inside of her.

"*Rem...*" Cassi covered her mouth with her hand. She bit her fingers to muffle a groan as I licked between those petals to taste more of her desire. "What's...what's gotten into you?"

"Need you." The words mumbled in her wetness as I ravaged her velvety delight. "Gotta get you ready."

"Oh, I'm ready." Her hands clutched the back of her knees, holding herself up for me. "I've been ready. I can't be apart from you for that long."

If only she had escaped when she'd had the chance.

Her legs pressed tightly together, but her puffy folds tempted me with a sweet promise. I could have taken her like this. The pants would have held her legs in the perfect place, unable to squirm away as I delivered her to every height and depravity I'd promised.

But *no*.

I needed something more. Something permanent. Visceral and primal.

I wanted to control her. Tame her. Seize her body and break her strength through complete and utter pleasure. I wanted to own her every breath, experience her every shiver, and draw every sharp gasp and moan from her lips.

I wanted to take her. I wanted to destroy her. I wanted to love her. I wanted to possess her.

And I longed for her to do the same for me.

I had no idea how long this insanity would last. The one and only true pleasure in my life would be the moment when I bared my soul to this woman and accepted whatever judgment or pain or hatred she'd feel for me.

I'd lose her forever.

But I wouldn't lose this night. This *feeling*. The exquisite torture in denying myself my own release while I pleasured her with long, laps of my tongue.

"You did miss me..." Cassi breathed. "Or just parts of me."

"Every part."

"Makes me wonder what would happen if I left for longer?"

My heart seized. She would, soon enough. It'd happen, but not tonight. Not for a minute, a second. Not even long enough for me to pull out of her tightness.

I *had* to be a part of her. Had to memorize every softness, every slick secret and fluttering heartbeat.

I pulled her from the swing, but there was no dignity in what we were doing tonight. No romance or sweetness. Just pure, adrenaline-fueled *mounting*.

Wild.

Surprised it hadn't come over me before. That I hadn't lost myself in that isolation before this moment. There was a reason I'd lived for so long by myself—cast away from towns and people and society. For five years I'd become one with the wildest and most primitive parts of the world. Living off the land. Fending for myself. Fighting off wild animals. Faced a grizzly and lived only to have a pack of wolves surround my home at night.

Nothing made a man stronger. More resilient. Harder. Fiercer.

And more desperate than ever to just *connect* with the only woman he'd ever loved.

Cassi didn't protest. Either she needed it too, or she knew that surrendering to me was the easiest, fastest, and best way to get filled with every inch of every promise I'd ever made.

She rested on her knees but dropped low to her elbows, stretching her curves and offering that plump, delicious ass that threatened to stroke me out while I stroked myself.

Her slit glistened in the dim light. Ready. Swollen. Eager to be filled and pumped and taken.

I gripped her hips and said a prayer because if *this* wasn't the ultimate fruit of a forbidden tree then I had no idea what else in this world could be as dangerous as a beautiful woman offering every inch of herself.

I wasn't a good enough man for this woman, but I was just animal enough to fuck her senseless and leave her begging for more.

My cock twitched as I jerked the thick length against her entrance. She bucked against me, and the slickness nearly tore me apart. I couldn't be gentle. Couldn't just *enjoy* and *feel*. This was a taking. A ravishing that would undo everything polite and lovely and sensitive.

No more words, only grunting.

No more foreplay, only rutting.

No more wondering if and when and how and why.

Only this.

Only her.

Only that tightness, the secret I'd already discovered but revealed a little more of her every time.

I thrust inside of her with one solid push, and the world split at the seams.

Light and dark blended in a single, roaring, conquering mount. The force knocked her forward, and the pleasure took me with it. Cassi groaned, but it wasn't enough. No sound, no breath, no twitch of her body was enough to satisfy me. I needed more. I needed her. Every way and any way.

She fell forward onto the porch. I collapsed over her, planting my legs to either side of her as her pants trapped her in a dizzying pleasure. My palms struck the porch and captured her shoulders beneath my chest. My body shadowed hers. Covered her. Wrapped over and inside of her.

And I still wasn't close enough.

I despised pulling out.

I celebrated thrusting in.

And I hated myself for doing it again and again, slamming harder into her as my body slapped against hers in a vulgar, sensual thrill.

Cassi tightened. She groaned, shocked and overwhelmed by the force of my hardness. I didn't offer pleasure. I threatened it. I didn't wish for her moans. I *created* them. She writhed in shock and delight and clutched at the wooden floorboards for any support the ground might have offered. She'd find none. I'd cruelly, *passionately* wrenched her out of this world and into a fantasy of my own lust.

This wasn't how I'd planned to take her, but nothing else felt right. Just as my life began to unravel and the secrets and lies coated everything in a film of deceit, *fucking* became my salvation. My only way to prove how recklessly I needed this woman. How I'd do anything, ruin everything, and destroy my own humanity to keep her under me, beside me, *with me.*

I loved her.

And I fucked her.

And I claimed her.

And she came for me again and again, struggling under my hips for a reprieve so I might have let her breathe and whisper my name and any other words neither of us should have said.

I gave her none of it.

Only cock. Only lies. Only my heart and all the trouble it had ever caused.

And only when she'd sweated and shivered and cried out in lovely torment under the onslaught of my hips did I finally let myself feel that terrible urge that made me the worst man in the world for her.

I came.

Hard. Fast. Pumping my hips harder against her ass until I bottomed out as deeply as my cock could reach. It wasn't a tingle or a rising swell of pressure. It was catastrophe and ecstasy, disaster and honesty.

A good man shared his pleasure. A bad man *stole* it. I jetted inside of her with every intention to mark her as mine. I'd have her remember this night and this moment and how desperately I wanted to be the only one she needed in this world. I wasn't, but it didn't stop me from *wishing.* From bucking my legs and filling her with warmth and passion and *hope.*

Hope wasn't mine to have.

Neither was she.

I rolled off of her. Cassi panted, flipping onto her back to suck in the first full breaths of air she'd taken since she'd arrived at the cabin.

My cock hadn't softened. She glanced at me, at *it*, and she...

Giggled.

"What's gotten into you?" She struggled to catch her breath. "You fucked me like we wouldn't be doing that again in twenty minutes."

"Try ten."

"Are you okay?"

I wasn't answering that. Wasn't thinking straight. Wasn't anything.

"Wanna run away?" I asked. "Far from here? Just me and you. No past. No problems. No worries. Just...*together*."

Far enough away and enveloped in so much pleasure she'd never again question that night, what'd had happened, what I'd done.

"And bring the kids?" She smirked.

Made it tougher, but manageable. "Sure."

"And my brothers?"

"It's looking less and less romantic, Sassy."

"There's plenty of romance right here at home." She stroked my tattoos. Her fingers danced over the inked sunflower. "You came back and look what happened."

Nothing yet, because the lies had mounted and the truth had been shielded from her.

Exhaustion overwhelmed me. Guilt punished what remained.

"Cas, I gotta tell you something."

"I know my family was rough." She slid to my side, covering my lips with her hand. "And I know that dinner was...terrible."

"Listen, Cassi…"

Her kiss warmed me. "This is how it was meant to be. You, back home. Me, here and all sticky and sweaty. Us, *together*. We were idiots back then. But I'm going to do everything I can to make it work this time, Rem." She bit her lip. "Even if it means the occasional food fight at family dinners. If I have to scrub some sweet potatoes out of the carpet to have you at my side, then I'll pack a sponge in my purse."

Cassi kicked off her pants and rolled over me, grinding that slippery, messy slit against my hardening cock. Her fingertips gently teased my beard.

"You are finally mine, Remington Marshall. And nothing could ever tear us apart."

She angled her hips, taking me inside of her once more. Her eyes closed, and an absolute beauty gentle rode herself to bliss over my hips.

I wished I could have believed her. Offered her a promise. Security. Honesty.

If the truth would ruin this, then I'd never speak a word.

The past would die in silence.

But how badly our future be destroyed?

16

Cassi

Sex with Remington Marshall was like having sex with the physical embodiment of bourbon, timber, and sweat.

Worshiped like a goddess.

Ravished like a lady.

Fucked like a slut.

Best of all worlds.

In bed, Rem was the lover I'd always imagined. Compassionate, kind, and devoted.

But when we returned to the real world, outside of the cabin and our own little forest on the mountain, everything changed. He'd started to withdraw. Avoided the kids. Refused to travel into town.

Was he pulling away?

Why was he so reluctant to seize the chance at a fresh start in Butterpond?

What was he still hiding from me?

I wasn't about to let it come between us.

Or him and the kids.

He'd felt guilty about Mellie's outbursts while I was gone—and even worse about the slight burn on her hand. She'd recovered, simply delighted for a chance to wear a bedazzled band-aid. It'd scarred Rem more. Not just the injury, but the words she'd spoken that she didn't understand.

It was almost adorable to see his confidence shaken by a three-year-old.

He needed some time with Mellie. Quality time. So I dragged him and the kids into Butterpond for a new event offered by the local library. It was a pretty happening place in the town. They had Quilting Mondays, Knitting Tuesdays, Embroidery Thursdays, and, the current favorite, Slow Cooker Sunday.

Unfortunately, Martial Arts Wednesdays was cancelled following a particularly heated sparring contest which had resulted in Mrs. Miller's shattered hip. The Silver Exercise program had recently reworked their mission statement from *TaekwonDO* to ...*Taekwon-probably-shouldn't*.

Rem stared at the library, hesitant to cross the red brick threshold. "The last time I was here..." He pointed to the dumpster adjacent to the building. "Tidus and I dropped an M80 into the can."

I nodded. "I remember. You frightened Mrs. Tulley's homing pigeons. Six of them fled across the state line."

Rem glanced to the overhead wires. "The others ended up eleven secret herbs and spices short of a KFC crispy bucket."

"Don't worry. No pigeons will be harmed today. This should be cute." I handed him the flyer. *Daddy-Daughter Painting.* The friendly bubble letters didn't excite him. "You and Mellie will love it. Right, Mellie?"

The toddler never ran, she bounced. Off of everyone and everything. She'd ricocheted off the library's brick half-fence and collided with Rem's legs. She tugged on his shirt to hop into his arms, but he didn't reach for her.

Hadn't really held her all week.

"Paint!" She beamed at him. *"Come on, Uncle Rem!"*

He didn't return her smile, and my heart broke. He stared at the library, the town, the whispering people as they passed us on the steps. He might have been gone for a few years, but everyone remembered Remington Marshall. That wasn't a good thing for either of us.

Robert Bunting and his two twin girls crossed the street towards the library, though he cautiously diverted the kids onto the sidewalk, choosing to enter through a second entrance, far from Rem.

Rem noticed.

Of course he noticed.

I frowned. "Mr. Bunting has no room to talk…and no liver either. He's spent the last fifteen years cheating on his wife with Jim Beam." I took Rem's hand. "Don't worry about them."

"You sure about this, Sassy?" Rem never sounded beaten. If anything, the reluctance made him all that more confident that what he did, where he hid, why he ran was the right thing. "I gotta give Mellie and Tabby the best start they can get. If I keep hanging around, what'll that do to them?"

"This is your *home.*" I mussed with Mellie's blonde curls. "And this is your niece who wants nothing more than to paint with you this afternoon."

He handed the flyer back. "It's *daddy*-daughter, Cas."

"They'll make an exception for an uncle, especially one who cares so much about his nieces."

Rem wasn't convinced. "You know what's going to happen the instant I step foot in there."

Yeah. If the little old volunteer librarians didn't drop dead, the shock would tangle their knitting and unravel Rem in gossip throughout Butterpond. Knit twice, purl once, and hide the women.

"Ignore them."

I pulled him close for a kiss, but Tabby stole him instead, puckering her own lips. He smirked and gave her two.

"You've been gone for a long time," I said. "They might not welcome you back overnight."

"I don't care what they think."

I arched an eyebrow. "Then why are you so worried?"

"I care what *you* think—and what will happen to your reputation."

"We played this game five years ago too, Rem." I winked. "Didn't scare me away then. Won't work on me now. Besides...I need the paycheck."

"And the truth finally comes out."

I pushed him towards the door. "Both of you. March. I'm ordering you to have fun."

"Ordering me?"

"That's right."

"Oh, no little girl." Rem opened the door for me with a wicked smile and no sense of his surroundings. "Think I'll have to punish that rebellious streak out of you..."

A horrified Mrs. Jenkins crossed herself as she hurried out of the library. She cast two indignant glances at us and tutted her disapproval.

Well, we'd be the hot topic at bridge club that night.

"I really can't take you anywhere, can I?" I gave his ass a subtle slap.

He intercepted the spanking and kissed my hand. "That was a mistake, Sassy. Tonight, I'm getting you back."

"Tenfold."

"Oh, at least twenty."

The library welcomed a dozen families into the rec room, exchanging a crisp twenty-dollar bill for an easel, a paint-stained smock, and entry into the ring of kids eagerly waiting for permission to begin wrecking the construction paper clipped to their workstations.

Mellie, as usual, ran full-speed, arms outstretched, braying like a donkey. Unfortunately, this time she collided with the one girl also spazzing her way across the carpet, somersault after somersault.

Both knocked heads and landed on their bottoms.

The little redheaded girl began to cry.

Mellie shushed the other girl with too much sass for her own good. "No crying! Don't be a baby!"

"Mellie!" I passed Tabby to Rem and stormed forward, ensuring the girls were only bruised, not broken. "You're supposed to say you're sorry for hitting her. Apologize. Now, young lady."

Mellie pointed at Rem. "Uncle Rem said only *babies* cry."

"Oh, *did* he?"

At least he looked ashamed.

I helped the other girl to her feet. Only one child in Butterpond had such fiery hair—tomato soup, Tidus always said. I searched for Sheriff Samson in the crowd and brushed the flecks of dirt off his granddaughter, Tina.

The Sherriff wasn't as mobile with the bum knee—injured after a late night, last call after the Rivets' playoff win. He masked the limp with a swagger that fooled no one except the couple punk kids under the age of twelve who happened to skateboard in the municipal office's parking lot.

"Whoopsie-daisy." Sherriff Samson swooped down, groaned as his back audibly cracked, and instead patted Tina's head. "You good, sweetpea?"

"Just had a little toddler head-on collision," I smiled. "I think they're okay."

"This is Emma Marshall's baby."

"Yep," I said. "I'm her nanny…"

Samson wasn't listening. His gaze passed to Rem.

Just my luck.

"You got the kids?" Samson asked.

Rem nodded. "Yeah."

"Brought her to *paint*?"

"That's right."

"Oddly wholesome for a boy like you, ain't it?"

"Men change, Sherriff."

The library was no place for the town's resident bad boy to face off against the Sherriff. I would not have the YA section become the OK Corral. Especially since the last five years had been kinder to Rem than Samson.

Rem had filled out, bulked up, and transformed into a hardened hunk of muscle and poise. In the same amount of time, Sherriff Samson had shrunk three inches, gained a gut, and threatened retirement after a flock of Canadian geese invaded the municipal center's parking lot, soiled his SUV, and attacked him every evening as he left the office.

No longer was Sherriff Samson chasing after Rem and Tidus as they transitioned from boyhood pranks and into the drugs that nearly ruined both of their lives. But that didn't mean a truce was struck. Neither man trusted the other.

"Thought the Paynes chased you out of Butterpond with whatever pitchforks were left in the rubble of the barn?" Samson asked.

Our equipment had been stored in a separate shed, but I wasn't getting in the middle of the pissing match without an umbrella. Rem bounced Tabby to his other arm and tried to maintain his stare while the baby stuck her fingers in his ears.

"Came back to help Em," he said. "Someone's gotta watch the kids while she gets better."

"Heroin, right?"

Of all the words for the librarians to hush. Rem stiffened, his jaw tight. "She's recovered. Clean for a couple weeks now."

"Hope it stays that way. A shame. First your father. Then you. Now her."

Rem didn't let it piss him off. "I've been sober a long time. My father's dead, buried, and rotting. But Em is getting help. She's beaten the addiction, no thanks to people like you who would kick her when she's down."

"Who do you think took the kids out of the house?"

Rem wouldn't hear it. "Well, I got the girls now, and Mellie wants to paint."

"*You?*" Samson's laugh filled the library. "Family man Remington Marshall. Responsible for *two* young kids. Surprised they haven't knocked over a preschool yet."

"I'm waiting until we can pull a heist on the Toys R Us in Ironfield." Rem's slick tongue would get us all in trouble. "Figured I'd teach them their ABCs—assault, battery, and counterfeiting."

I interrupted before the librarians were summoned. They were old, but they were damn accurate with their canes. These ladies didn't shush—they struck, right behind the knees.

I took Tabby away before Rem's fist clenched her as well. "I'm the girls' nanny, but Rem's been really good with them."

Samson's tone gentled for me. "At least they have *some* good influences then. Hate to see a third generation of Marshall end up in the gutter like the rest."

Rem endured enough. He poked Samson's chest in a way that would get Rem maced if the sheriff could have found his pockets under his gut.

"Look." Rem's voice lowered—just enough of a grunt to accuse him of threatening Butterpond's two-member police department. "I know my family's name isn't worth the spit to say it. But those girls aren't *me*. They're innocent. They don't know anything about their momma or uncle except both read 'em bedtime stories and feed 'em chicken nuggets. You will *not* insult them." He stepped closer. A challenge. "I don't got a lot to be proud of, but those girls mean more to me than a night in the lock-up for punching you square in the balls."

"*Okay...*" I pushed them apart. "I think we should take the girls to paint now."

"Best thing you ever did for this town...and for her..." Samson pointed at me. "Was leaving."

"Well, now I'm back." Rem held his arms out. "What are you going to do about it?"

"Hopefully, nothing." Samson narrowed his eyes. "I did a favor for you, boy. Five years ago, when Bill Payne wanted you locked up for that fire. I did you a *favor*."

A favor? I frowned, but Rem didn't let me ask the question.

"No. You did the *Paynes* a favor," Rem said. "Don't act like it was for me."

"You aren't that noble, Marshall. Go and pretend that you're some martyr, but I know the truth. You were no good then, you're no good now, and the entire town of Butterpond—including this pretty lady— were better off with you gone."

A step too far for both of us, but I didn't get to defend my own honor.

A shocked librarian cried over the room. "She's covered in *paint!*"

And that was my cue.

I didn't have to ask. Didn't even need to look.

I just *knew*.

That *punch in the gut, this is going to take forever to clean, does paint come out of a car seat* instinct that all people inherited when working with small children.

The crowd parted as I rushed inside the rec room.

It was worse than I'd thought.

Mellie had plunked down on the carpet with her shirt off, but I couldn't tell. A thick layer of red, blue, yellow, and green paint smeared over her arms, chest, and fingers. The child had become a goddamned macaw, and only once the room had panicked did she stop slapping the paint over herself. A drizzle of blue dripped from her fingertips.

"Oh, *Mellie*..." I covered my mouth. "What did you do?"

The gaze of every parent seared through me. The judgment was next. *Why was she left unattended? Who would allow their child to behave in such a way? Who raises an abstract artist when that trend is so early 2000s?*

I knelt down, but I didn't have enough wetnaps in my purse to fix this one.

Mellie grinned at her uncle and gave him a cheeky wave. "Look! I'm Uncle Rem!"

"What?" I asked.

She proudly pointed to the colors on her arms and then at him. "*Look!*"

Rem wore a short-sleeved shirt, tight against his chest, abs, and biceps. So far, it had entertained the moms dropping off their husbands and daughters for the event. But peeking from the sleeves and extending down his arms...the snake tattoo.

Bright and vibrant, the reds, yellows, and greens inked a complete sleeve into his skin.

Mellie had painted herself to look like her uncle.

"*Hey*." Rem's smile horrified the parents more than the painted child. "That's kinda neat!"

"Rem," I whispered.

He sounded so goddamned *proud* it broke my heart. "She wanted to look like *me!*"

Sherriff Samson grumbled, shaking his head as he kept his granddaughter out of the utter mess that'd spilled from Mellie's exuberance. A rolling glop of red had escaped the newspaper lining, and the splattered blues and greens stained the paper. One wayward kick from Mellie, and the paper tore, ruining the carpet beneath the child.

Mellie was a mess. The paints were spilled. The librarians fumed.

But Rem looked so *happy*.

At least...for a moment.

"She gave herself *tattoos*?" One of the librarians gasped in disbelief. "What sort of child is this?"

Another mother scoffed. "What kind of home is she living in?"

"Not one I'd let my kid visit." A father agreed.

Sherriff Samson stepped close, eying a now somber Mellie and quieted Rem. "I asked myself...what would happen if Rem Marshall took in two little girls. How could a man who'd lived his life without regard for any other person ever care for a toddler?" His voice lowered. "Emma might be bad, but you're worse. You gotta think about what sort of influence you have on these girls...all three of them."

Rem didn't answer. He knelt before Mellie and rubbed the semi-dry paint from her chest. It didn't come off. He swore.

"Shit."

Tabby giggled in my arms. "*Tit!*"

That didn't help matters. Rem scooped Mellie up, ignoring the wet paint that stuck to his shirt. He stalked out of the rec room.

Damn it. I shushed Tabby as she delighted the room with a variety of her uncle's favorite words. The librarians watched in horror.

"I'm sorry..." I hurried to the door. "Please, bill me for the expenses and cleanup. Send it to the farm. I'll take care of it..."

I didn't wait for an answer, chasing after Rem as he hauled Mellie to the park behind the library. He plunked her down in front of a water pump and attempted to splash the chillingly cold water over the paint. Mellie fought him. He held her steady. Neither was happy.

"It's not coming off." He struggled to keep his voice even. "What the hell is in this paint?"

"It's nothing a good scrub in the bath won't fix." I sucked in a breath. "And if she's...*tinted* for a couple days, that's fine."

"It's *not* fine." Rem kicked the pump, scared the kids, and spouted a leak in the mechanism. "Damn it!"

"Rem, she was just playing. This happens. Usually...not in public or with such vibrant colors, but..." I shifted Tabby to another hip and took his hand, bringing him close. "It's just a part of being a kid. We'll clean her up. Ignore what Samson said—he was always an idiot who stuck his nose into everyone's business."

"You don't understand. Mellie *has* to get cleaned up. She can't have any paint on her tomorrow."

"Why?"

Of all the times to keep a secret.

Of all the days to not trust me.

What was it with this man and refusing to let me into his heart?

"Tomorrow is Emma's hearing. The court is meeting to determine if she can regain custody." Rem couldn't look at me or the girls. "Tomorrow, they might be going home."

17

Rem

Pretty sure I couldn't douse a kid in turpentine.

I plunked Mellie into the tub instead, drummed up some bubbles, and debated getting the paint stripper to peel the not-so-temporary tattoos off my niece.

Mellie giggled and picked at the blue stain under her fingernails. She waved her hands at me and sighed.

"Mess. Mess. Mess."

"You said it." I filled a Tupperware container with water and tipped it over her head. "Look out. *Tidal wave.*"

Mellie puffed her cheeks and held her breath while the water dumped over her hair.

Green hair. Red hair. Yellow hair.

I'd inadvertently tie-dyed the kid. The courts probably wouldn't want the girl showing up in any color but their normal hue.

Mellie didn't care. She pinched both her nose and the nose of her favorite tub buddy. The toy needed to be stuffed down the drain. Bath-time Barbie was becoming Black-Mold Barbie. CPS wouldn't like that either.

I'd get her a new one if she went back to Em's.

When.

When she went back to Em's.

The thought weighed me down so heavy I worried about leaning over the water. Already felt like I was drowning. Guilt. Hope. Rage. Resignation.

God, I was a bastard. I should have been *thrilled*. Emma had recovered. She'd stayed sober for three months. That was a fucking amazing accomplishment—something the girls could be proud of.

Wished I had that much to offer them. All I could do was dump some water over their heads with a beat-up Tupperware container.

"*Tidal wave!*" I teetered the container in my hand. "*Whoa!*"

Mellie scrunched up. Unfortunately, she wanted to protect Barbie's nose and forgot about her own. She sucked in a breath just as the water passed over her face. Her laughter turned to coughs, and she hacked up half of the water.

"Uh-oh." I waited while she sputtered. "Are you okay?"

She shook her head.

"Just water up your nose?"

The coughing subsided. "Yeah."

"Good."

I dumped another container of bathwater over her with a splash. Mellie giggled, kicking in the tub and creating more multi-colored bubbles.

"Uncle Rem!"

"What?" Another waterfall. "I thought you liked...*tidal waves.*"

She laughed. "Stop!"

"Don't you want to get clean?"

Another splatter. She splashed me back. "No fair!"

"Nothing's fair during...*tidal wave!*" Two dunks this time. "You just gotta hold your nose."

Another splash. Mellie practically dissolved into giggles. A giggle would have been easier to clean. Getting the paint off her body was a goddamned Herculean task.

Tabby shouted from the living room. Soon, the bathroom door burst open and she toddled inside, muttering a furious story of babble and gibberish under her breath. Cassie followed.

And reluctantly spoke to me.

"Tabby wanted to see what the commotion was."

"Bath!" Tabby pointed excitedly at the tub. "Bath!"

Sure. Two and a half weeks ago, the kids were allergic to water. I bargained with a one-year-old, selling my soul to get her butt to stay put in the tub with a bribe of chocolate. My range of talents now included hunting, tracking, carpentry, and protecting a candy bar from some shampoo.

"You'll get a bath later." I poked her chubby belly. "Right now, your sister looks like a Picasso."

"*Pikachu?*" Mellie gasped.

"Sure." I dunked another ladle of water over her. "Give me an arm, Mellie. I gotta scrub you down."

Mellie scrunched up her nose. "I like it."

So did I, until I realized no one else in the library thought the paint tattoos were as adorable as me.

"Well, we gotta get you clean."

"Why?"

I glanced at Cassie. She was no help. Then again, I'd blindsided her with the court date. At least she wouldn't get angry around the kids. Hopefully Mellie would have a nightmare tonight and sleep in our bed. Cassi wouldn't suffocate me with a pillow in sight of the kids.

"Tomorrow..." I swallowed. The words were harder to spit out than I thought. "You get to see Mommy."

Mellie leapt to her feet. Half of the water surged out of the tub and onto me and the clean towels I'd set out for her. She made a break for it, but the excited dance slowed her down. I plunked her into the tub while she squealed.

"Mommy!" She celebrated by kicking her feet and knocking every shampoo and soap into the bath with her. Everything, including me and the towels and the water and the soaps, tinted a strange shade of blue. "I miss Mommy!"

Tabby pounced in the puddles, unsure of the cause for such excitement but pleased by the mess at her feet. She stomped twice before slipping. Cassie caught her as she fell, but Tabby wiggled enough so she could sit in the dampness and slap it with her hands.

"Okay, so we gotta scrub you down and get you clean," I said. "Sound good?"

"Yep!"

A half-hour and two drained and re-filled tubs later, the kid was still shaded like monopoly money, but she seemed essentially cleaned. Good enough for court.

She buzzed around the cabin with a doll, letting Tabby toddle behind, and we set to making dinner.

Silently.

Cassi hadn't spoken. Hadn't really looked at me.

I knew it was coming. I braced myself for it.

What was I supposed to say?

She tossed some chicken in the oven, but she lowered the knife to the cutting board halfway through the broccoli. That was fine. Mellie had an aversion to *green*. After today, I shared it.

"When were you going to tell me?" Cassi stared at the counter. "Was I just going to wake up one day and assume the toddlers had moved out?"

"Would it have worked?"

"Don't you dare joke about this."

Fair enough. "What do you want me to say?"

"How about...*the kids' court case is on Thursday, and we should get ready for it*?"

"Topic never came up."

A lame excuse. Cassi knew it. She thumped her hand on the counter and gave her fingernails a rat-a-tat-tat against the wooden cutting board. Probably would have been smart to move the chef's knife away from her.

"You *lied* to me," she said.

"You didn't ask."

"Don't play that game, Rem," Cassi said. "You didn't tell me—*deliber-*

ately. Why?"

Because since the minute my life got babyjacked, I'd been wondering when I'd be on my own again.

Counting days. Estimating the time.

Letting the little ankle-biters get under my skin and into my heart.

"I never thought Emma would recover." The truth hurt. "Now she has, and she has a right to take them home. I didn't want you to worry about the custody issue."

"You should have told me."

"Probably."

Her voice hardened. "No. You *should* have told me."

"Yeah."

Cassi exhaled. "Think she's ready to take them back?"

I had no idea. It had taken me a hell of a lot longer to kick my additions—and I had to run a lot farther away to avoid the temptations. But Emma did her rehab. She passed the blood and piss tests. She was sober when I'd talked to her. What else was there to discuss?

"That's not my decision," I said.

"But you know your sister."

"I'm not a judge."

"Rem."

The cabin suddenly felt far too small for a conversation this huge. "It's not up to me. I'm not CPS. Christ, I'm not their father."

"Do you want to be?"

I snorted, hand running through my hair, trying to find the closest exit, closest highway, closest *anywhere* that wasn't my not-so-isolated mountain. "Just stop, Cas. I'm not going there."

"Why not?"

"Because it's a stupid fucking question."

She straightened, her lips puffing into a kissable pout. "Excuse me?"

"You really think those kids are any better here with me than they are with their mother?"

She didn't blink. "Yes. I do."

Christ, she was naïve. How hadn't I seen it before? "Cas, you're smarter than that."

"So now I'm stupid too?"

"I'm not a good guardian to these girls, and you know it."

"Why not?"

"Do you need a reason besides the gallon of paint that'll be clogging my septic system? Don't be polite. Don't play pretend. Don't bullshit me. I'm a terrible uncle, a shit parent, and everyone in this town is right about me."

"I can't believe you're letting them get into your head."

"Jesus. Look at the kids. *Listen* to the kids. They're swearing. They're getting in trouble. Mellie wants to emulate *me*. What sort of three-year-old wants tattoos?"

"She doesn't want *tattoos*," Cassi said. "She wants to be like *you*."

"And that's the problem. I am the worst example for these kids. Always have been, always will be."

"You said you've changed."

"Do you think that'll matter when they're old enough to know the kind of man their uncle is? When they hear the stories? Realize he's got the same problems, the same tendencies as their mother? When they realize it's because of *me* that their name is continuously dragged through the mud?"

"You're their *family*." Cassi tried to take my hand. I didn't let her close. "You can't change family, believe me. But there is nothing stronger in this world. Even when they punch holes through the walls with each other's heads. Even when there's no room in the house to take care of a family member who's been seriously wounded. Families make it work."

Yeah. Some of them.

Families like the Paynes, which, until five years ago, had been a model family. They'd loved each other. They'd cared for each other. And they'd taken in kids like me to share that wealth of warmth and comfort and support. *Nothing* was more important than protecting that *goodness*.

And that's why I didn't belong anywhere near it.

I didn't recognize the catch in my voice. "They deserve a better family than me."

"*Why?*" Her question turned plea. "Rem, *why* are you treating yourself like this? Don't let what my brothers or the Sherriff say change how you feel about those girls. You aren't a terrible person. Five years ago, you were wild, a bad boy with a bad reputation who liked trouble. Now?" She moved before me, her hands on my chest. "Now you're a good man who is *hurting*. You don't want the girls to go."

"Cassi, for Christ's sake, I can't even take care of them by myself. I need *you* here to help."

"There's nothing wrong in asking for help..." Her words softened. "Just like there's nothing wrong in loving them."

"And that's why I want what's best for them. Emma's recovered. She wants her family, a family I don't want to ruin...and don't look at me all doe-eyed. You know who I am—who I *really* am."

Cassi whipped from zero-to-pissed-off in the time it took to pull her hair into a ponytail.

Dinner was forgotten. The fight had only just begun.

"Yeah, I know you," she said. "You're the one who broke my heart five years ago because you were too scared to take responsibility for your life and your decisions."

"No. I left because I was afraid I'd ruin you, your life, and your family if I stayed. I would have destroyed your future...same as I'll destroy Mellie and Tabby's."

Cassi huffed. "So that's it then. You aren't even going to try?"

"They're not my kids."

"They're still your family. And if you have any doubt in your mind that Emma—"

"There's none. Emma is *fine*. Better than fine. I talked to her. I talked to her sponsor. She's clean. She's sober. She's got her life back on track."

"So then what?"

What else was there? "What do you mean?"

"When they go home?" Cassi narrowed her eyes. "What will you do?"

"What *should* I do?" I extended my arms. "I gave them food and a roof over their head."

"You gave them more than that."

"Yeah, a new colorful vocabulary and potential lead poisoning from that paint."

Cassi raged but her voice stayed even, trying not to alarm the kids. I didn't have the same tact.

"You know you did more for those little girls than that. Will you visit them?"

What the hell did it matter? The less they saw of me, the better they'd be. "I'll send gifts. See them at the holidays. Doesn't matter."

"I can't believe you." She nearly laughed. "You don't even want to be a part of their life?"

I *never* said that.

But I knew it was the right thing to do.

"You're running again, aren't you?" Cassi stared at me, her voice weakening. "You're not even going to *try*. I thought you were better than that."

"I'm not."

"*Why?*"

She wanted the truth?

Fine.

She'd pulled it from me, tortured me with my own guilt. If she wanted to know why I was such a fucking bastard, then I'd tell her.

We'd see if she still felt the same way after.

"I'm the one who got Emma hooked on the junk."

Cassi's breath escaped in a slight *oh*.

She quieted, staring at me with that look of utter mortification I knew I'd have to face sometime.

Why bother sugarcoating it?

Why bother hiding it?

It wasn't the worst thing I'd done, and it wasn't the worst secret I'd kept. But it revealed too much to the woman who'd so foolishly trusted me.

"It was my needle," I said. "I came home four years ago for your mother's funeral. I hid in the back. I didn't talk to anyone. Didn't try to find you or your brothers. But I had to pay my respects to the woman who was like a second mother to me. And the only way I could face this town or your family or that woman who didn't deserve to be in that casket was if I broke my own damn sobriety. So I did. And Emma…"

I'd been too stoned to even realize what had happened.

"I didn't know Emma would take it," I said. "And I didn't know she was pregnant."

"Rem…"

"She found my stash at her house while I crashed on her couch. And she got pissed. Raged at me. She took it away. I thought she was trying to get me clean, but I was pissed. I hated what I'd become. How weak I was. I knew better than to go near an Oxy addict with that shit, but…"

Cassi sunk against the counter, her words a whisper. "Rem, it's not your fault."

"Of course it is." I glanced to the kids. "That's why I had to take the girls. It was my fault their mother got as bad as she did. I had to do something to make up for the past."

"Then *stay* with them. Be a part of their lives. Just love them, Rem. There's nothing wrong with that."

But nothing I ever did would be *right* for those kids.

I knew it. The Paynes knew it. The town knew it.

Cassi was the only one who couldn't see it.

So I knew what had to be done. To protect them. To protect *her*.

Cassi deserved the truth. All of it. Why I ran. What I'd done. Who I'd protected.

Even if it hurt everyone and destroyed everything.

A lie spared her pain.

The truth would be unforgivable.

And both would forever deny me the woman I loved.

18

Cassi

Without the kids, the cabin was silent.

No TV. No laughter. No annoyingly shrill iPad game that tweeted birds and flashed lights and prompted a toddler to bang you over the head with the device when the batteries died.

Worst of all?

It was quiet. It was peaceful.

It was lonely.

So *incredibly* lonely.

Made worse by Rem as he'd completely isolated himself from the pain after a quick hug and kiss outside the courthouse.

He'd bagged the girls things in the middle of the night, packed Em's car while we talked on the steps, and declined the chance to go to her house for a celebratory pizza lunch.

As if he couldn't stand to look at the kids. Or his sister.

Or me.

For two days, he'd hidden away in the workshop, obsessing over a project no one had ordered and he hadn't let me see.

He was pulling away.

It wasn't even subtle.

Something had flicked in his head. That trigger to run when it got tough, to hide when his feelings were exposed, and to avoid any opportunity to *forgive* himself and his past.

Whatever that past was.

Whatever other secrets he'd refused to tell me.

Trust was hard to give when I'd already been burned by this man. But if he didn't trust himself, if he thought so little of his character and soul, then how was I to help him?

Or to protect myself?

I knew better than to let Remington Marshall back into my heart.

Problem was…he'd always been there.

Night had fallen before Rem came back to the house to eat. He rummaged in the fridge, emerged with a juice box, and stared at the little cartoon critter on the carton. Mellie had refused to touch the reduced sugar apple juice until Rem doodled funny faces on the cartoon apples. He stared at a buck-toothed smiley, gripped it tight…

Then silently threw it in the garbage.

"Haven't seen you all day." I lowered my phone and tried to meet his gaze. Didn't work. "Marius is doing well. The doctors say it'll be a couple weeks, but they're already thinking about the prosthetic."

"Good."

He gave me nothing else.

"They have a family house near Walter Reed—for long-term recovery patients. Might be something we could do until he's ready to come home."

"You gonna go?"

I hadn't decided yet. "That depends."

"On what?"

"On you."

Rem opened a beer but didn't drink. He leaned against the sink, staring out the window into the night. "Got a call from a buddy at the logging site."

"In Canada?"

"Yeah."

My stomach dropped. "What'd he say?"

"Job's there if I want it."

"All the way across the continent?"

"Yeah."

Everything soured. Rem said nothing else. Without the Disney movies or baby cooing or constant toddler jabber, nothing silenced my anger.

I ground my teeth. "Think that will be far enough?"

He glanced at me. "From what?"

"From whatever it is that's terrifying you."

"I'm not afraid of anything."

"Sure, you are." I gave up, pushing away from the counter. "You're afraid of doing what's *right*."

He caught me before I left the room, but I batted his hand away. Rem stared, his chestnut eyes dark and flat, as if he hadn't slept at all. Maybe he hadn't. Certainly hadn't touched me. Or kissed me. Or Held me. Not for two nights.

"I know you're hurting." My honesty stung. "I'm hurting too. Let me help you."

"I don't need help."

It would have been funny if it wasn't so damned tragic. "I think you said that five years ago too."

"Let it go, Cas. What's done is done."

"That's not true. If it were *done*, then all these feelings and questions would be resolved. But they're not."

It was his turn to walk away. I didn't let him out the door.

"What the hell happened to you, Rem? What changed to make you this way?"

If he took offense, he didn't show it. "This *is* who I am. Who I've always been."

"You're lying to me. You've *been* lying to me. Everything you've ever done is a lie."

He didn't deny it. "I've never wanted to hurt you, Cassi. Did all I could to prevent it."

"Hiding things *is* hurting me. Not trusting me *is* hurting me. You didn't tell me about Em's problem. You didn't tell me about the court date." And he *still* didn't react. "It's like you're so damn terrified to get close to me."

Rem looked away. "You know how I feel about you."

"And it never mattered. You were always going to run. The first chance you got, you were going to bolt out that door and out of my life. As soon as you got rid of the girls, you'd planned to leave."

Silence. The accusation hung heavy in the air.

And he didn't deny it.

"I can't stay here," he said.

"Why not?"

"Doesn't matter."

"It's happening *again*." I hated these words. "You're shutting down, Rem. You would destroy everything we have so you don't need to face those feelings."

"What do we have?" Rem's resigned whisper killed me. "Honestly. What future can I give you?"

My heart refused to break twice.

The pieces just fell back into the gaping pit that was my foolishness.

"I'm not good for you, Cassi."

He'd been saying it—repeating it—chanting it like a self-deprecating mantra for a week.

I didn't believe it. Hell, I wasn't even sure *he* believed it.

But there it was. Ripping us apart.

Stealing minute after minute, hour after hour, year after year of our happiness.

"You think you're a bad influence on the kids?" I asked.

"Yeah."

"I don't believe it."

"You will. Give it time."

He sounded like *everyone* else. Everyone who'd refused to give him a chance, who couldn't see beyond the reputation. They'd all warned me to stay away from him. To never sneak out to meet him. To do all I could to never fall for him.

Maybe they were right.

My father never forgave him. Jules refused to try. Even Tidus had freaked when I'd accidentally revealed our relationship.

If the entire town of Butterpond could read Rem for the bastard that he was, and if Rem insisted that he was as terrible as they said...

Maybe they weren't the blind ones.

Maybe I was the only fool stupid enough to think I could change him.

Except I still didn't believe a single word.

He'd lied before. What was stopping him from lying now?

"You haven't been honest with me since the day I stepped foot in this cabin," I said. "Since the day I came here loaded with boxes, stunned that a man like you would even consider opening his home for those little girls."

Rem nodded. "I told you."

"Yeah, well, I didn't listen." I sucked in a breath. "And that was my choice. I let myself get close. I let myself think I could resist you and deny my feelings and not wonder about all the time we lost."

His voice lowered. "It's my fault. I chased you. I hoped...it'd be different."

"You know what I think?" I didn't wait for his answer. "I think it was a *mistake* that you left me then, and it'd be even bigger one to go now."

"Why?"

"Something hurt you, Rem. You needed help then, and I couldn't give it. But I can help you now—and you can help me."

"What are you talking about?"

"Take me with you."

"*What*?"

"Take me with you. Wherever you're going. Me and you. We'll be together. Start a new life."

Rem rubbed his face, suddenly exhausted and pained. "Cassi, I'm trying to make this easy on you."

"You *always* take the easy way out, Rem. This time, I'm doing it too. I've wanted to get away from Butterpond for months now. What better opportunity than now?" The hope in my voice destroyed me. "We could go together, stay together. Just...be *together*."

"You can't," he said.

"Why?"

"What the hell are *you* running from?" His words sharpened. "Jesus, Cas. You've got family here. Friends. Your entire life. You love them, they love you. Don't take that for granted."

"You think you aren't loved?"

"That doesn't matter to me."

"You know my family loved you like another son." I swallowed, hard. "You know that *I* love you."

Rem knew how to twist the knife. "You shouldn't."

"That's my problem."

"I'm not a good man."

"And I'm a foolish woman who thinks five years apart was long enough. Don't make it any longer."

Rem crossed his arms. His eyes darkened, studying me.

Tearing through me.

"You'd really come with me?" Rem asked.

"In a heartbeat."

"All the way to the Canadian wilderness?"

"Sounds like fun."

"Leave Butterpond? Pack up. Start a new life."

"Of course."

He stepped closer, a thin smile on his lips. "Yeah? *What about Marius*?"

A gut punch. I sucked in a breath that did nothing to suppress the guilt.

"Who's gonna take care of Marius?" he whispered. "Who will take care of the rest of your brothers? They got no one now. No idea what to do with their lives. How they're supposed to start a life on the farm none of them wanted." Rem knew he was right, and it made him insufferable. "Yeah, they're gonna fight. And they'll get pissed off. And they'll make mistakes. But it's worth the effort to forgive them."

"They're adults. They can handle themselves." Even I hardly believed it. My chest heaved. Tight. Aching. "And Marius...he can get a nurse or someone to watch over him..."

"Cassi, you've already made your choice."

Rem reached for me, brushing a hand against my cheek. I didn't push him away, even when the tears teased over his fingers.

"I know you're staying," he said. "You would never leave your brothers. Not when you want to protect them. That's what you do. Protect. Care. *Love*. And that's the reason I run. If I want to protect the ones I love from what I've done, then the only thing I can do is *leave*."

"Saying it doesn't make it true, Rem."

"You wanted me to be honest. So I'm honest."

"No." I pulled away and dried my cheeks with my hands. "You've never been honest a day in your life, Rem. You're hiding secrets. You're telling lies. One day you might be honest with me, but it won't matter then. Not if you refuse to be honest with yourself."

The worst part of breaking up wasn't losing the man I loved.

It was knowing that no matter how hard I'd tried, how many days would pass, and how many times I'd cursed his name, I'd never get over him.

Heartbreak wasn't fair the first go round.

This time, I didn't have much of a heart left.

19

Rem

Beer didn't taste good unless Cassi took a swig first, scrunched her nose, and demanded an IPA.

Great women loved their shitty beer.

I hadn't been blackout drunk in four years. Figured now was the time to give it a go. Christen one bad decision with a worse one.

I'd rather be drunk and alone than sober and ruining the lives of the people I loved.

I hated the cabin now. Too quiet. Too dark. Too many rooms and too many little memories. Cassi's ponytail holder in the bathroom. Mellie's forgotten shoe in a closet. Tabby's unnoticed milk dribbe on the back of the couch.

Didn't need to find traces of them in my house. I couldn't get them out of my head. My body was on Tabby's schedule—breakfast, play, lunch, nap, dinner, bath time, bed time, and then peace. Mellie's stupid clean-up song played on loop in my brain, clawing through useful thoughts like where to measure the cut and how to fit the joist.

And Cassi...

I hurt everywhere. Head. Heart. Body.

Five years ago, I learned the past could hurt. Humiliation hurt. Resentment hurt. Regret hurt.

Now?

The future would be just as painful.

So I hid in the workshop—from myself, from her memory, from everything and anything—and I found absolutely no relief. No hiding from this shame. All I could do was work it away. Finish my project. Head back to the logging camp. Grow the beard out again. And just...

Stay far away.

Running could solve any problem. The further I ran, the easier it'd be to start over. To forget what I gave up. To ignore who I'd hurt.

For the first time, it seemed like a shit idea.

Three beer bottles lined up at my feet, and I cautiously sketched a measurement on the section of timber. Something this important had to be measured *precisely*, and not just because it was the only thing in my world that mattered anymore, but because of who would use it. Each piece needed to be exact, every line, every angle, every potential side she could touch.

The timber lined with the saw blade, but my phone rang before I could make the cut.

Wouldn't have been the first time I considered tossing my phone onto the band saw.

Emma's name blazed on the screen. If it were anyone else, I'd have let it go. Something honorable must have remained in me.

I answered with a grunt. "Hey."

Emma practically vibrated with energy, blitzing through the phone and jabbering with a manic enthusiasm.

Should I have been worried?

Or maybe that's how Emma sounded when she was happy and healthy?

"So you aren't coming over for dinner?" Emma asked.

It was easier that way. "No."

"The kids miss you."

"They'll be fine."

"I'm making you a plate."

In the background, Tabby began to fuss. Her high-pitched, *pay-attention-I'm-not-dying-but-goddamn-it-someone-better-take-care-of-this-shit* cry.

Emma sighed. "This baby. She's awfully opinionated."

"What's wrong?"

"Oh nothing. She's probably hungry. Not wet. Not too hot. Not starving. Just being a little prima donna, huh, Tabs?" Emma turned sly. "She says she wants her Uncle Rem to come over for dinner."

I ignored that. "She's saying that her socks are crooked."

"*What?*"

"She doesn't like it if her socks turn around. Fix her socks, she'll stop fussing."

"That's crazy."

"She's your kid."

"Why don't you come over and eat?"

I stood, stepping over the rest of the timber. The project's frame now waited for the final few pieces. I needed another beer before I could look at it again.

"I'm not in a *family dinner* mood," I said.

"You used to love them."

"Yeah. When I ate at the Paynes."

"So why can't the Marshalls start their own tradition?"

That'd be easy. "What are you making?"

"Brinner."

There was all the evidence I needed. "*Brinner?*"

"Yeah. Pancakes. Bacon. Sunny side up eggs."

Mellie would never sit at that table. "You gotta scramble them."

"So you will come over?"

"No, but you gotta scramble the eggs."

"Why?"

"Because Mellie doesn't like her food looking at her. Sunny side up to her is like the Eye of Sauron to the fucking hobbits. She won't go near it."

Emma's tone shifted. "Anything else I should know about *my* children?"

Plenty, and nothing that I could list off. Wasn't like I had a running tally of the foods they loved—strawberries, pineapple, and chicken nuggets. Or the foods they hated—spinach, spaghetti with any white sauce, and beef that wasn't ground up. Or the stories they liked before bed—Elmo fine, Doctor Seuss's *Marvin K Mooney Will You Please Go Home* had been torn up in a bout of rage.

Bath time required bubbles and no less than two toys.

Play time demanded access to both crayons and a bouncy ball.

Mellie fell asleep immediately in the car. Tabby needed to be cuddled late at night on the couch before bed.

I'd learned so much. Personality quirks. Likes, dislikes, things that scared them, things that made them giggle.

And those girls loved to giggle.

I changed the subject.

"Thanks for the offer," I said. "But I'm in the middle of something."

"Oh. Is your girlfriend there?"

"Cassi?"

"Yeah."

I paused. "No."

Emma's annoyed sigh was practically prophetic. "What the hell did you do this time?"

The phone was getting annoying. There was a reason I hardly used it. My fingers ached while I clutched the damn thing. "I didn't *do* anything."

And that was the biggest problem.

"You already lost her once, jackass. Did you break up with her again?"

"It's complicated."

Emma hooted. "Bullshit. You're a goddamned coward."

I gritted my teeth, but I wasn't about to cuss out my sister when she was only a couple months out of rehab. Supposed to be *supportive* and *compassionate* and not hope that she'd choke on her phone.

"She's dealing with shit with her family," I said. "Marius got hurt overseas."

"Oh, no. He was so cute."

"Hopefully, you'll find him cute with one less leg."

"...Probably."

"Cassi is helping her family now. Went home. We broke it off."

"Oh. Did *you* lose a leg?"

I frowned. "No."

"So, you still got two functional ones?"

"Yeah."

"Then why don't you march your skinny ass down to the farm and help her too. She'll need it."

"Oh, Christ, Em—"

"Don't you take that tone with me, Remington. You know goddamned well what you're doing, and I'm sick to death of it. At least my vice came in a little baggie. Yours is stuck between those lopsided ears."

"I did what I thought was right."

"You let her get away."

"I let her *go*."

"Oh, you are so freaking magnanimous."

Now my temper flared. The Marshalls had a family rule. Someone else starts it, you finish it. Probably why the rest of the town hated us.

"Look, you know she's better than me," I said.

"Says who?"

"Says *everyone*."

Emma snorted. "And why would they say that?"

"Because we're trash, Emma. For Christ's sake."

A steely silence. I regretted the words.

"Are you calling my little girls *trash*?"

I practically heaved. "No. Absolutely not."

"Then you better take those words back right fucking now."

"Em, you know as well as I do that those girls are better than us. They deserve more than what we had. So does Cassi."

"And you think you can't give that life to these kids or to Cassi without sitting up all alone on your mountain?" The realization hit her pretty quick. "Fuck, you're leaving, aren't you?"

"Yeah."

"Great. So instead of telling that girl you love her, you're going to run far away, never speak to us again, and pretend none of this exists."

"That's the plan."

"You're such a selfish asshole."

Goddamn it. I flung the beer bottle at the wall. The glass shattered. I reached for a new beer, but my fingers grazed a jagged piece near my chair. Blood blossomed over my hand. I swore. A handkerchief caught most of the blood. The cut wasn't bad, but it should've been worse, just to punish me.

Emma sighed. "Is this about that ridiculous fire?"

"Yes."

"You told me what happened back then, but I don't know if it's worth believing."

"Why would I lie?"

"Because you *never* tell the truth, not when a lie means you could bask in your own worthlessness for a while longer."

"I'm not doing this for me. I've never done *anything* for myself."

"Except deliberately hurt yourself." Emma snorted. "At least I used a drug, Rem. I never used other people."

"I'm protecting everyone else—especially the Paynes."

"Why?"

"Because they gave me a roof, food, and work when I needed it. And I don't want to see anything destroy that family. I left before the truth came out."

Emma's voice softened. "What about *our* family?"

"We didn't have a family."

"Yeah…" She hesitated before swearing once more. "But you had *me*."

"What?"

"You know, I could have used my brother these last couple years. It's been kinda rough, Rem."

"You didn't need me. Christ, I'm the one who made you this way. Rehab did more for you than I ever did."

"But I needed you there. I needed you to *tell me* to get help."

Shit.

I wobbled on my feet. Four beers in an hour with nothing on my stomach except shame. I gripped the timber frame and steadied myself.

"Em, I'm..."

"Don't bother." Her words slapped like a hand to my cheek. "Doesn't matter now. I wouldn't even know if you're being sincere or not. You'd blame yourself for everyone else's sins again."

"I'm trying to do what's right." Even I didn't believe it. "I'm...trying to be a good man."

Emma's voice layered thick with disappointment and resignation. "That's the stupidest thing I've ever heard. You want to be alone, *fine*. You want to pretend this is the only way. *So be it*. I'm glad you're leaving. Glad you're gonna get away from my kids."

"Emma—"

"I'd hate to have them grow up and see their uncle for who he really is." She grunted. "Or worse—get hurt by him."

"I would never—"

"You already are. Don't you see? Being alone doesn't make you a good man." Her words fell to a whisper. "Go live in your lies. No one will miss a selfish bastard if he's living alone."

She ended the call.

I didn't blame her.

My hand ached. I checked the handkerchief. Bloody, but not dangerous. Needed to be wrapped though. I pushed off the timber to head back to the house.

Stopped.

A streak of blood stained my newest project.

And the sight sickened me.

The crib was meant to be something transitional for Tabby. When she got bigger, I'd take it apart and turn it into a "big-girl" bed that she'd love. Something beautiful and perfect and the only thing that I ever thought I could offer such a sweet little girl.

Not a hug. Not a cuddle. Not a song when her tummy ached or a quick *tidal wave* in the tub.

I wasn't the guy who'd ever be good enough to kiss a boo-boo, hold her hand at the bus stop, or chase away the first boys who'd start hanging around her or Mellie.

But I could do *this*.

I could make them something they needed. Something they could use. Something sturdy and strong that would last them forever.

It wasn't enough.

I ignored my bleeding hand and collapsed to the floor, my back to the crib.

A lie was a lie.

Alone was alone.

And nothing I did would ever change what had been done.

I'd punished myself for those past deeds, and I'd tried to protect everyone else by closing off.

It worked. Too well.

I didn't want to hurt anyone.

But I didn't want to be so goddamned alone.

20

Cassi

My suitcase still didn't close.

Duct tape would do the trick until I got another set of luggage.

Until I had a place to go. Somewhere I could run where it wouldn't hurt anymore.

Too bad I couldn't go back in time.

At least my brothers had learned to politely rap on the door before barging into my room. All it took was one late-night intrusion while my hands were busy under the blankets, and my humiliation awarded me privacy. Still wasn't able to look Tidus in the eyes though.

Tidus entered first. Reluctantly, he made way for Jules too.

I didn't have much to say to either of them. They talked anyway.

"Doctors called." Jules sat on my bed, grimaced, then stood and gestured to the bed as if asking permission. A step in the right direction. Now if he'd stop using my conditioner, we'd be set. "Marius is moving out of the ICU tomorrow. Transferring to a different wing in the hospital."

"I know." I set my suitcase near the door. "I talked to Marius this morning."

"Oh."

I arched an eyebrow. "And when was the last time you talked to Marius?"

Jules shrugged. Tidus cleared his throat.

"*Yeah*," I said. "Well, I'm glad you heard it from the *doctors* instead of your *brother*."

Jules rubbed his face. Exhaustion marred my eldest brother's features. The grey in his temples had started to spread. Not much, but more than had been there before he'd started calculating the cost of the equipment we needed to get the farm operational.

"Marius and I aren't..." Jules must have hoped that I'd finish his thought. Nope. I wasn't covering for their petty fights anymore. "It was easier when he was still unconscious."

"Yeah, forgiveness is a bitch," I said.

Tidus glanced at the suitcase. He read my mind, as usual. "What the hell are you doing?"

"What do you mean?"

"We're your brothers. We're supposed to be miserable. But I don't like seeing my sister upset."

I crossed my arms. "I'm not upset."

Jules frowned. "Liar."

"I'm fine."

Tidus agreed. "Liar."

"What do you want from me?" I gestured to my old room, my bed, my own corner of Butterpond where nothing ever changed, people never forgave each other, and the water tasted a little oily. "I'm *fine*."

"Where's Rem?" Jules asked.

Oh, he wanted to open *that* can of worms? "Since when do you care?"

"Since you started to care about him."

My turn. "*Liar*."

"Well," Tidus swore. "Guess we're all big sacks of shit lying to each other, aren't we?"

Jules nodded. "Guess so."

"Well, what happened?" Tidus awkwardly asked the questions neither of them wanted to be answered. "I thought...things were going well."

Was that before or after the entire town berated Rem? "It was going good until you accused him of taking advantage of me. You remember...when you insulted him in front of the family and the little girls he was raising?" The words ached. I gave up. "Doesn't matter. You were right. Happy now?"

"If you think I'm happy that you're upset—"

"Forget it." I batted Jules and his dusty feet away from my area rug and leaned against the window. "I knew he was bad news five years ago."

"And now?" Jules asked.

"He's even worse."

"Do you really believe that?"

"Don't you?"

Jules smirked. "Well, yeah. But I always thought he was one paycheck short of becoming a criminal and one cigarette too many to be a choir boy." He paused. "But *you* never believed that."

Tidus teased me, his voice pitched chipmunk high. "*He's changed, guys. He's different now.*" I pitched a water bottle at his head. He caught it with a grin. "What do you *really* think, Sassy?"

If I spoke it out loud I'd need a pint of Ben and Jerry's to get through the conversation and then another to wash down the bitterness.

"I think he's a good man and a complete idiot," I said.

Jules didn't argue. "There it is."

"I'm serious. He's hellbent on living this life of isolation, like he's ashamed of himself or what he's done. He doesn't think he's a good influence on the girls—he won't even go over to Emma's and visit them. He's constantly lying to hide what happened in the past…"

I stared outside, over the farm, admiring the landscaping and hedge work Jules had done. It looked nice. Neat. Like how Dad used to have it. When life was simpler, and I had all the time in the world to let myself get hurt.

"He's more of an idiot now than he was five years ago," I said. "Like he has a *reason* to act so selfishly."

Tidus tossed the water bottle to me. I took a quick swig. It didn't stop the inopportune hiccups.

"Look, Cas, there's a lot you don't know about Rem." Tidus cracked his knuckles. Nervous. Looked like he'd wanted a smoke, but Quint had stuffed his cigarettes down the garbage disposal in the heat of a fight. "He *is* a good guy—he really is. Deep down. I know Jules doesn't believe it, but I wouldn't be the man I am today without him."

I believed him.

I *wanted* to believe Tidus.

But what good did it do now?

"It doesn't matter." I puffed a lock of hair out of my face. "Who can even remember five years ago?"

Jules raised his hand. Tidus smacked his shoulder.

"He doesn't want to change," I said. "He doesn't want to make this work. He says he's running to protect us, but he won't say from what. So fine. I won't make him stay. I put my life on hold for him once. I can't do it again."

Jules nodded to the suitcase against the wall. "So you're leaving too?"

"What do you think I should do?"

"There's a farm here that could use some work."

"I've been working the farm, Jules. Maybe not cutting back the trees and tilling any dirt, but..." God, why did the tears have to come *now*? Everything was always so much easier if I didn't talk about it. Maybe Rem had it right. "I took care of Dad day in and day out. I made his meals. I helped him shower. I gave him his medicine. I was with him when he *died*. Maybe I didn't plant corn, but I held this farm together for as long as I could." My throat tightened. "And none of you were here to help."

Tidus looked away, but, for the first time, Jules didn't. He took my hand, tugged me close, and kissed my forehead.

"We're here now, Cas," he said.

And it made it better.

And worse.

And so much harder.

Jules still gave me the option. "What will you do?"

I sucked in a reluctant breath. "Why would I stay? Dad's gone. Every day is a struggle. No one is happy, and I'm trapped in the middle. Don't I deserve a chance to have a life too?"

Tidus was better with a fist-to-jaw than a heart-to-heart. "That's our fault, Sassy. We can make it better for you. Make the effort."

"You wouldn't just leave, would you?" Jules remained stoic, but I heard the worry. "You're the only one who knows where Dad kept anything. Without you, I wouldn't have found the five-grand taped under the mattress."

Tidus scowled. "*Whoa, whoa, whoa.* You found five grand? Where is it?"

"I put it in the tax fund."

"What *tax fund*?"

Jules lost his patience. "You like this house?"

"It's okay."

"You like the land?"

"I've seen better."

"Well, right now it's all you got, and if you don't want Sawyer County to own all of it, yeah. We need a tax fund."

Tidus without a cigarette in his mouth tended to talk more than he should. "We don't got a working hot water heater that can handle six people in a house, but *that's just fine*. We'll freeze our dicks off while you hoard money."

I groaned. "Tidus."

"Sorry. Freeze our *asses*. Gender-fucking-neutral."

"*This* is what I mean!" I meant to redo my pony tail. Nearly ripped my hair out instead. "This constant bickering. All the time. Can you blame me for wanting to leave? For needing to get away from this negativity? If this keeps up, every fruit and vegetable we grow will be just as bitter as all of you!"

"So that's it?" Jules crossed his arms. "You're gonna look us in the eye, bitch about Rem taking off, and then follow his example."

"Why not?"

Jules tightened his jaw. "One word. *Marius*."

Son of a bitch. I knew he'd throw that in my face. Just like Rem. Just like them all.

They assumed I'd just drop everything to take care of the family.

No fights. No protest. Not even a simple question asked in honest and good faith—*Hey, Cassi, do you think you could help Marius while he recovers*?

I'd done it before, so I must have wanted to do it again. I must have wanted to sacrifice and scrimp and save and put everything on hold for a family that refused to stay together.

They wouldn't talk unless I locked them in a room. They wouldn't work together unless they meant to destroy my relationship with the only man I'd ever loved. They wouldn't even pray together over their injured brother, suffering in the hospital with a devastating prognosis.

Something had to change.

And it started *now*.

I grabbed my suitcase and tossed it at Jules.

He ducked, but the luggage bounced off his side and rattled to the ground. The tape didn't hold. It popped open.

Empty.

"I'm not going anywhere, you jackasses." I met both of their stunned gazes. "But I'm *not* taking care of Marius."

The silence crackled. I let it pass with a single, steady breath.

"*We* are going to take care of Marius," I said. "*Together*. Not just me, but *everyone*. We're a goddamned family. We might hate each other, but for Christ's sake, we're not going to abandon one and other."

Tidus didn't hesitate. He swept me into a hug and swore.

"Thank Christ," he said. "Now I don't have to stalk you through Ironfield."

Jules wasn't good with anything emotional, but he gave me a smile. "You're right. We should all pitch in. Take care of Marius...and take care of you."

"I'm fine," I lied.

"I know what you want to do."

"Create a schedule for the showers?" I smirked. "Claim my own shelf in the pantry?"

Jules frowned. "You want to stop Rem."

The room suddenly felt a little too tight. I hardly had room to pace, let alone bare my soul.

"I can't stop Rem," I said. "It's his decision."

"Even if it's the wrong one?"

"I don't want to hurt him anymore than he's already hurting. He's ashamed of himself, and he thinks he's a bad influence on me. I can't watch him destroy his life. The life we might have had together."

"Do you love him?" Tidus asked.

"Always and forever." A lump formed in my throat. "But telling him won't work. He has to figure it out for himself. He needs to heal. Forgive the past. I can't do that for him."

Hard to be alone in a house filled with five brothers.

Hard to be sad when each of them did their best to cheer me up.

Hard to let go of everything I'd ever wanted, the love I'd dreamed about, and the future I'd deserved.

Absence might have made the heart grow fonder.

But abandonment just made it break.

21

Rem

THE PHONE RANG.

And rang.

And rang.

My head raged against the damn kiddie jingle—Cassi's idea of a joke, replacing my rington with some sort of Telli-Tubby-Elsa-Disney-Wheels-On-The-Wiggles shit. Hell if I knew the name of the song. It was loud. It was pissing me off. And it was half past *fuck you* in the morning.

I fumbled for the phone and grumbled a profane greeting.

No one answered.

But a kid was crying in the background.

No.

Two kids.

I bolted up in the bed, squeezing the phone.

"*Emma?*" The groggy cleared from my voice. No longer drunk, but an hour short of a massive fucking hangover. "You there?"

Nothing. More crying.

My gut turned, and it wasn't the alcohol. I pushed myself from the bed and headed to the bathroom. A cold splash of water did nothing to fix my face—tired, worn, and hating the one staring back.

"Em?" I raised my voice. "Are you there?"

Her mumbling was breathy and slurred. "Rem…"

Shit. What the hell had happened?

"What's wrong?"

She groaned something, smacked her lips, and went silent, a labored breath echoing from her side of the call.

"Son of a bitch."

I wanted to tell myself she was sick.

A flu. Strep throat. Fever.

But I wasn't stupid. I recognized the sounds because I'd been there before. Four years ago. In the same damn spot, in the same damn way, trapped in that same fucking spiral.

Emma had relapsed.

And the kids were crying.

"I'm coming!" I shouted into the phone.

I doubted she could hear me. Doubted even more that she'd care. But I did. It soothed me. Calmed my racing heart despite that utter fucking *terror* that iced my veins.

I tripped over my bags in the bedroom. Christ. I'd almost left today.

Decided to stick around because I had a couple last beers in the fridge and because...

Didn't matter why.

Didn't matter that I thought about Cassi. That I regretted every minute she wasn't warming my bed. Didn't matter that I knew I'd broken her heart. Again.

I couldn't let myself wonder *what if*.

What if I apologized? What if she took me back?

What if we had a chance?

At least that indecision had kept me in Butterpond. Had I been traveling...had I left the state...

Emma was out. The kids were alone.

No more *what ifs*.

I pulled on a pair of jeans and tossed a flannel shirt over my shoulders. Loathe as I was to do it, I dialed the Sherriff while tugging on my shoes.

The emergency line had forwarded to Samson's personal cell. It took him a good minute to answer.

His greeting was just as uncouth. In another life, a less fun life, we might have gotten along.

"It's Remington Marshall," I said.

"Aw shit."

"Evening to you too." I gritted my teeth as I bolted for the truck. "Look, I got a problem."

"It's the middle of the damn night, Marshall."

"It's Emma." I bit the words. "She's in trouble."

"As usual."

"Don't fuck with me." The truck roared to life. It wasn't safe to speed down the pitch-black mountain. I floored it anyway. "I'm heading there now. Might need an ambulance."

"That bad?"

"I know you think we're trash, that we're no good, that we're some sort of scourge on the town because our daddy drank at home instead of at Renegades with the good ol' boys...but she's in trouble."

"Got no problem helping someone who needs help, Marshall." Samson huffed. "Only got a problem with a smart, capable boy who ran away because he thought it'd make him a man."

"Don't let Emma suffer for it."

"Neither of us would let that happen. I'll call for an ambulance."

I didn't thank him. He didn't expect it. I ended the call and sped down the mountain, headlights blasting over the bumpy and potholed roads.

I was twenty minutes from town.

Twenty minutes of a thumping heart.

Twenty minutes of cold sweat.

Twenty minutes of imagining the words I'd need to explain to a three-year-old why her mommy wasn't waking up.

And if she died...

I slammed a hand on the steering wheel.

No. I wouldn't let the worst-case scenario rot in my brain.

The kids cried as I pulled in the driveway. Heard them from *outside* the house, but it was a shitty rental. The one level ranch kept them warm, but it needed a coat of paint, better windows, a new roof, and someone on the inside who could stay sober for two damn weeks at a time.

I expected worse. The living room was in toddler-order—blankets and pillows randomly tossed on the floor. A box with crayon doodles in the corner. A rainbow assortment of blocks scattered over the carpet, just waiting for an unsuspecting foot. The furniture was second-hand, and the carpets stained, but the only problem was the reeking stench of too many cigarettes. Emma only gave up one vice at a time, apparently. Not great around the little kids.

"Emma?" I called through the house. "Where are you?"

The girls wailed from the back of the house. I hurried down the hall, crashing through the door to my sister's bedroom.

My sister had collapsed on the bed, wearing only a bra, jeans, and one shoe. The needle was on the nightstand. Who needed dignity when they had drugs?

Mellie sobbed on the floor beside her mother. I scooped her up, earning a higher pitched shriek until I shushed her.

"It's okay. It's Uncle Rem. I got ya."

Mellie, red-faced and panting, pointed at Emma. "*Mommy!*"

My heart broke. I pushed Mellie's head onto my shoulder, away from the sight. "I know. It's okay."

I leaned down and gave Emma a push. Getting ashen, but she was still alive.

Was that better or worse?

I pulled Mellie from the room and set her on the floor in the hallway. Poor thing wasn't even wearing pants. Just an oversized t-shirt, panties, and one sock. She was shivering. Crying. Snotty. Hiccupping.

What the hell had she been through?

"Mommy's gonna be okay. She's sleeping." I smoothed her hair. "Let's check on Tabby."

My chest ached. Tabby wailed from her crib. Filthy. She'd soiled her diaper sometime during the afternoon or night, but Emma hadn't been sober enough to change her.

I picked her up anyway, trying my hardest to soothe the tiny girl, flushed pink, uncomfortable, and scared. Tabby's chubby little arms wrapped around my neck, and she buried her face against me.

Mellie dove at me too, her hug tight around my legs.

What the hell had I done?

I let them go.

Hadn't considered Emma's health or stability. Hadn't checked in on her.

I wasn't even going to say good-bye.

I thought nothing could hurt more than packing their little clothes and toys and sending them back to their real home.

Except *this*.

This tortured me.

How could I have let this happen to them? The two innocent girls already bore the last name of Marshall. One strike in the book before even hitting preschool.

They deserved so much better than a dirty home, an unstable parent, and an uncle too terrified of his mistakes to see what he could give them.

A good life.

A healthy life.

A *loving* life...

Together.

I knelt, welcoming Mellie into my arms. My ass hit the floor, but it didn't matter. The girls snuggled hard into me, and I squeezed them back.

"I'm sorry…" My words choked with tears I wouldn't let fall. Not now. "I'm here, guys. I won't leave you. I'm gonna be right here for you. I promise. I'm not going anywhere."

I owed it to them.

I owed it to myself.

I owed it to the past I'd escaped.

And I owed it to the future I'd make. A future with the girls.

"*Cassi*?" Mellie sniffled into my chest. "I want *Cassi*."

I pulled her close, kissing her head. Outside, red and blue lights flashed. Sherriff Samson.

The night was only going to get worse for them.

"I know, sweetheart." I held them tighter. "I miss her too."

But not for long.

I'd made enough mistakes. Lived enough lies. Ruined enough hearts.

It was finally time for me to fix it. All of it.

It started with the kids.

And it ended with Cassi.

No…

With Cassi, we'd finally *begin*.

22

Cassi

A POUNDING SHOOK THE HOUSE AND WOKE ME AT SIX IN THE MORNING.

That wasn't unusual. A lot of strange noises came out of the Payne farmhouse.

Quint's concerts in the shower. Julian's menagerie of chain saws and lawn mowers he'd constantly fix on the porch just below my window. Tidus's never-ending feud with the hundred year old floorboards.

And Varius...

I wished I heard him more. It was Jules who kept checking on him, making sure he was just quiet and not measuring out the rope.

This pounding wasn't the usual foot through the drywall. It was a knock. And if the unfortunate bastard rapping at the door wanted to live, he should've prayed that I'd reach the porch before Tidus and his accompanying hangover.

I stumbled down the stairs, patting at my chest to make sure I at least had a sports bra on under the tank top. The hair was another story. The pink scarf did its best, but the curls were quietly consuming everyone and everything in their path. If I got lucky, they'd devour the jackass pounding at the door so early in the morning.

A yawn conquered me. My head butted against the frame as I pulled the chain away and swung the door wide.

"Hi!" Mellie sauntered into my living room as if appearing out of thin air. Her hair was a mess, she yawned as hard as me, and she rocked a pink pajama shirt with orange leggings. "This is for you."

She handed me a sticker that read *Ironfield Regional Hospital.*

My stomach sunk.

"Mellie...what..."

Rem poked through in the doorway. He motioned with a finger over his lips and nodded to the sleeping Tabby on his shoulder.

Exhaustion hardened his features. Dark circles shadowed under his eyes. His lips had thinned in an undercurrent of rage. He stood barechested and silent. The baby slept in his arms, wrapped in his flannel shirt, strategically knotted to create the world's most redneck onesie. Both girls seemed to be okay, but my stomach dropped.

His expression revealed everything.

"Oh no. What happened?"

Rem didn't hesitate. His chestnut eyes narrowed on me, honest and completely sincere.

"I love you, Cassi Payne."

I gripped the door. "*What?*"

"I love you, Sassy. I shouldn't have let you go."

I blinked. Sucked in a breath. Frowned. "...*What?*"

"I love you."

Words I'd been dying to hear, but not like this. Not at the crack of dawn while I worried about the two exhausted little girls and the secrets they shared with Rem.

"What happened?" I asked. "Rem, the girls..."

He didn't hesitate, even as the shame destroyed him from the inside out. "Got a call from Em in the middle of the night."

"Is she okay?"

"She was once I got her to the hospital."

A worst fear then. He confirmed it.

"Overdose," he said. "She's okay. But the girls were alone. Emma called me before she passed out, and I got there before any harm was done. Mostly. The kids were scared. I didn't grab a change of clothes for them before I left for the hospital. I waited for Emma to stabilize, and then..." He shrugged. It nudged Tabby but didn't wake her. "I came here."

"I'm so sorry, Rem."

"I shouldn't have left them." His honesty shocked me. "And I never should have left you."

What was he trying to do to me? "Rem, I can't do this right now..."

He closed the door behind him. His watchful eye ensured Mellie had only crept into the living room to collapse on the couch.

"Cassi...two weeks ago, I wanted the girls to go back with Emma. I thought she'd recovered. And I thought...I could handle it. But it *hurt* to lose them. It *hurt* to stay in the cabin all alone, wondering why Emma could get her life together and move on while I was stuck in the past. I missed then. And I missed you."

I hadn't had time to cobble those defenses back up before honesty eroded them away. "I missed you too."

"I thought I'd be a bad influence on the girls. A detriment to their life."

"Only if you keep running."

He took my hand. "I get that now. You showed me that. You saw the man I could become."

My heart raged. I should have pushed him out. Should have stopped him from speaking the sweet words. Should have closed myself to him.

But would that have made me any less of a liar than Rem?

"You always were that man." My words weren't gentle. Only wish I could have punctuated them with a smack across his shoulder. "You didn't need me to prove it."

"But I did. I needed you, Cas. I needed the kids. I had to see what this could be."

"And what's that?"

"A *family*."

My knees couldn't take much more of this. I backed away, groping a hand against the wall behind me. But the wall didn't hold me steady.

Rem did.

"I've wanted a family above all else. I want to be a family to the girls... an uncle, a father, whatever they need." He smiled at me. How didn't I melt right through the wall? "And I want to be the man for you. I want in your life. I want to be at your side. No more hiding. No more running. I love you, Cassi Payne. I've always loved you. And now I need you in my life."

"*Rem...*"

I stood, stunned and bewildered and choked by every terrible word I should have shouted and every lovely and desperate secret I'd whispered across the pillows.

The words stuck in my throat. I had nothing to say that would be as sweet as his declarations...except maybe the offer of syrup.

"Do you..." My head spun. "Do you want some pancakes?"

Rem exhaled, a deep, shattering breath. What remained was a gentle smirk. "Yeah. Sounds good."

Did it?

Or did it sound like yet another heart-breaking mistake?

I led the biggest complication in my life into the living room, surrounded Tabby with pillows on the couch next to her sister, and had no better answers by the time I'd reached the stove.

Despite the words and revelations and sweet declarations swarming in my head, I remembered the pancake recipe after staring at the fridge for a solid minute to identify the eggs.

What the hell was I supposed to do?

My heart demanded that I rush into his arms, steal his kisses, and offer myself right there on the kitchen floor. I couldn't focus on the labels. I'd dumped what I believed to be flour into a liquid which seemed to be milk as Jules limped into the kitchen, covered in grease, grass stains, and thorns.

He bled *purple* as he groped for the fridge. The crimson streak he left behind wasn't as appetizing as the leftover pizza he'd stolen from Tidus's box. The slice never made it to his mouth. Jules stared at Rem.

Rem handed him a dishrag, but nothing could rub away the violet stain covering his arms, neck, face. "What the hell happened to you?"

My brother glanced to me and knew better than to say anything. "Fucking blackberries."

"What?" I asked.

"There's a blackberry patch infesting where the second field used to be. I tried to clear it out. The berries won."

One crisis at a time. I stared into the bowl of gloopy mix, trying to remember what the hell I was making. "Want some...breakfast?"

"No." Jules stole a banana from Varius's pantry shelf and tempted his own damnation with a bite. He should have left in silence. The concept was foreign to him. "What the fuck is he doing here?"

"Shh." I smacked his arm and pointed to the living room. "The kids are sleeping."

"What the hell are *they* doing here?" Jules checked his watch. "How long was I stuck in that goddamned bush?"

Rem headed for the coffee pot, the one object in the house unchanged in the last five years. Dad had always kept the coffee, coffee pot, non-dairy creamer, and a coffee-stained paper plate to hold a stirring spoon in the same corner of the kitchen. Rem shoveled the grounds into the pot, thought better of it, and added another scoop.

We should have added whiskey to it.

"Emma overdosed last night," Rem said.

Jules exhaled. "She okay?"

"Will be."

"And you're here because..."

"I came to apologize to Cassi."

Jules approved of this. "Good. Cause you've been a monumental dick. Got any more apologies lined up?"

"Probably more than I could give."

"Why not start?"

I sighed. "Jules, he had a rough night."

"And you had a rough five years, Cassi." Jules pointed at me. "And a rougher two weeks when he broke your heart *again*."

Rem had never backed down from a challenge. "I'm gonna win her back."

"Great. So you can complicate her life even more."

"No. So I can make it *better*." Rem's dark eyes followed me. "I loved her then, and I love her now. I'm not going anywhere. If she wants me...I'll be here. Waiting. For as long as she needs."

Goddamn it. I dropped the whisk in the batter.

Should I have yelled?

Kicked him out of the house?

Rushed into his arms?

A quiet resentment poisoned my words. "How dare you, Remington Marshall. First you chase me. Then I fall in love with you. Then you push me away, tell me lies, and spout some garbage about not being a good enough man for me and the kids." I couldn't look at him without hurting, so I scolded the floor at his feet. "You *ran*, Rem. Again. How can I be sure that this was the last time?"

"Because I'm not leaving Butterpond," he said. "I'm taking the kids. I'm staying to look after Emma. And if you have me, I'm gonna love you."

"How can you stand there and say that you love me?" My eyes prickled with tears, but I would *not* cry. "You still refuse to tell me the full truth."

"That's because I can't."

"Why not?"

"Because it isn't *my* truth to tell."

"What the hell does that mean?" I gave up, my patience cracking under the weight of all his supposed *honesty*. "This is your *last* chance, Rem. I need to know what you're hiding from me. Why you ran five years ago."

"Cas…"

"What the hell happened that night? Why did you hurt this family? Why didn't you stay to help us after the fire?" I sucked in a worthless breath. "Either you tell me the truth…or I will walk away now. I won't be lied to anymore, Rem."

"I don't want to lie." Maybe the first honest thing he'd ever said. "But can't we let this go? It's been so long. It doesn't matter now."

"It matters to me. And it should matter to you."

"*Why?*"

"So we can both *forgive* it."

Hard steps squeaked the kitchen floor. Tidus emerged from the stairs, hair tussled and no shirt. At least he'd remembered pants this morning.

But my brother didn't crack a smile or his knuckles. He refused to meet our gazes.

Something weighed on him. He nearly dropped to his knees.

"There's nothing to forgive." Tidus spoke through clenched teeth. "Don't blame Rem for what happened."

Rem's warning was quick. "No."

"What are you talking about?" Jules asked.

"The barn fire wasn't his fault."

Rem stepped forward. "Tidus, shut your mouth."

My brother ignored him, his eyes focusing only on me.

"Rem didn't start the fire," Tidus said. "I did."

23

Cassi

The farm hadn't changed much since we were kids—all that was missing was the barn.

We didn't have any animals, and we hadn't grown any crops, but with Rem at my side...it felt like we'd traveled back five years.

I wasn't sure if that was good or not.

Jules had agreed to watch the kids—or, at the very least, ensure a bleary-eyed Quint didn't accidentally sit on them when he stumbled out of the kitchen with his Coco Pebbles. Rem had taken my hand and led me outside.

To talk, he'd said.

I still couldn't speak a single word.

Rem guided me behind the chicken coop. I peeked in on Helena, the eggless wonder. She pecked at the earth, content, plump, and standing by her life-choices one gobble of seed at a time.

He stopped in the center of the field and squeezed my hand. "Remember this spot?"

All of a sudden, I remembered a lot of things. Some good. Most bad. "Should I?"

"This was where I threatened to run you over with the lawn tractor." Rem smirked. "You stood your ground."

"And you ran over my shoe."

"Your foot wasn't in it."

"You still mulched my favorite boot."

"Yeah." He snickered, tugging my hand to keep walking. "We kept finding flecks of pink rubber all over the damn farm during our chores."

And Rem had always been diligent with the chores. He'd work with Tidus in the mornings. Help water the animals with Jules. Muck the stables with whoever got stuck on animal duty that afternoon. Mowed the grass with Dad. Harvested the crops with Quint and Varius.

Even helped me water the little sunflower garden Mom and I had planted.

Until that day with the barn, Rem had been another member of the family, putting in the blood, sweat, and tears required to make the farm successful.

And he never did it because Dad threw money his way. And it wasn't because his friends were stuck doing chores before they could go get in trouble.

Rem had worked the farm because he'd wanted to help.

He'd wanted to be a part of the family.

I still couldn't breathe. Rem was careful, walking slow with me, unable to answer the questions I couldn't voice yet.

"Right here?" He planted his feet and leaned against a fence in desperate need of repair and paint. He pointed into the pasture. "Right here was where I watched you ride that black mare."

"Olivia."

"I watched you one day, just riding. You didn't see me. Don't think you saw anything but wind and grass. You and Olivia just flew across the field, and I thought…I've never seen anyone so beautiful in my life."

"Me or the horse?"

"I think you know."

"At this point?" Confusion and desperation rocked my soul. "I don't know anything anymore."

"I fell in love with you that day." Rem frowned as the fence nearly collapsed under the weight of his arms. Old wood that'd gone too long without repair. "I was standing here thinking…someday, I'm gonna marry her."

My heart lurched, but Rem didn't say anything more. He walked away, his pace slow until I reached his side once more.

What was he doing to me?

Did he want to drive me to my knees? Start a panic attack?

Was he trying to make me dive into his arms and never let go?

Cause I was close. And it scared me.

He walked me over the fields, pausing at every place of significance for him. Where we'd shared our first kiss behind the shed. Our fight near the cow trough where he'd landed face first in the water. The secret tree where we'd meet under the cover of darkness while everyone slept. Even Tidus didn't know about that.

In a matter of minutes, we'd walked through our life. Places where we fell in love. Hideaways where we'd fought. Shadows where we'd teased each other, tormented each other, and tried to hide all of our feelings.

He stopped at the edge of the field where the grass shaded a lighter color. Rusted equipment and junk now littered the corner of the farm where the barn once stood.

"And this is where everything fell apart." Rem's voice lowered. "I never meant for it to happen this way, Cas."

"I don't understand. *What* happened? Why would Tidus set fire to the barn? Why would you take the blame?"

"Because I had to."

"That doesn't make sense."

Rem stared over the farm. "Your family was my family, Cassi. My dad lived only to drink, and the bottle gave out same year as his liver. My mom followed him to the grave. I was on my own, but your parents welcomed me to the farm. Every day. They fed me. They let me stay the night when my folks were fighting. Gave me my first job. Without them...I might have ended up a lot worse. They kept me from going too far. From losing myself."

"But the fire..."

"I didn't want anything to hurt your family. I'd already led Tidus down the wrong path. You think he'd have those tattoos if it wasn't for me? The smoking? The drinking? The drugs?"

"He's cleaned up now," I said.

"Because I left. Because I wasn't there every day, encouraging him." He didn't hide the truth anymore, even if it broke our hearts. "I was the one who got us in trouble. We pissed around. We got arrested. Hell, we almost got expelled from high school. Tidus was a good kid, and it was my fault he had that...*streak* in him. I was mad at the world, but he had everything. And because of me, he never saw how *good* it was."

"That doesn't explain *why*."

"There was a lot you didn't see back then, Sassy. A lot we hid from you, to protect you. You think the fighting is new? It started long before the fire. Tidus never got along with your father."

It didn't surprise me. "No one got along well with Dad. He worked them too hard."

"Because he thought he was saving us. When he looked at Tidus, he saw my influence. Your dad pushed too hard. Punished him for every ounce of trouble we got into. Then he started doubting Tidus. Accused him of lying. The older we got, the less your dad trusted him, and Tidus resented that."

My chest ached for the brother I'd thought I knew the best. "He never said anything."

"No one was listening." Rem shrugged. "Except me. And it shouldn't have been me."

"What happened?"

"One day, your mom's migraine meds went missing. The benzos. Your dad blamed Tidus. Roughed him up when he denied it. Never once believed Tidus when he said it wasn't him."

I couldn't blame Dad. Back then, I'd have assumed any missing drugs to be in Tidus's pocket too. "Who took them?"

"No one. They were just missing. But Tidus was embarrassed to be called out like that. He got mad. Real mad. He didn't snap because of the pills, but because of everything. Years of your dad railing on him. Beating his ass. Refusing to listen. So Tidus got pissed, lost his temper, and…"

Same story, time and again. "He lost control."

"I caught him in the barn, lit cigarette in his hand. He didn't even say a word. Just flicked the cig into the hay. Then he lit another one."

Rem rubbed his beard and combed a frustrated hand through his hair. I squeezed his shoulder, but I don't think it helped the memory.

"I leapt on him before he could toss the second one," he said. "We fought until we were bloody. He broke my nose. I bashed his head against the barn door. It took a concussion before he realized what he'd done. Then…he panicked. The fire was already out of control. We got most of the cows out, but after that…it had to burn."

I hugged myself. "It was chaos. Middle of the night. Everyone was panicked. Terrified."

"It sobered me up, right then and there. I saw everything. It was my fault Tidus had ended up the way he was. He'd taken on his vices because of me. And I never tried to help him, only wanted to get in more trouble."

"So you took the blame?"

"If your father had known Tidus set the fire, he'd have kicked him off the farm and out of the family. It would have destroyed you guys. Torn you apart. I couldn't let it happen. The Paynes were the only real family I ever knew, the only ones I'd ever loved. And you did so much for me, all the while I pissed away my chances and made it harder for everyone, including Tidus."

I wished I could have held him, but my feet didn't move. "You were a kid, Rem."

"And I became a man that day. I took responsibility. I said it was me. I told Tidus to shut his mouth, turn his damn life around, and to help his old man instead of fighting all the damn time. I told him I wanted to keep your family together—to spare them the pain that would have come from the truth." His words hollowed. "And I left that night."

"Without saying goodbye," I whispered. "Without telling me the truth."

"I had to, Cas. I wasn't anywhere near good enough for you then. I couldn't take care of you. Couldn't support you. Couldn't even keep myself clean. You deserved someone better." He brushed my cheek with his hand. "So I'm going to be better for you."

The tears threatened to roll over my cheeks. "Do you know how long I spent loving you and hating you and missing you and trying to get over you?"

"Same amount of time I loved you, hated myself, missed you, and regretted leaving."

"I would have understood."

"Maybe. I did so much to protect your family that I forgot to start one of my own. And I want to change that now. I want you, Cas. Me. You. The girls, for as long as they need. I wasn't born into a family, but your parents gifted one to me. Now it's my turn. I want to create that family with you."

I bit my lip, but the words tumbled out anyway. "You always had one here, Rem. I never stopped loving you."

His smile washed away my fear and anger and hesitance. "I can help with the farm. Work it with Jules and your brothers. Restore it to how your Dad imagined it. We can do it together, Sassy. Rebuild over the bad memories and make new ones. Better ones."

I slipped into his arms. "What sort of memories?"

"The best kind."

"Me and you?"

"If you'll have me," he said.

"If you think I'm letting you get away from me this time..."

"Got some rope in the truck if you want to tie me down."

I grinned, sneaking closer for a kiss. "I can do one better."

"That so?"

"Oh, Remington Marshall…" I nibbled on his bottom lip. "I'm going to make it so good for you that I'll be surprised if you could even walk, let alone escape me."

"I'm not going anywhere, Sassy." He winked. "Except down."

"That a promise?"

"It's a vow, if you'll say yes."

"Might need some convincing."

Rem swept me into his arms and headed for the shed. I squealed, but he silenced me with a kiss. "I'll prove how much I love you if I have to fuck you all day and night."

"Think that'll be enough?"

He kissed me again.

"It's a start."

EPILOGUE

Rem

THE SUNLIGHT HINTED THROUGH CASSI'S BEDROOM WINDOW, KISSING her warm, dark skin.

Not a bad sight in the morning, made even better by her ridiculously small twin bed. I didn't mind. Just kept her closer to me. Wrapped in my arms. Safe under me while I moved within her all night.

I kissed that lovely shoulder. Tickled my fingers down her graceful arm. Woke her as I shifted her against my chest.

She'd hardly batted her eyes open, but she offered her body.

I slipped inside that tightness with a guttural groan. Her whispered gasp was the only sound I'd ever wanted to hear in the morning.

Tight. Our bodies fit together in delirious perfection. Nothing rushed. Nothing heated. Nothing desperate.

She was mine. I was hers.

And I claimed her body with every stroke just as she claimed mine with the little bump of her hips.

She shook first, tensing over my length with fingertips curled into the pillows. I followed, spilling every drop of seed as deep into her as I could get.

And we rested together. Soundless. Warm. Peaceful.

Like it could have been for so long.

Like it would be from here on out.

Her door clattered open and slammed against the wall. Cassi jumped, covering herself with the blanket. Fortunately, Mellie was too excited to hear.

"Pancakes!" She screeched, her fists drawn to her chin like breakfast was a wicked machination. "Want pancakes!"

And now so did the rest of the house.

Mellie scurried down the hall and hollered for breakfast. Cassi giggled, pushed from the bed, and quickly wound a robe around her lovely body.

"And here I thought the only early riser was you." Her eyebrow arched at the tent accidentally pitched in the bed. "Better put that way. You have a big day ahead of you, Mr. Marshall."

I needed a shower and a cup of coffee before I could comprehend it. "Just amazed Jules went for the idea."

"He's wanted that barn rebuilt for months," Cassi winked. "Who better to help him construct it than the man who…" She shrugged. "Well, the man who watched it burn."

"Cross your fingers." I slipped from the bed and pulled on jeans before any wayward children or protective brothers happened to barge into the room. "I heard this zoning officer is a hardass. Citing some new regulations or some bullshit. Barn might be too close to the property line to rebuild or something."

Cassi pouted. "It was there before. Stood there for a hundred years."

"I'm only repeating what Emma said. Her new boyfriend's worked some construction jobs in the area. Said the whole zoning department is fuc—*heyyyy*. You're back!"

Mellie waited at the door, impatiently pleading with opened arms for her pancakes.

"*Please!*" She begged while hopping on one foot. "I'm *hungry!*"

"Better get you food before you waste away." I snatched her up and hauled her over my shoulder, winking at Cassi. "Meet you downstairs?"

Cassi smirked. "You're getting to be a natural at that now."

I gave Mellie's tush a smack as she giggled. "Not yet. Soon though."

The kid giggled, squirmed, and kicked me in the gut.

No better way to start the morning.

No better way to wake up. No better woman. No better kids.

No better family.

~

THE PANCAKES CAME, WENT, AND HALF OF THEM ENDED ON THE FLOOR. Wasn't even Mellie this time. Quint's ADD rattled him off the ways without the addition of maple syrup. A little scrubbing and a nap later—both for Quint and the girls—and all I had to deal with was Jules stalking the porch.

"Where the hell is this zoning officer?" Jules checked his watch, eyed the storm clouds, and jerked a thumb towards the fields. "The farm is already a solid layer of mud from the rain last night. If he doesn't get here soon, we'll all sink out there."

I bounced Tabby on my lap as she attempted to bolt and toddle away. I should have let her go. The surprise in her diaper wasn't the first impression Jules and me needed to give this county zoning guy.

I didn't bother heading inside. Tabby and me were pros now. I laid a blanket over the porch and grabbed the kid, diaper bag always at the ready.

Jules paced again, avoiding the mess. He checked his phone. "I'm gonna call that office."

"It's local government," I said. "They move at a different pace."

"They said eleven. It's twelve. Why didn't this asshole call?"

"Because...local government."

"Isn't that what we pay taxes for?" He dialed the phone. Wouldn't get him anywhere, but it cooled him down. "Christ, I'm paying this bastard's salary. He can't even show up on time?"

I tucked the dirty diaper in a spare bag and slid and fresh one under Tabby's butt. Should have kept the wipes out.

A slinking, huffing figure stormed up the driveway—half-mud, half-homicidal rage.

For some random asshole at the zoning office, the dude rocked a skirt. His legs went to his chin, his dress hugged the right curves, and even the mud complimented that cinnamon skin.

This couldn't have been the zoning officer. I didn't know the lady. But she was *pissed*.

"Jules," I said.

He ignored my warning.

"You know, this is what's wrong with the world," he said. "I'm trying my goddamned hardest to get this farm up and running. How am I supposed to work if the taxes are killing me, the regulation is binding my hands, and now this zoning bullshit tells me where I can and can't build on my own damn property?"

I eyed the woman stomping her foot behind him. "*Jules...*"

"This is *our* land. It was my father's land. His father's land. And *his* father's land." Jules slammed a hand against the siding of the house. "They built this home with their bare hands. Then they worked the land every day of the year. Sunup to sundown. And there wasn't any *municipality* telling them what they could and couldn't do on their own land."

I gestured to the woman caked in mud as she grew more pissed by the second. "Julian."

"Now I have some hotshot wannabe politician telling me what to do? Probably some fatass who never even set *foot* on a farm. Never worked a day in his life, sitting behind some desk in a cushy office, getting off on every rejected building application. Know it took me two weeks to even *get* an appointment with this asshole? He's too goddamned incompetent show up on time."

"Julian!" I grabbed Tabby off the blanket and stood. "I think *he* is here."

Jules turned, took one look at the woman coated in mud, and burst out laughing.

Pretty sure this was how the Paynes would inevitably lose their farm.

"What the hell...who are you?" Julian stared at the woman. "What happened to you?"

"Someone...." The woman seethed, practically melting the mud from her body. It stained her business suit, her purse, and her bare feet. What the hell had happened to her shoes? "There's a...it was *locked...*"

Jules grabbed Tabby's blanket and offered it to her. She refused, fists balled at her side, the rage choking her.

Livid.

Yep.

She was about to go nuclear.

"The gate was *locked*." She pointed down the path. "I had to get out...open it...mud everywhere..." She peeked at her wiggling toes, coated in mud and bits of grass. "My shoes...*sucked in. And you*." She hissed at Jules. "Are you Julian Payne?"

"Yeah. Who the hell are you?"

"Your *appointment*." She gritted her teeth. "And I would have been here sooner if *someone* hadn't locked the gate. I fell into the mud then had to claw my way here."

Jules shook his head. "Look, swamp thing. I'm sorry you got a little dirty, but I got an appointment with Micah Robinson, not..."

And here I thought I made bad choices. Jules made worse decisions. A lot worse.

"...Not his *secretary*."

The woman started to laugh, though I got the feeling she didn't find his statement that funny.

"You know, honey," she said. "I was doing you a favor."

"Were you?"

"Coming out in person. Seeing the farm. Meeting this Julian Payne everyone keeps talking about." Her rage seemed to manifest in a torturous retribution. "But I can tell you right now what the decision will be regarding your barn."

"Oh yeah?"

"Yeah...it's gonna get denied. Hard." She wiped the mud from her face and stormed away. "Don't bother helping me with the gate. I think I got it."

"Don't let it knock you on your ass on the way out, sweetheart."

Tabby gave an excited wave. "Buh-bye!"

"That's right, kid." Jules snorted. "Bye-bye."

He yanked out his phone and put the call on speaker as he dialed the zoning office.

"What the hell are you doing?" I asked. "Ratting her out?"

"Who the hell is this *Micah Robinson*?" Jules nearly crushed his cell in his fist. "I had to send him half a dozen emails to even schedule this meeting. Least he can do is tell me he's cancelling the appointment."

"He didn't cancel." I pointed to the woman marching away. "He sent her."

"He sent his *secretary*." Jules waited while the phone rang a dozen times. "Damn it. He won't even answer!"

The voice mail message began. A pre-recorded, gentle voice graciously offered an excuse for the absence.

A *woman's* voice.

"This is Micah Robinson, Sawyer County Zoning Department." Her words dripped sweetness instead of mud. "I'm out of the office for the day, but please leave your name and number, and I'll return your call shortly. Or, you can email me, at..."

Jules ended the call and sucked in a breath.

I owed him a moment of silence for the farm he'd just killed.

"So..." I said. "That was...Micah."

Jules exhaled and nearly deflated. "*Yeah*."

I nodded. "Micah's a *woman*."

"*Yeah*."

"Micah is..." I pointed with Tabby's hand. She giggled. Jules did not. "That woman, stomping away."

"Of course, she is."

"*So...*"

Jules collapsed onto the porch's top step as the rain fell in a sudden torrent. He watched his only chance at a barn angrily storm off his property, her soaking wet dress clinging to her curves.

"This..." Jules spoke mostly to himself. "This is going to get really complicated."

I hauled Tabby into my arms and brought her inside while the rain gusted onto the porch in sheets.

Jules stayed in the rain. Probably for the best.

Cassi waited for me in the kitchen as she mixed a jug of lemonade with Mellie. She peeked out the window, watching the woman in the distance.

"What happened?" she asked. "Was that the zoning officer?"

I lowered Tabby to the ground. She toddled to Cassi, grabbed her leg, and plunked down on her foot.

"After some debate...we have concluded that that woman was, in fact, the zoning officer."

"What'd she say?"

"Before or after Jules inadvertently locked her off the property, got her stuck in a mud puddle, then insulted her?"

It didn't surprise her. "Do we get the barn?"

"Not looking good."

I couldn't stand to see her upset. The pitcher of lemonade clunked on the table. I pulled her as close as I could get with both ankle-biters hugging alternate legs.

"Hey…" I tucked a curl behind her ear. "Don't worry about the barn."

"We need it," she said. "The farm's gotta get up and running. Jules is working so hard. If we get it built, maybe the others will see. Maybe they'll come around. Stop fighting. Start…acting like a family again."

"They don't need a barn for that." I traced a finger over her chest, to her heart. "That's why they got you. As long as you're taking care of them, no one should worry."

"I suddenly have a lot to take care of…" She hummed. "These two girls."

"They're little. Don't take up much room."

"Marius."

"You're alternating weeks with the others to stay in DC with him."

"And you…"

"Me?" I smirked. "There's only one thing you can do for me."

"Not in the middle of the kitchen with the girls here."

I conceded that. "Okay…two things."

"And what's that?"

I leaned in and captured her a kiss. "Tell me you love me."

"On one condition."

"Name it."

"You tell me first."

That wouldn't a problem. I'd never stop saying it.

"I love you, Sassy."

How had I ever run from her smile?

"I love you too."

THE END

COMING SOON!

Coming February 2018!
P.I.T.A. - An Enemies To Lovers Romance
A Payne Brothers Romance

> He's sexy.
> He's charming.
> He's fantasic in bed.
> Too bad he's a total
> Pain In The Ass.
>
> Coming February 2018
> P.I.T.A
> An Enemies To Lovers Sextravaganza
> A Payne Brothers Romance

Never knew a woman could be so beautiful...
...so tempting
...so amazing
And such a pain in my ass.

I need her to save my farm.
She expects a favor in return.

I didn't just make a deal with the devil.
I slept with her too.

Coming February 2018!

Click Here to sign up to my mailing list for more updates!

or

Text: SOSIE
to
245-87

To receive a text message alert when PITA goes live!

ABOUT THE AUTHOR

Keep tabs on me through Facebook

Join my mailing list to receive updates, news, special sales, and opportunities for advanced reader copies of upcoming novels!

You will **only** receive emails from me and about me—no promoting other authors and cluttering your box!
I'll send **1-2 emails a month** when I have a new release!

You can also receive a **text message** when a new book is live!

Text: SOSIE
to
245-87

Subscribe to text message alerts! Get a text right to your phone! No more wading through all those author emails that clog your inbox. Never miss one of my books again!

I'll only text when a new book is released!
(No more than one or two times a month)

Or
You can always email me at:
sosiefrost@gmail.com

ALSO BY SOSIE FROST

Bad Boy's Series

Bad Boy's Baby

Bad Boy's Redemption (Previously Bad Boy's Revenge)

Bad Boy's Bridesmaid

Touchdowns and Tiaras

Beauty And The Blitz

Once Upon A Half-Time

Happily Ever All-Star

Standalone Romances

Sweetest Sin - A Forbidden Priest Romance

Hard - A Step-Brother Romance

Deja Vu - An Amnesia Romance

While They Watch - A Sexy BDSM Romance

ACKNOWLEDGMENTS

Short and sweet <3

To my readers:

Thank you all so much for waiting for this latest release. I'm touched by the support, messages, emails, and well-wishes I've received these past few months.
I do it all for you guys. :)

And to Kelley:

Thank you again for all your words and wisdom and edits.
Especially the edits.
I don't know what I'd do with you.
<3

Made in the USA
Columbia, SC
10 October 2020